They found her, after some questing and probing in new snow, swept the fresh fall from the ice, and looked down upon her, a girl in a mirror, a girl spun from glass.

Not a drop fell from the ice until they had carried her back to Bromfield and stowed her in the chill, bare mortuary of the priory. Then the glittering edges began to soften and slide.

The girl lay remote and pale within her lucid shroud, and yet grew steadily more human and closer to life, to pain and pity and violence, and all the mortal lot of mankind.

It was past ten, and High Mass in progress, when the shell of ice had dwindled so far that the girl began to emerge, the tips of thin, pale fingers and stretched toes, her nose, as yet only a minute pearl, and the first curling strands of hair, a fine lace on either side of her forehead.

Cadfael bent, aware of her open eyes, still thinly veiled with ice. Their colour seemed to him the soft, dim purple of irises, or the darkest grey of lavender flowers.

The VIRGIN in the ICE

The Sixth Chronicle
of Brother Cadfael

ELLIS PETERS

FAWCETT CREST • NEW YORK

A Fawcett Crest Book
Published by Ballantine Books
Copyright © 1982 by Ellis Peters

Previously published in Great Britain in 1982 by Macmillan London
Limited

Library of Congress Catalog Card Number: 82-14500

ISBN 0-449-20537-1

This edition published by arrangement with William Morrow and
Company, Inc.

Manufactured in the United States of America

First Ballantine Books Edition: May 1984

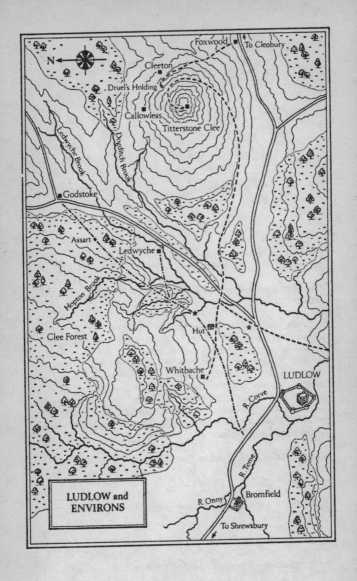

N

Foxwood ■ To Cleobury

Cleeton ■

Druel's Holding ●

Callowleas ■

Titterstone Clee

Ledwyche Brook

Dogditch Brook

Godstoke ■

Assart

Ledwyche ■

Hopton Brook

Clee Forest

Hut ■

Whitbache ■

LUDLOW

R. Corve

R. Terne

R. Onny   Bromfield

To Shrewsbury

**LUDLOW and
ENVIRONS**

1

It was early in November of 1139 that the tide of civil war, lately so sluggish and inactive, rose suddenly to sweep over the city of Worcester, wash away half its livestock, property and women, and send all those of its inhabitants who could get away in time scurrying for their lives northwards away from the marauders, to burrow into hiding wherever there was manor or priory, walled town or castle strong enough to afford them shelter. By the middle of the month a straggle of them had reached Shrewsbury, and subsided thankfully into the hospitable embrace of monastery or town, to lick their wounds and pour out their grievances.

They were not in too bad case, apart from the old or sick, for the winter had not yet begun to bite hard. The weather-wise foretold that there was bitter cold in store, heavy snows and hard and prolonged frosts, but as yet the land lay dour, cloudy and mild, with capricious winds, but clear of frost or snow.

'Thanks be to God!' said Brother Edmund, the infirmarer, devoutly. 'Or we should have had more burials on our hands than three, and they all past their three score and ten.'

Even so, he was hard put to it to find beds in his hospice for all those who needed them, and there was thick straw

laid down in the stone hall for the overflow. They would
live to return to their spoiled city before the Christmas
feast, but now, exhausted and apathetic with shock, they
needed all his care, and the abbey's resources were
stretched to their limits. A few fugitives with distant rel-
atives in the town had been taken into the houses of their
kin, and were warmly provided. A pregnant woman near
her time had been taken, husband and all, into the town
house of Hugh Beringar, the deputy sheriff of the shire,
at the insistence of his wife, whom he had brought here to
the security of the town, complete with her women, mid-
wife, physician and all, because she, too, looked forward
to giving birth before the Nativity, and had a welcome for
any who came in the same expectation, and in any kind of
need.

'Our Lady,' remarked Brother Cadfael ruefully to his
good friend Hugh, 'had no such reception.'

'Ah, there is but one of *my* lady! Aline would take in
every homeless dog she saw in the streets, if she could.
This poor girl from Worcester will do well enough now,
there's nothing amiss with her that rest won't mend. We
may yet have two births here for this Christmas, for she
can't well be moved until she's safely over her lying-in.
But I daresay most of your guests will soon be shrugging
off their fears and heading for home.'

'A few have left already,' said Cadfael, 'and more of the
hale ones will be off within days. It's natural they should
want to get home and repair what they can. They say the
king is on his way to Worcester with a strong force. If he
leaves the garrison better found, they should be safe over
the winter. Though they'll need to draw stores from east-
wards, for their own reserves will all have been carried
off.'

Cadfael knew from old experience the look, the stench,
the desolation of a gutted town, having been both soldier
and sailor in his young days, and seen service far afield.
'And besides wanting to reclaim what's left of their store
before Christmas,' he said, 'there's the spur of the winter
coming. If the roads are cleared of bad customs now, at
least they can travel dry-shod and warm enough, but another month, another week it may be, and who knows
how deep the snow will be?'

'Whether the roads are cleared of bad customs,' said

2

Beringar in wary reflection, 'is more than I should care to say. We have a pretty firm hold here in Shropshire—thus far! But there's ominous word from east and north, besides this uneasiness along the border. When the king is all too busy in the south, and his mind on where his Flemings' next pay is to come from, and his energy mostly wasted in wavering from one target to another, ambitious men in remoter parts are liable to begin to spread their honours into palatines, and set up kingdoms of their own. And given the example, the lesser fry will follow it.'

'In a land at war with itself,' agreed Cadfael sombrely, 'you may take it as certain that order breaks down, and savagery breaks out.'

'Not here, it shall not,' said Hugh grimly. 'Prestcote has kept a close rein, and in so far as it falls to me as his man, so will I.' For Gilbert Prestcote, King Stephen's sheriff of Shropshire, was planning to keep Christmas in the chief manor of his own honour, in the north of the county, and the castle garrison and the rule of law throughout the southern half of the shire would be left in Beringar's hands. This attack on Worcester might be only a foretaste of further such raids. All the border towns were at risk, as well from the precarious loyalties of constables and garrisons as from the enterprise of the enemy. More than one lord in this troubled land had already changed his allegiance, more than one would do so in the future, some, perhaps, for the second or third time. Churchmen, barons and all, they were beginning to look first to their own interests, and place their loyalty where it seemed likely to bring them the greater profit. And it would not be long before some of them came to the conclusion that their interests could be served just as well by flouting both contendants for the crown, and setting up on their own account.

'There was some talk of your castellan in Ludlow being none too reliable,' observed Cadfael. 'For all King Stephen set him up in the honour of Lacy, and trusted Ludlow castle to him, there have been rumours he was casting his eyes towards the empress. Touch and go with him, as I heard it, if the king had not been close and with a sharp eye on him.'

Anything Cadfael had heard, Hugh had certainly heard. There was not a sheriff in the land who had not all his in-

3

telligencers alerted, these days, and his own ear to the ground. If Josce de Dinan, in Ludlow, had indeed been contemplating defection, and thought better of it, Hugh was content to accept his present steadfastness, but with reservations, and was watching him still. Distrust was only one of the lesser horrors of civil war, but saddening enough. It was well that there could still be absolute trust between tried friends. In these days there was no man living who might not suddenly have acute need of a steady and stout back braced against his own.

'Ah, well, with King Stephen on his way to Worcester with an army, no one is going to lift finger or show face until he draws off again. But for all that, I never stop listening and watching.' Hugh rose from the bench against the wall of Cadfael's workshop, brief refuge from the world. 'Now I am going home to my own bed, for once—even if I am banished from my wife's by my own arrogant brat. But what would a devout religious like you know about a father's tribulations!'

What, indeed? 'You must all come to it,' said Brother Cadfael complacently, 'you married men. Third and unwanted where two are lost in admiring each other. I shall go to Compline and say a prayer for you.'

He went first, however, to the infirmary, to check with Brother Edmund on one or two patients who were slow in their recovery from their wanderings, being feeble from age or poverty and hunger, and renew the dressing on a knifewound which was ill to heal, and only then went to Compline, there to pray for many more, besides his friend, his friend's wife, and his friend's child to come, this winter child.

England was already frozen into a winter years long, and he knew it. King Stephen was crowned, and held, however slackly, most of England. The Empress Maud, his rival for the throne, held the west, and came with a claim the equal of Stephen's. Cousins, most uncousinly, they tore each other and tore England between them, and yet life must go on, faith must go on, the stubborn defiance of fortune must go on in the husbandry of the year, season after season, plough and harrow and seed, tillage and harvest. And here in the cloister and the church, the sowing and tillage and harvest of souls. Brother Cadfael had no fear for mankind, whatever became of mere men.

4

Hugh's child would be a new generation, a new beginning, a new affirmation, spring in midwinter.

It was on the last day of November that Brother Herward, sub-prior of the Benedictine monastery of Worcester, appeared at chapter in the fraternal house of Saint Peter and Saint Paul at Shrewsbury, where he had arrived the previous night, and been entertained in Abbot Radulfus' own lodging as a cherished guest. Most of the brothers had no knowledge of his coming, and wondered who this could be, brought in courteously by their own abbot, and seated at his right hand. For once Brother Cadfael knew no more than his fellows.

The abbot and his guest made a sharp contrast. Radulfus was tall, erect, vigorous, with strong, austere features, magisterially calm. When needed, he could blaze, and those scorched drew back advisedly, but his fire was always in control. The man who entered beside him was meagre, small and slight of body, grey of tonsure, still tired after his journey, but his ageing eyes were direct of gaze, and his mouth set into lines of patience and endurance.

'Our brother, Sub-Prior Herward of Worcester,' said the abbot, 'has come to us with an errand in which I have been unable to help him. Since many of you here have been active in serving those unfortunates who came to us from that city, it is possible that you may have heard from them something which may be to the purpose. I have therefore asked him to repeat his request here to all.'

The visitor rose, to be better seen and heard by all present. 'I am sent to make enquiry after two noble children who were in Benedictine care in our town, and fled from it when the attack fell upon us. They have not returned, and we have traced their steps as far as the borders of this county and there lost them, It was their intention to make for Shrewsbury, and therefore, since our order is responsible for them, I came to find out whether they ever reached here. Father Abbot tells me that to his knowledge they never did, but it may be that some others among the fugitives may have seen them or got word of them in their travels, and spoken of them here among you. I should be grateful for any news that might lead to their safe recovery. And these are their names: the girl

5

Ermina Hugonin, almost eighteen years of age, who was in the care of our sister convent in Worcester, and her brother Yves Hugonin, who was in our charge, and is only thirteen. They are orphaned of both parents, and their uncle and natural guardian has long been overseas in the Holy Land, and is only now returned, to be met by the news of their loss. It will be understood here,' said Brother Herward wryly, 'that we feel ourselves greatly to blame for having failed in our charge, though to say truth, we are not wholly at fault. As this thing befell, it was taken out of our hands.'

'In such confusion and peril,' agreed Radulfus ruefully, 'it would be much to ask of any man that he should order all successfully. But children of such tender age . . .'

Brother Edmund asked hesitantly: 'Are we to understand that they left Worcester alone?' He had not meant to sound either incredulous or censorious, but Brother Herward bowed his head meekly to the implied reproach.

'I would not wish to excuse myself or any of my house. Yet it fell out, perhaps, not quite as you suppose. That attack came in the early morning, but on the south side it was held, and we did not hear how grave it showed, or how great the force coming against us, until later, when they came about, and broke in by the north. It so happened that the boy Yves was visiting his sister, and they were quite cut off from us. The Lady Ermina is, dare I say, a headstrong young woman. In such a case, though the sisters thought best to gather in their church and abide the issue there, trusting that even these marauders—for I must tell you many were already drunk and wild—would respect their cloth, and do them no more harm than to steal, perhaps, their more valuable furnishings— the sisters, I say, held that faith required them to remain, but the Lady Ermina thought otherwise, and would slip away out of the town, as so many did, and make away into some safe and distant refuge. And since she would not be dissuaded, and her brother held with her, the young nun who was her tutor there offered that she would go with them, to see them safe into shelter. When all the raiders were gone, and we had put out the fires, and seen to the dead and wounded, only then did we get word that they had escaped out of the city and intended to reach Shrewsbury. There were well provided, though without horses,

6

since all were seized at sight. The girl had her jewels, and store of money, and wit enough not to let them be seen on the way. And sorry I am to say it, it was well that she would go, for these men of Gloucester did not respect the sisters as they had hoped and trusted, but ravaged and burned, stole away some, the youngest and best-favoured among the novices, and bitterly misused the prioress who tried to prevent. The girl did well to venture, and I pray she and her brother, and Sister Hilaria with them, are safe in shelter somewhere this moment. But alas, I do not know.'

Brother Denis the hospitaller, who knew every soul who came within the gates, said regretfully: 'I grieve to have to tell you, but quite surely they never arrived here. We have had no such party. But come with me and speak with every fugitive we are still sheltering here in the guest-hall, and the few in the infirmary, in case they can tell you anything of use. For of course we knew nothing of these young people until now, and therefore have not asked about them.'

'Or again it may be,' suggested Brother Matthew the cellarer, 'that they knew of some kinsman or tenant or old servant here in the town, and therefore have passed us by, and are now within the walls.'

'It is possible,' agreed Herward, brightening a little. 'But I think Sister Hilaria would prefer to bring them here, to our own order for protection.'

'If there are none here who can help,' said the abbot briskly, 'the next move is certainly to consult the sheriff. He will know who has been received within the town. You did mention, brother, that the uncle of this young pair is newly come home from Palestine. There are channels he may use to approach the authorities here. How is it that he is not pursuing this enquiry in person? For surely he cannot cast the blame all on you.'

Brother Herward heaved a great sigh that first stiffened his little frame, and then let it collapse dispiritedly into limpness. 'Their uncle is a knight of Angevin blood —they are his sister's children—by name Laurence d'Angers. Newly home from the Crusade he is, but to Gloucester, to join the forces of the empress. It is also true that he did not arrive there until after this onslaught, and bears no blame for it, as he took no part in it. But no

7

man from Gloucester dare show his face now in our city. The king is there with a great force, and an angry man, like every ruined burgess of the town. The search for these children is deputed to our house, perforce. Nevertheless, this is a quest for creatures absolutely innocent, and I shall so present it to the sheriff.'

'And you shall have my voice,' Radulfus assured him. 'But first, since none here can provide us news . . ?' He looked enquiringly round the chapter-house, and found only shaken heads. 'Very well, we must enquire among our guests. The names, the youth of the parties, the presence of the nun, may yield us some useful word.'

Nevertheless Cadfael, filing out from chapter among the rest, could not believe that anything would come of such enquiry. He had spent much of his time, in recent days, helping Brother Edmund house and doctor the exhausted travellers, and never a word had been said of any such trio encountered on the way. Travellers' tales enough there had been, freely spilled for the listening, but none of a Benedictine sister and two noble children loose on the roads with never a man to guard them.

And the uncle, it seemed, was the empress's man, as Gilbert Prestcote was the king's man, to the hilt, and bitterness between the factions was flaring up like a torch in tinder over the sack of Worcester. The omens were not good Abbot Radulfus would lend his own persuasions to the envoy's, and this very day, too, but what countenance the two of them would get for Laurence d'Angers was a dubious speculation.

The sheriff received his petitioners courteously and gravely in his own apartment in the castle, and listened with an impassive face to the story Herward had to tell. A sombre man, black-browed and black-bearded, and his natural cast of countenance rather forbidding than reassuring, but for all that a fair-minded man in his stern fashion, and one who stood by his word and his men, provided they kept the standards he demanded of them.

'I am sorry,' he said when Herward had done, 'to hear of this loss, and sorrier still that I must tell you at once you will be seeking your party in vain here in Shrewsbury. Since this attack took place I have had word brought to me of every soul from Worcester who has entered the town, and these three are not among them. Many have already left again for home, now that his Grace has reinforced the garrison in Worcester. If, as you say, the uncle of these children has now returned to England, and is a man of substance, can he not undertake the search in person?'

It was Herward's weakness that he had withheld, up to that point, all but the name of that nobleman, putting off the evil moment. And as yet the name meant nothing, beyond a knight with the credit of the Crusade shedding lustre upon him, newly arrived from the Holy Land, where a relatively secure peace held at this time. But no help for it, the truth would out.

'My lord,' owned Herward, sighing, 'Laurence d'Angers is willing and anxious to make search for his nephew and niece, but for that he requires your countenance, or the special dispensation of his Grace the king. For he returned home as an Angevin owing allegiance to the Empress Maud, and has attached himself and his men to her forces at Gloucester.' He hurried on, to have all said while speech was allowed him, for the sheriff's level brows had drawn together into a steely bar above eyes now narrowed and bright in understanding. 'He had not arrived in Gloucester until a week after the attack, he took no part in it, knew nothing of it, cannot be held responsible for it. He came only to discover that his kin were lost, and all his desire is to find them and see them into safety. But it is impossible for a man of Gloucester to come near Worcester now, or to enter the king's lands except by special safe-conduct.'

'So you,' said Prestcote after a daunting pause, 'are acting on his behalf—the king's enemy.'

'With respect, my lord,' said Herward with spirit, 'I am acting on behalf of a young girl and a boy of tender years, who have done nothing to make them enemies to king or empress. I am not concerned with faction, only with the fate of two children who were in the charge of our order until this evil befell. Is it not natural that we should feel responsible for them, and do all we can in conscience to find them?'

'Natural enough,' allowed the sheriff drily, 'and moreover, as a man of Worcester yourself you're hardly likely

9

to feel any great warmth towards the king's enemies, or want to give them aid or comfort.'

'We suffered from them, like the rest of Worcester, my lord. King Stephen is our sovereign, and as such we acknowledge him. The only duty I feel here is to the children. Consider what must be the dismay, the anxiety, of their natural guardian! All he asks—all we ask for him—is leave to enter the king's lands, not in arms, and search for his niece and nephew without hindrance. I do not say such a man, however innocent of this murderous raid, and even with his Grace's safe-conduct and countenance, would be utterly safe among the men of our shire or yours, but that risk he is willing to take. If you will give him safe-conduct, he pledges himself to pursue this quest, and no other end. He will go unarmed, and with only one or two attendants to help him. He will take no action but to find his wards. My lord, I entreat it of you, for their sake.'

Abbot Radulfus added his own plea, very restrainedly. 'From a Crusader of unblemished repute, I believe such a pledge may be accepted without question.'

The sheriff considered, darkly and in frowning silence, for some minutes, and then said with chill deliberation: 'No. I will issue no safe-conduct, and if the king himself were here and minded to grant it, I would urge him to the contrary. After what has happened, any man of that faction found in any part of my territory will be treated as a prisoner of war, if not as a spy. If he be taken in any ill circumstances, his life may be forfeit, and even if on no wrong errand, his liberty. It is not a matter of his intent alone. Even a man so pledged, and true enough to his pledge, might take back with him knowledge of castles and garrisons that would stand the enemy in good stead later. Also, and above all, it is my duty to combat the king's enemies and reduce their forces wherever chance offers, and if I can pluck away a good knight from them I will do it. No affront to Sir Laurence d'Angers, whose reputation, as far as I know it, is honourable enough, but he shall not have his safe-conduct, and if he ventures without it, let him look to his head. No doubt he did not come home from Palestine to rot in a prison. If he risks it, it is his own choice.'

'But the girl Ermina,' began Herward in dismayed appeal, 'and her brother, a mere child—are they to be left unsought?'

'Have I said so? Sought they shall be, to the best I can provide, but by my own men. And if found, they shall be delivered safely to their uncle's care. I will send out orders to all my castellans and officers, to look out for such a company of three, and make due enquiries after them. But I will not admit the empress's knight to the lands I administer for the king.'

It was all they would get from him, and they knew it by voice and face, and made the best of it.

'It would help,' suggested Radulfus mildly, 'if Brother Herward gives you some description of the three. Though I do not know if he is well acquainted with the girl, or the nun, her tutor . . .'

'They came several times to visit the boy,' said Herward. 'I can picture them all three. Your officers should enquire after these—Yves Hugonin, thirteen years old, heir to a considerable portion from his father, is not over-tall for his age, but sturdy and well-set-up, with a round, rosy face, and both hair and eyes dark brown. I saw him the morning this coil began, in bright blue cotte, cloak and capuchon, and grey hose. For the women—Sister Hilaria will be known best by her habit, but I should tell you that she is young, not above five and twenty, and well-favoured, a slender woman and graceful. And the girl Ermina . . .' Brother Herward hesitated, gazing beyond the sheriff's shoulder, as if to recall more perfectly someone but seldom seen, yet vividly impressed on his vision.

'She will be eighteen very shortly, I do not know the precise day. Darker than her brother, almost black of hair and eye, tall, vigorous . . . They report her quick of mind and wit, and of strong will.'

It was hardly a detailed description of her physical person, yet it established her with surprising clarity. All the more when Brother Herward ended almost absently, as if to himself: 'She would be reckoned very beautiful.'

Brother Cadfael heard about it from Hugh Beringar, after the couriers had ridden out to the castles and manors, and carried the word to the towns, to be cried publicly. What Prestcote had promised, that he performed to the letter before he took himself off to the peace of his own

11

manor to keep Christmas with his family. The very announcement of the sheriff's interest in the missing siblings should cast a protecting shadow over them if anyone in this shire did encounter them. Herward had set off back to Worcester with a guarded party by then, his errand only partially successful.

'Very beautiful!' repeated Hugh, and smiled. But it was a concerned and rueful smile. Such a creature, wilful, handsome, daring, let loose in a countryside waiting for winter and menaced by discord, might all too easily come to grief.

'Even sub-priors,' said Cadfael mildly, stirring the bubbling cough linctus he was simmering over his brazier in the workshop, 'have eyes. But with her youth, she would be vulnerable even if she were ugly. Well, for all we know they may be snug and safe in shelter this moment. A great pity this uncle of theirs is of the other persuasion, and cannot get countenance to do his own hunting.'

'And newly back from Jerusalem,' mused Hugh, 'no way to blame for what his faction did to Worcester. He'll be too recent in the service to be known to you, I suppose?'

'Another generation, lad. It's twenty-six years since I left the Holy Land.' Cadfael lifted his pot from the brazier, and stood it aside on the earth floor to cool gradually overnight. He straightened his back carefully. He was not so far from sixty, even if he did not look it by a dozen years. 'Everything will be changed there now, I doubt. The lustre soon tarnished. From which port did they say he sailed?'

'Tripoli, according to Herward. In your unregenerate youth I suppose you must have known that city well? It seems to me there's not much of that coast you haven't covered in your time.'

'It was St Symeon I favoured myself. There were good craftsmen in the shipyards there, a fine harbour, and Antioch only a few miles upriver.'

He had good cause to remember Antioch, for it was there he had begun and ended his long career as a crusader, and his love affair with Palestine, that lovely inhospitable, cruel land of gold and sand and drought. From this quiet, busy harbour in which he had chosen at last to drop anchor, he had had little time to hark back to those

12

remembered haunts of his youth. The town came back to him now vividly, the lush green of the river valley, the narrow, grateful shade of the streets, the babel of the market. And Mariam, selling her fruit and vegetables in the Street of the Sailmakers, her young, fine-boned face honed into gold and silver by the fierce sunlight, her black, oiled hair gleaming beneath her veil. She had graced his arrival in the east, a mere boy of eighteen, and his departure, a seasoned soldier and seafarer of thirty-three. A widow, young, passionate and lonely, a woman of the people, not to everyone's taste, too spare, too strong, too scornful. The void left by her dead man had ached unbearably, and drawn in the young stranger heart and soul into her life, to fill the gap. For a whole year he had known her, before the forces of the Cross had moved on to invest Jerusalem.

There had been other women, before her and after. He remembered them with gratitude, and with no guilt at all. He had given and received pleasure and kindness. None had ever complained of him. If that was a poor defence from the formal viewpoint, nevertheless he felt secure behind it. It would have been an insult to repent of having loved a woman like Mariam.

'They have alliances there that ensure peace now, if only for a time,' he said reflectively. 'I suppose an Angevin lord might well feel he's more needed here than there, now it's his own liege lady in the lists. And the man bears a good name, from all I hear. A pity he comes when hate's at its height.'

'A pity there should be cause for hate between decent men,' agreed Hugh wryly. 'I am the king's man, I chose him with my eyes open. I like Stephen, and am not likely to leave him for any lure. But I can see just as plainly why a baron of Anjou should rush home to serve his lady every whit as loyally as I serve Stephen. What a bedevilment of all our values, Cadfael, is this civil war!'

'Not all,' said Cadfael sturdily. 'There never was, for all I could ever learn, a time when living was easy and peaceful. Your boy will grow up into a better ordered world. There, I've finished here for tonight, and it must be nearly time for the bell.'

They went out together into the cold and dark of the garden, and felt on their faces the first flakes of the first

13

snow of the winter. The air was full of a drifting unease, but the fall was light and fitful here. Further south it set in heavily, borne on a north-westerly wind, dry, fine snow that turned the night into a white, whirling mist, shrouding outlines, burying paths, blown into smooth, breaking waves only to be lifted and hurled again into new shapes. Valleys filled to a treacherous level, hillsides were scoured clean. Wise men stayed within their houses, clapped to shutter and door, and stopped the chinks between the boards, where thin white fingers reached through. The first snow, and the first hard frost. Thank God, thought Cadfael, hastening his steps as he heard the Compline bell begin to sound, Herward and his company will be far on their way home now, they'll weather this well enough.

But what of Ermina and Yves Hugonin, astray somewhere between here and Worcester, and what of the young Benedictine sister who had offered, in her gallant innocence, to go with them and see them safe into sanctuary?

2

On the fifth day of December, about noon, a traveller from the south, who had slept the night at Bromfield Priory, some twenty-odd miles away, and had the good fortune to find the highroad, at least, in passable condition, brought an urgent message into Shrewsbury abbey. Prior Leonard of Bromfield had been a monk of Shrewsbury until his promotion, and was an old friend of Brother Cadfael's, and familiar with his skills.

'In the night,' the messenger reported, 'some decent fellows of that country brought in a wounded man to the priory, found by the wayside stripped and hacked, and left for dead. And half-dead he is, and his case very bad. If he had lain out all night in the frost he'd have been frozen stiff by morning. And Prior Leonard asked would I bring word here to you, for though they've some knowledge of healing, this case is beyond them, and he said you have experience from the wars, and may be able to save the man. If you could come, and bide until he mends—or until the poor soul's lost!—it would be a great comfort and kindness.'

'If abbot and prior give me leave,' said Cadfael, concerned, 'then most gladly. Footpads preying on the roads so close to Ludlow? What are things come to, there in the south?'

'And the poor man a monk himself, for they knew him by his tonsure.'

'Come with me,' said Cadfael, 'and we'll put it to Prior Robert.'

Prior Robert heard the plea with sympathy, and raised no objection, since it was not he who must ride out all those miles in haste, in what was now the shrewd grip of winter. He took the request in his turn to the abbot, and came again with his approval granted.

'Father Abbot bids you take a good horse from the stables, for you'll need him. You have leave for as long as may be necessary, and we'll send and have Brother Mark come in from Saint Giles in the meantime, for I think Brother Oswin is not yet practiced enough to be left in charge alone.'

Cadfael agreed, fervently but demurely. A willing and devoted soul, but hardly competent to look after all the winter ailments that might crop up in his tutor's absence. Mark would leave his lepers on the outskirts of the town with regret, but God willing it need not be for very long.

'What of the roads?' he asked the messenger, who was stabling his own beast as Cadfael chose his. 'You made good time here, and so must I back.'

'The worst is the wind, brother, but it's blown the high-road almost clear in all but a few bad places. It's the by-ways that are clean buried. If you leave now you won't fare too badly. Better going south than north, at least you'll have the wind at your back.'

Cadfael took some thought over filling his scrip, for he had medicines, salves and febrifuges not to be found in every infirmary cupboard, and the commoner sorts Brom-field could provide. The less weight he carried, the better speed he would make. He took stout boots and a thick travelling cloak over his habit, and belted the folds se-curely about his waist. If the errand had not been so grim, he would have relished the prospect of a justified trip back into the world, and the rare permission to take his pick of the stables. He had campaigned in wintry condi-tions as well as in burning sun, the snow did not daunt him, though he was shrewd enough to respect it, and treat it with caution.

All those four days since the first snow the weather had followed a fixed pattern, with brief sunshine around noon,

16

gathering cloud thereafter, fresh snow falling late in the evening and well into the night, and always iron frost. Around Shrewsbury the snowfalls had been light and powdery, the pattern of white flakes and black soil constantly changing as the wind blew. But as Cadfael rode south the fields grew whiter, the ditches filled. The branches of trees sagged heavily towards the ground under their load, and by mid-afternoon the leaden sky was sagging no less heavily earthwards, in swags of blue-black cloud. If this went on, the wolves would be moving down from the hills and prowling hungrily among the haunts of men. Better to be an urchin under a hedgerow, sleeping the winter away, or a squirrel holed up snugly with his hoarded stores. It had been a good autumn for nuts and acorns.

Riding was pleasure to him, even riding alone and in the bitter cold. The chance seldom came his way now, it was one of the delights he had given up for the quiet of the cloister and the sense of having discovered his true place. In every decision there must be some regrets. He hunched his back solidly against the malice of the wind, and saw the first driven flakes, fine as dust, whirl by him and outpace his horse, while he felt nothing in his shroud of cowl and cloak. He was thinking of the man who waited for him at the end of this journey.

Himself a monk, the messenger had said. Of Bromfield? Surely not. If he had been one of theirs they would have named him. A monk loose and alone about the roads in the mid of the night? On what errand? Or in flight from what, before he fell into the mercies of robbers and murderers? Others must have ranged through the same countryside, in flight from the rape of Worcester, and where were they now? Perhaps this cowled wanderer had made his way painfully out of the same holocaust?

The snow thickened, two fine curtains of spume driving past him one on either side, cloven by his sturdy body and waving away ahead of him like the ends of a gauze scarf, drawing him forward. Perhaps four times on this ride he had exchanged greetings in passing with other human creatures, and all of them close to home. In such a season only the desperate travel.

It was dark by the time he reached the gatehouse of Bromfield, crossing the foot-bridge over the little River

Onny. His horse had had enough by then, and was blowing frostily, and twitching irritable shoulders and flanks. Cadfael lighted down gladly between the torches in the gateway, and let a lay brother take the bridle. Before him the familiar court opened, straighter than at Shrewsbury, and the shapes of the monastic buildings gilded here and there by the flame of a torch. The church of Saint Mary loomed dark in darkness, large and noble for such a modest foundation. And striding out of shadows across the court came Prior Leonard himself, a long, loose-jointed heron of a man, pointed back anxiously advanced, arms flapping like wings. The court under his feet, surely swept during the day, already bore a smooth, frail coating of snow. By morning it would be crisp and deep underfoot, unless the wind that brought it removed half of it again to hurl it elsewhere.

'Cadfael?' The prior was near-sighted, he had to peer and narrow his eyes even by daylight, but he groped for a hand that came to meet his, and held and knew it. 'Thank God you could come! I fear for him . . . But such a ride . . . Come within, come within, I have provision made for you, and a meal. You must be both hungry and weary!'

'First let me see him,' said Cadfael briskly, and set off purposefully up the slope of the court, leaving his broad bootprints plain in the new-fallen whiteness. Prior Leonard strode beside him, long legs curbed to his friend's shorter pace, still talking volubly.

'We have him in a room apart, for quietness, and watched constantly. He breathes, but snoringly, like a man with a broken head. He has not spoken word or opened eye since they brought him. Bruises darken on him everywhere, but those would heal. But a knife was used on him, he has bled too much, though the wound is stanched now. Through here—the inner room is less cold . . .'

The infirmary stood a little apart, sheltered from the wind by the mass of the church. They went in, and shut the heavy door against the malice of the night, and Leonard led the way through to the small, bare cell where a little oil-lamp burned beside a bed. A young brother rose from his knees at their entry, and drew from the sick man's bedside to make room for them.

The patient lay under piled covers, stretched on his

18

back like a man coffined. Certainly he breathed, with a groaning effort, but the intake of breath barely lifted the blanket over his breast, and the face upturned on the pillow was motionless, eyes closed, cheeks hollow and blue beneath thrusting bones. His head was bandaged, covering the tonsure, and the brow beneath the wrappings was swollen and bruised, so misshapen that one eye was sunken in folds of battered flesh. No telling how he would look in health, but Cadfael judged that he was well-made, and certainly not old, probably no older than thirty-five.

'The marvel is,' whispered Leonard, 'that no bones are broken. Unless, indeed, his skull . . . But you'll examine him thoroughly, later . . .'

'No better time than now,' said Cadfael practically, and shed his cloak and went to work, setting down his scrip on the stone floor. There was a small brazier burning in a corner, but for all that, when he slid his hands under the covers and felt at flank and thigh and foot, the unresponsive flesh was everywhere deadly cold. They had wrapped him well, but it was not enough.

'Lay stones over your hob in the kitchen,' said Cadfael, 'get them hot and wrap them in flannel. We'll pack him round with warmth, and change them as they cool. This is not the cold of winter, but the chill of man's mishandling, we must get him out of it, or he never will wake. I've known men shattered by horror or cruelty turn their backs on the world and die, when there was nothing mortal ailed their bodies. Have you made shift to get any food or drink into him at all?'

'We have tried, but he cannot swallow. Even a trickle of wine only runs from his mouth again.' A broken mouth, battered by fists or cudgels. Probably he had lost teeth. But no, Cadfael drew back the upper lip delicately, and the strong white teeth showed, even, clenched and large.

The young brother had slipped away silently to see about heating stones or bricks in the kitchen. Cadfael turned back the covers, and viewed the naked body from head to foot. They had left him so, under a linen sheet, to have only a clean, smooth surface touching his many bruises and broken grazes. The knife-wound under his heart was bandaged close. Cadfael did not unbind it; no need to doubt that every wound had been scrupulously

19

cleaned and dressed. But he slid his fingers under the upper folds, and felt along the bones beneath.

'It was meant to finish him. But the knife struck the rib, and they did not wait to make certain. In health this must be a fine man—see the build of him. Three or four at least did this to him.'

He did what he could for the many injuries that showed some angry signs of festering, drawing on his stock of salves tried over years, but let the lesser and clean abrasions alone. They brought the heated stones, two or three eager young brothers hovering anxiously, and packed the battered form round with them, close but not touching, and trotted away devotedly to heat more. A good hot brick at the long, bony feet; for if the feet stay cold, all stays cold, said Cadfael. And then the bludgeoned head. He unwound the bandages, Leonard supporting the man's shoulders. The tonsure emerged unmistakable, thick, bushy brown hair framing a pate scarred by two or three still oozing wounds. So thick and strong the hair, of such vigorous growth, that even the ring of it might well have saved him a broken skull. Cadfael felt delicately all round the cupola of bone, and could not find a hollow that gave to his touch. He drew breath in cautious hope.

'His wits will have been shaken up into confusion, but I do believe his skull is whole. We'll bind it up again for his comfort in lying, and for warmth. I can find no break.'

When all was done, the mute body lay as before; hard to detect any change that did not stem from the handling of others. But the warm stones zealously renewed as they cooled had had their effect. His flesh felt softer and human to the touch, capable of healing.

'We may leave him now,' said Cadfael, staring down at him with a considering frown. 'I'll watch with him through the night, and get my sleep tomorrow by daylight, when we see better how he fares. But I say he'll live. Father Prior, by your leave, I'm ready now for that supper you promised me. And before all, for I'm too stiff to fend for myself, get a stout youngster to haul off these boots.'

Prior Leonard himself waited on his guest at supper, and freely admitted his relief at having a more experienced physician at hand. 'For I never had your knowledge, nor

20

the means of acquiring it, and never, God knows, have I had so wretched and broken a creature left at my door. I thought I had a dead man on my hands, before ever I brought him in and tried to stop the bleeding, and wrap him against the frost. And how he came by this usage we may never get to know.'

'Who brought him in?' asked Cadfael.

'A tenant of ours near Henley, Reyner Dutton, a good husbandman. That was the first night of snow and frost, and Reyner had lost a strayed heifer, one of the venture-some kind that will wander and break loose, and he was out after her with a couple of his lads. They stumbled on this poor soul by the wayside, and left all to carry him here to shelter as fast as they could. It was a wild night, driving squalls and stone blind when they came. I doubt if he can have lain there long, or he would not be living now, as cold as it was and is.'

'And these who helped him had seen nothing of any footpads? Met with no hindrance themselves?'

'Nothing. But there was no seeing more than a dozen paces, men could pass close and never know it. Likely they were lucky not to meet the same fate, though three of them, perhaps, would be enough to daunt any footpads. They know this countryside like their own palms. A stranger would have had to lie up somewhere and wait till he could see his way. In these drifts, and with such a wind blowing, and the snow so dry and fine, paths appear and vanish twice in a day and more. You could walk a mile, and think you knew every landmark, and see nothing you recognised on the way back.'

'And this sick man of ours—no one knows him here?'

Prior Leonard stared startled and embarrassed sur-prise. 'Why, yes! Did I never make that plain? Well, my messenger was enlisted in great haste, there was no time to make a long tale of it. Yes, this is a Benedictine brother of Pershore, who came on an errand from his abbot. We have been treating with them for a finger-bone of Saint Eadburga, whose relics, as you know, they possess, and this is the brother who was entrusted with bringing it here to us in its reliquary. He delivered it safely some days ago. The night of the first of the month he arrived here, and stayed to witness the offices when we installed it.'

21

'Then how,' demanded Cadfael, gaping, 'did he come to be picked out of the snow and brought back to you naked only a day or two later? You're surely grown somewhat careless with your guests, Leonard!'

'But he left us, Cadfael! The day before yesterday he said he must prepare to leave early in the morning, and be on his way. And as soon as he had breakfasted yesterday he left, and I do assure you, well provided for the first part of his journey. We know no more than you how he came to be stricken down still so close to us, and you see he cannot yet speak, to make all plain. Where he has been between yesterday's dawn and the thick of the night no one knows, but certainly not where he was found, or we should be tolling for him, not trying to heal him.'

'Howbeit, at least you know him. How much do you know of him? He gave you a name?'

The prior hoisted bony shoulders. What does a name tell about a man? 'His name is Elyas. I think, though he never said, not long in the cloister. A taciturn man—in particular, I think, he would not speak of himself. He did eye the weather somewhat anxiously. We thought it natural, since he had to brave the way home, but now I fancy there was more in it than that, for he did say something of a party he had left by Foxwood, coming from Cleobury, some people he encountered there in flight from Worcester, and urged to come here with him for safety, but they would push on over the hills for Shrewsbury. The girl, he said, was resolute, and she called the tune.'

'Girl?' Cadfael stiffened erect, ears pricked. 'There was a girl holding the rein?'

'So it seemed.' Leonard blinked in surprise at such interest in the phenomenon.

'Did he say who else was in her company? Was there a boy spoken of? And a nun in charge of them?' He realised ruefully the folly of any such attitude to this relationship. It was the girl who called the tune!

'No, he never told us more. But I did think he was anxious about them, for you see, the snow came after he reached us, and over those bleak hills . . . He might well wonder.'

'You think he may have gone to seek them? To find assurance they had made the crossing safely, and were on a

22

passable way to Shrewsbury? It would not be so far aside from his way.'

'It could be so,' said Leonard, and was mute, searching Cadfael's face with a worried frown, waiting for enlightenment.

'I wonder, I wonder if he found them—if he was bringing them here for refuge!' He was talking to himself, for the prior was left astray, patiently regarding him. And if he was, thought Cadfael silently, what, in God's name, has become of them now? Their only helper and protector battered senseless and left for dead, and those three, where? But as yet there was no proof that these were the hapless Hugonins and their young nun. Many poor souls, girls among them, had fled from the despoiled cry of Worcester.

Headstrong girls, who called the tune? Well, he had known them crop up in cottage no less than in castle, in croft and toft, and among the soil-bound villein families, too. Women were as various as men.

'Leonard,' he said earnestly, leaning across the table, 'have you had no proclamation from the sheriff about two young things lost from Worcester in the company of a nun of the convent there?'

The prior shook a vague but troubled head. 'I don't recall such a message, no. Are you telling me that these . . . Brother Elyas certainly felt some anxiety. You think these he spoke of may be the ones being sought?'

Cadfael told him the whole of it, their flight, the search for them, the plight of their uncle, threatened with capture and prison if he ventured across the king's borders in quest of them. Leonard listened in growing dismay. 'It could be so, indeed. If this poor brother could but speak!'

'But he did speak. He told you he left them at Foxwood, and they were bent on crossing the hills still towards Shrewsbury. That would mean their venturing clean over the flank of Clee, to Godstoke, where they would be in the lands of Wenlock priory, and in good enough hands.'

'But a bitter, bleak way over,' mourned the prior, aghast. 'And that heavy snow the next night.'

'There's no certainty,' Cadfael reminded him cautiously. 'Barely a suspicion. A quarter of Worcester fled this way to escape the slaughter. Better I should keep watch on this patient of ours than waste time on speculation. For only he can tell us more, and besides, him we already have, he was laid at our doors, and him we must keep. Go to Compline, Leonard, and pray for him, and I'll do as much by his bed. And if he speaks, never fret, I'll be awake enough to catch his drift, for all our sakes.'

In the night the first sudden but infinitesimal change took place. Brother Cadfael was long accustomed to sleeping with one eye open, and both ears. On his low stool beside the bed he drowsed thus, arms folded, head lowered, one elbow braced on the wooden frame of the bed, to quicken to any move. But it was his hearing that pricked him awake to stoop with held breath. For Elyas had just drawn his first deeper, longer, eased breath, that went down through his misused body from throat to stretched feet, groaning at the disturbed pains that everywhere gored him. The horrid snore in his throat had softened, he drew air, painful though it was, down into his midriff hungrily, like a starving man grasping at food. Cadfael saw a great quiver pass over the mangled face and part the swollen lips. The tip of a dry tongue strove to moisten, and shivered and withdrew from pain, but the lips remained parted. The strong teeth unclenched to let out a long, sighing groan.

Cadfael had honeyed wine standing in a jug beside the brazier, to keep warm. He trickled a few drops between the swollen lips, and had the satisfaction of seeing the unconscious face contort in muscular spasm, and the throat labour to swallow. When he touched a finger to the man's lips, again closed, they parted in thirsty response. Drop by drop, patiently, a good portion of the drink went down. Only when response failed at last did Cadfael abandon the process. Cold, oblivious absence had softened gradually into sleep, now that a little warmth had been supplied him both within and without. A few days of lying still, for his wits to settle again right way up in his head, thought Cadfael, and he'll come round and be on his way back to us. But whether he'll remember much of what befell him is another matter. He had known men, after such head injuries, revive to recall every detail of their childhood and past years, but no recollection whatever of recent injury.

He removed the cooling brick from the foot of the bed, fetched a replacement from the kitchen, and sat down to resume his vigil. This was certainly sleep now, but a very uneasy sleep, broken by whimpers and moans, and sudden shudders that passed all down the long body. Once or twice Elyas laboured in evident distress, throat and lips and tongue trying to frame words, but achieving only anguished, indecypherable sounds, or no sounds at all. Cadfael leaned close, to catch the first utterance that should have meaning. But the night passed, and his vigil had brought him nothing coherent.

Perhaps the sounds that measured out the cloistral day were able to reach some quiet core of habit even within the sufferer's disrupted being, for at the note of the bell for Prime he fell suddenly quiet, and his eyelids fluttered and strove to open, but closed again wincingly against even this subdued light. His throat worked, he parted his lips and began to attempt speech. Cadfael leaned close, his ear to the struggling mouth.

'. . . madness . . .' said Elyas, or so Cadfael thought he said. 'Over Clee,' he grieved, 'in such snows . . .' He turned his head on the pillow, and hissed with the pain. 'So young . . . wilful . . . He was lapsing again into a better sleep, his disquiet easing. In a voice thread-fine but suddenly clearly audible: 'The boy would have come with me,' said Brother Elyas.

That was all. He lay once again motionless and mute.

'He has the turn for life,' said Cadfael, when Prior Leonard came in to enquire after the patient as soon as Prime ended, 'but there'll be no hurrying him.' An earnest young brother stood dutifully by to relieve him of his watch. 'When he stirs you may feed him the wine and honey, you'll find he'll take it now. Sit close and mark me any word he says. I doubt if you'll have anything more to do for him, while I get my sleep, but there's a ewer for his use if he needs it. And should he begin to sweat, keep him well covered but bathe his face to give him ease. God willing, he'll sleep. No man can do for him what sleep will do.'

'You're content with him?' asked Leonard anxiously, as they went out together. 'He'll do?'

'He'll do very well, given time and quietness.' Cadfael was yawning. He wanted breakfast first, and a bed after, for all the morning hours. After that, and another look at the dressings on head and ribs, and all the minor hurts that had threatened suppuration, he would have a better idea of how to manage both the nursing of Brother Elyas and the pursuit of the lost children.

'And has he spoken? Any sensible word?' pressed Leonard.

'He has spoken of a boy, and of the madness of attempting to cross the hills in such snows. Yes, I believe he did encounter the Hugonin pair and their nun, and try to bring them into shelter here with him. It was the girl who would go her own way,' said Cadfael, brooding on this unknown chit who willed to venture the hills in both winter and anarchy. 'Young and wilful, he said.' But however mad and troublesome they may be, the innocent cannot be abandoned. 'Feed me,' said Cadfael, returning to first needs, 'and then show me a bed. Leave the absent for later. I'll not quit Brother Elyas as long as he needs me. But I tell you what we may well do, Leonard, if you've a guest in your hall here making for Shrewsbury today. You might charge him to let Hugh Beringar know that we have here what I take to be the first news of the three people he's seeking.'

'That I'll certainly do,' said Prior Leonard, 'for there's a cloth merchant of the town on his way home for the Christmas feast, he'll be off as soon as he's eaten, to get the best of the day. I'll go and deliver him the message this minute, and do you go and get your rest.'

Before night Brother Elyas opened his eyes for the second time, and this time, though the return to light caused him to blink a little, he kept them open, and after a few moments opened them wide in blank wonder, astonished by everything on which they rested. Only when the prior stooped close at Cadfael's shoulder did the brightness of recognition quicken in the sick man's eyes. This face, it seemed, he knew. His lips parted, and a husky whisper emerged, questioning but hopeful:

'Father Prior . . ?'

'Here, brother,' said Leonard soothingly. 'You are here with us, safe in Bromfield. Rest and gather strength, you have been badly hurt, but here you are in shelter, among friends. Trouble for nothing . . . ask for whatever you need.'

'Bromfield . . .' whispered Elyas, frowning. 'I had an errand to that place,' he said, troubled, and tried to raise

26

his head from the pillow. 'The reliquary . . . oh, not lost . . ?'

'You brought it faithfully,' said Leonard. 'It is here on the altar of our church, you kept vigil with us when we installed it. Do you not remember? Your errand was done well. All that was required of you, you performed.'

'But how . . . My head hurts . . .' The sighing voice faded, the dark brows drew together in mingled anxiety and pain, 'What is this weighs on me? How am I come to this?'

They told him, with cautious gentleness, how he had gone forth again from the priory, to make his way home to his own abbey of Pershore, and how he had been brought back broken and battered and abandoned for dead. At the name of Pershore he grasped gladly, there he knew he belonged, and from there he remembered he had set forth to bring Saint Eadburga's finger-bone to Bromfield, avoiding the perilous route by Worcester. Even Bromfield itself came back to him gradually. But of what had befallen him after his departure he knew nothing. Whoever had so misused him, they were gone utterly from his disturbed mind. Cadfael leaned to him, urging gently:

'You did not meet them again? The girl and boy who would press on over the hills to Godstoke? Foolish, but the girl would go, and her young brother could not persuade her . . .'

'What girl and boy were these?' wondered Elyas blankly, and drew his drawn brows more painfully close.

'And a nun—do you not recall a nun who travelled with them?'

He did not. The effort at recall caused him agitation, he dragged at memory and produced only the panic desperation of failure, and in his wanderings state failure was guilt. All manner of undischarged obligations drifted elusive behind his haunted eyes, and could not be captured. Sweat broke on his forehead, and Cadfael wiped it gently away.

'Never fret, but lie still and leave all to God, and under God, to us. Your part was done well, you may take your rest.'

They tended his bodily needs, anointed his wounds and grazes, fed him a broth made from their austere stores of meat for the infirmary, with herbs and oatmeal, read the

27

office with him before bed, and still, by the knotting of his brows, Brother Elyas pursued the memories that fled him and would not be snared. In the night, in the low hours when the spirit either crosses or draws back from the threshold of the world, the sleeper was shaken by recollection and dream together. But his utterances then were broken and mumbled, and so clearly painful to his progress that Cadfael, who had reserved to himself that most perilous watch, bent his energies all to soothing away the torment from his patient's mind, and easing him back into healthful sleep. Cadfael was relieved before dawn, and Elyas slept. The body rallied and healed. The mind wandered and shunned remembrance.

Cadfael slept until noon, and arose to find his patient at rest in wakefulness as he had not been in sleep, very docile, without much pain, and well tended by an elderly brother with long experience of nursing the sick. The day was clear, and the light would last well. Though the frost was unbroken, and without doubt there would be fresh snow in the night, at this hour the sun and the remaining hours of daylight tempted.

'He's well enough cared for,' said Cadfael to the prior. 'I may leave him for a few hours with an easy mind. That horse of mine is rested now, and the ways none so bad until the next fall comes or the wind rises. I'll ride as far as Godstoke, and ask if these truants ever reached there, and whether they've moved on, and by what road. Six days it must be now since he parted from them, at Foxwood you said. If they came safely to the lands of Wenlock priory they may well have made their way either to Wenlock or Shrewsbury by now, and all the coil over them will be done. Then we can all breathe freely.'

3

Godstoke, sunk in its deep, wooded valley between the hills, was held by the priory of Wenlock, a third of the manor farmed in demesne, the rest leased out to life tenants, a prosperous settlement, and well-found in stores and firing for the winter. Once over the bleak hills and into this sheltered place, a party of fugitives could rest and be at ease, and make their way onward at their own pace, moving from manor to manor of the prior's wide-ranging properties.

But these fugitives had never reached Godstoke. The prior's steward was quite certain.

'We got word already they were being sought, and though we had not great call to suppose they would be heading this way, any more than by Ludlow or any other road, I've had enquiry made everywhere. You may take it as sure, brother, that they did not reach us.'

'The last known of them,' said Brother Cadfael, 'was at Foxwood. From Cleobury they were in company with a brother of our order, who urged them to come on with him to Bromfield, but they would continue north over the hills. It seemed to me they must make for you.'

'So I would say also,' agreed the steward. 'But they did not come.'

Cadfael considered. He was not perfectly familiar with

29

these parts, yet he knew them well enough to make his way. If they had not passed here, small profit in searching beyond. And though it would be possible to work backwards along the way they should have taken to reach this place, and look for traces of them between here and Foxwood, that would certainly have to wait for another day. This one was already too far spent. Dusk was closing in faintly, and he had better make his way back by the nearest way.

'Well, keep watch in case some word reaches you. I'm for Bromfield again.' He had come by the most used roads, but they were less than direct, and he had a good eye for country. 'If I make straight south-westerly from here, I take it that's the way the crow flies for Bromfield. How are the tracks?'

'You'll be threading part of Clee Forest if you try it, but keep the sunset a little on your right hand and you'll not go wrong. And the brooks are no stay, nor have been since the frost set in.'

The steward started him off in the direction he should go, and saw him out of the wooded hollow and on to the narrow, straight track between gentle hills, turning his back upon the great, hunched bulk of Brown Clee, and his left shoulder on the grimmer, more rugged shape of Titterstone Clee. The sunlight had long withdrawn, though the sun itself had still some way to sink, and hung in a dull red ball behind veils of thin grey cloud. The inevitable nocturnal snow should not begin for an hour or two yet. The air was very still and very cold.

After a mile he was in the forest. The branches still held up roofs of frozen snow, trailing long icicles where the noon sun had had room to penetrate, and the ground underfoot, deep in leaf-mould and needles, was easy riding. The trees even created a measure of warmth. Clee was a royal forest, but neglected now, as much of England was surely being neglected, left to rot or to be appropriated by opportunist local magnates, while king and empress fought out their battle for the crown. Lonely country, this, and wild, even within ten miles of castle and town. Assarts were few and far between. The beasts of the chase and the beasts of the warren had it for their own domain, but in such a winter even the deer would starve without some judicious nursing from men. Fodder too precious to be wasted by the farmer might still be put out by the lord to ensure the survival of his game in a bad season. Cadfael passed one such store, trampled and spread by the hungry beasts, the snow patterned with their slots all around. The hereditary forester was still minding his duties, no matter which of the two rival rulers claimed his estate.

The sun, seen briefly between the trees, hung very low now, evening had begun to gather like an overhanging cloud, while the ground below still had light enough. Before him the trees drew apart, restoring an hour of the failing day. Someone had carved out an assart, a clearing of narrow garden and field about a low cottage. A man was folding his two or three goats, herding them before him into a wattled enclosure. He looked up alertly at the rustle of crisp snow and frozen leaf under hooves. A sturdy, squat husbandman no more than forty years old, in good brown homespun and leggings of home-tanned leather. He had made a good job of his lonely holding, and stood erect to face the traveller as soon as he had penned his goats. Narrowed eyes surveyed the monastic habit, the tall and vigorous horse, the broad, weathered face beneath the cowl.

'God bless the holding and the holder,' said Cadfael, reining in by the wattle fence.

'God be with you, brother!' His voice was even and deep, but his eyes were wary. 'Whither bound?'

'To Bromfield, friend. Am I going right?'

'True enough to your road. Keep on as you are, and in a half-mile you come to the Hopton brook. Cross it, and bear a little to your left over the two lesser brooks that run into it. After the second the track forks. Bear right, level along the slope, and you'll come out to the road beyond Ludlow, a mile from the priory.'

He did not ask how a Benedictine brother came to be riding this obscure way at such an hour. He did not ask anything. He spread his solid bulk across the gateway of his enclosure like a portcullis, but with courteous face and obliging tongue. It was the eyes that said he had somewhat within to cover from view, and also that he was storing every sight and sound to be delivered faithfully elsewhere. Yet whoever hewed this holding out of the forest could be nothing less than a practical, honest man.

31

'Thanks for your rede,' said Cadfael. 'Now help me with another matter if you can. I am a monk of Shrewsbury, now nursing a brother of our order from Pershore, in the infirmary of Bromfield priory. Our sick brother frets over certain people he met on their way to Shrewsbury from Worcester, in flight from the sacking of the city. They would not turn west with him for Bromfield, they would hold northwards this way. Tell me if you have seen hide or hair of such.' He described them, in doubt of his own intuition until he saw the man cast one swift glance over his shoulder towards his cottage, and again confront him unblinking.

'No such company has come my way in this woodland,' he said steadily. 'And why should they? I'm on the way to nowhere.'

'Travellers in strange country and snow may very well find themselves on the road to nowhere, and lost to anywhere,' said Cadfael. 'You're none so far from Godstoke, where I've already been enquiring. Well, if any or all of these three should come your way, give them the word that they're sought by all the shire and the abbeys of Worcester and Shrewsbury, and when they're found they shall have safe escort wherever they would be. Worcester is re-garrisoned now, and anxious about its strays. Say so, if you meet with them.'

The wary eyes stared him thoughtfully in the face. The man nodded, and said: 'I will say so. If ever I do meet with them.'

He did not move from his place before the gate until Cadfael had shaken his rein and moved on along the track, yet when Cadfael reached the shelter of the trees and turned to look back, the cottager had vanished with some speed into his house, as if he had an errand that would not wait. Cadfael rode on, but at a slow, ambling walk, and once well out of sight, halted and sat listening. The small, cautious sounds of movement behind him were his reward. Someone light-footed and shy was following him, trying at the same time to hurry and to remain unheard. A sly glance over his shoulder afforded him a fleeting glimpse of a blue cloak that whisked aside into cover. He idled, letting the pursuer draw nearer, and then suddenly reined aside and turned to look back openly. All sounds ceased instantly, but the leaning branches of a beech sapling quivered and shed a few flakes of powdery snow.

'You may come forth,' said Cadfael mildly. 'I am a monk of Shrewsbury, no threat to you or any. The goodman told you true.'

The boy stepped out of hiding and stood in the open ride, legs braced well apart, ready to run if he saw fit, or stand his ground sturdily. A small, stocky boy with a round shock-head of brown hair, large unwavering brown eyes, and a formidably firm mouth and chin belying the childish fullness of his cheeks. The bright blue cotte and cloak were somewhat soiled and crumpled now, as if he had slept wild in the woods in them, as perhaps he had, and there was a tear in one knee of the grey hose, but he still wore them with the large assurance of his own nobility. He had a little dagger at his belt, the sheath ornamented with silver, sign enough of his worth to have tempted many a man. He had fallen into good hands at this recent stay, whatever had happened to him earlier.

'He said . . .' The boy advanced a step or two, reassured. 'His name is Thurstan. He and his wife have been good to me. He said that here was one I could trust, a Benedictine brother. He said you have been looking for us.'

'He said truly. For you, I think, must be Yves Hugonin.'

The boy said: 'Yes. And may I come with you to Bromfield?'

'Yves, very heartily you may, and a warm welcome you'll get from all those who are out hunting for you. Since you fled from Worcester your uncle d'Angers is come back from the Holy Land, and reached Gloucester only to hear you were lost, and he's been sending about to have you sought all through this shire. Main glad he'll be to get you back whole and well.'

'My uncle d'Angers?' The boy's face wavered between eagerness and doubt. 'In Gloucester? But . . . but it was men from Gloucester . . .'

'It was, we know, but none of his doing. Never trouble your head over the divisions that keep him from coming himself to find you, nor you nor I can help those. But we're pledged to return you to him safe and sound, and that you may rely on. But the search is for three, and here

33

we are fobbed off with but one. Where are your sister and her governess?'

'I don't know!' It came almost in a wail. The boy's resolute chin shook for a moment, and recovered gallantly. 'I left Sister Hilaria safe at Cleeton, I hope she is safe there still, but what she would do when she found herself alone . . . And my sister . . . My sister is the cause of all this! She went off with her lover, in the night. He came for her, I am sure she sent him word to fetch her away. I tried to follow them, but then the snow came . . .'

Cadfael drew breath in mingled wonder, dismay and relief. Here was at least one of the three safely netted, another might be snug if distracted at Cleeton still, and the third, even if she had committed a great folly, seemed to be in the hands of someone who held her dear, and presumably meant her nothing but good. There might yet be a happy ending to all. But meantime, it bade fair to be a very long and confused story, and here was dusk falling, the rim of the sun already dipped, and several miles to go, and the best thing to be done was to get this one back to Bromfield, and make sure he did not wander away to be lost again.

'Come, let's get you home before night falls on us. Come up before me, your light weight won't worry this fellow. Your foot on mine, so . . .' The boy had to reach high. His hand was firm and eager in Cadfael's, he came up with a spring, and settled himself snugly. His body, at first tensed, relaxed with a great sigh.

'I have thanked Thurstan, and said farewell to him,' he said in a soft, gruff voice, reviewing his own behavior scrupulously. 'I gave him half what was left in my purse, but it was not very much. He said he did not want nor need it, and I was welcome, but I had nothing else to give him, and I could not go and never leave a token.'

'There may be a time, some day, to visit him again,' said Cadfael comfortably. The boy had been well brought up, and felt his status and its obligations. There was much to be said for the monastic education.

'I should like that,' said the child, wriggling himself warmly into the hollow of Cadfael's shoulder. 'I would have given him my dagger, but he said I should need it, and what would he do with such a thing, when he dared not show it for fear of being thought to have stolen it.'

34

He seemed to have put away for the present his worries over the two women he had somehow mislaid in the snow, in his gratitude at being relieved of anxiety on his own account. Thirteen years old, they said he was. He had a right to be glad when someone else took charge of him.

'How long have you been there with them?'

'Four days. Thurstan said I'd best wait until someone trusty came by, for there are stories of footpads about the hills and the woods, and in this snow, if I set out alone, I might get lost again. I was lost, two whole days,' said Yves, staring remembered terrors firmly in the eye. 'I slept in a tree, for fear of wolves.' He was not complaining, rather doing his best not to boast. Well, let him talk, easing his heart of loneliness and fright like a man stretching his feet to a good fire after a dangerous journey. The real story he had to tell could wait until proper attention could be paid to it. If all turned out well, he might be able to point the way to both the missing ladies, but what mattered now was to reach Bromfield before complete darkness fell.

They went briskly wherever the forest thinned and the lingering light showed their way clearly. The first floating flakes of new snow drifted languidly on the air as they came down to the Hopton brook, and crossed it on solid ice, Cadfael lighting down to lead the horse over. From that point they bore somewhat to the left, though veering gradually away from the course of the brook, and came to the first of the little tributaries that flowed down into it, from the long, gentle slope on their right hand. Every stream was still, frozen now for many days. The sun was gone, only an angry glow remained in the west, sullen under leaden greyness. The wind was rising, the snow beginning to sting their faces. Here the forest was broken by scattered holdings and fields, and occasionally a sheep shelter, roughly propped with its back to the wind. Shapes began to dissolve into a mere mottle of shadows, but for fugitive gleams of reflected light from surfaces of ice, and the bluish mounds where untrodden snow had drifted deep.

The second brook, still and silent like the rest, was a shallow, reed-fringed, meandering serpent of silver. The horse disliked the feel of the ice under him, and Cadfael dismounted again to lead him over. The wide, glassy surface shone opaque from every angle, except when looking directly down into it, and Cadfael was watching his own foothold as he crossed, for his boots were worn and smooth. Thus his eye caught, for a moment only, the ghostly pallor beneath the ice to his left, before the horse slithered and recovered, hoisting himself into the snowy grass on the further side.

Cadfael was slow to recognise, slower to believe, what he had seen. Half an hour later, and he would not have been able to see it at all. Fifty paces on, with a thicket of bushes between, he halted, and instead of remounting, as Yves expected, put the bridle into the boy's hands, and said with careful calm: 'Wait a moment for me. No, we need not turn off yet, this is not the place where the tracks divide. Something I noticed there. Wait!'

Yves wondered, but waited obediently, as Cadfael turned back to the frozen brook. The pallor had been no illusion from some stray reflected gleam, it was there fixed and still, embedded in the ice. He went down on his knees to look more closely.

The short hairs rose on his neck. Not a yearling lamb, as he had briefly believed it might be. Longer, more shapely, slender and white. Out of the encasing, glassy stillness a pale, pearly oval stared up at him with open eyes. Small, delicate hands had floated briefly before the frost took hold, and hovered open at her sides, a little up-raised as if in appeal. The white of her body and the white of the torn shift which was all she wore seemed to Cadfael to be smirched by some soiling colour at the breast, but so faintly that too intent staring caused the mark to shift and fade. The face was fragile, delicate, young.

A lamb, after all. A lost ewe-lamb, a lamb of God, stripped and violated and slaughtered. Eighteen years old? It could well be so.

By this token, Ermina Hugonin was at once found and lost.

4

There was nothing to be done here at this hour, alone as he was, and if he lingered, the boy might come to see what kept him so long. He rose from his knees in haste, and went back to where the horse stamped and fidgeted, eager to get back to his stable. The boy was looking round for him curiously, rather than anxiously.

'What was it? Is there something wrong?'

'Nothing to fret you.' Not yet, he thought with a pang, not until you must know. At least let's feed you, and warm you, and reassure you your own life is safe enough, before you need hear word of this. 'I thought I saw a sheep caught in the ice, but I was mistaken.' He mounted, and reached round the boy to take the reins. 'We'd best make haste. We'll have full darkness on us before we reach Bromfield.'

Where the track forked they bore right as they had been instructed, a straight traverse along the slope, easy to follow. The boy's sturdy body grew heavier and softer in Cadfael's arm, the brown head hung sleepy on his shoulder. You at least, thought Cadfael, mute in his anger and grief, we'll put out of harm's way, if we could not save your sister.

'You have not told me your name,' said Yves, yawning. 'I don't know what to call you.'

37

'My name is Cadfael, a Welshman from Trefriw, but now of Shrewsbury abbey. Where, I think, you were bound.'

'Yes, so we were. But Ermina—my sister's name is Ermina—she must always have her own way. I have far more sense than she has! If she'd listened to me we would never have got separated, and we should all have been safe in Shrewsbury by now. I wanted to come to Bromfield with Brother Elyas—you do know about Brother Elyas?—and so did Sister Hilaria, but not Ermina, she had other plans. This is all her fault!'

And small doubt, by now, that that was true, Brother Cadfael reflected wretchedly, clasping the innocent judge who lay warm and confiding in his arm. But surely our little faults do not deserve so crushing a penalty. Without time to reconsider, to repent, to make reparation. Youth destroyed for a folly, when youth should be allowed its follies on the way to maturity and sense.

They were coming down on to the good, trodden road between Ludlow and Bromfield. 'Praise God!' said Cadfael, sighting the torches at the gatehouse, yellow terrestrial stars glowing through a fragile but thickening curtain of snow. 'We are here!'

They rode in at the gate, to be confronted by a scene of unexpected activity in the great Court. The snow within was stamped into intricate patterns of hooves, and about the stables two or three grooms, certainly not of the household, were busy rubbing down horses and leading them to their stalls. Beside the door of the guest-hall Prior Leonard stood in earnest conversation with a lithe young man of middle height, still cloaked and hooded, and his back turned, but it was a back Cadfael knew very well by now. Hugh Beringar had come in person to probe into the first news of the lost Hugonins, and brought, by the look of it, two or three more officers with him.

His ear was as sharp as ever, he turned towards the arrivals and came striding before ever the horse halted. The prior followed, eager and hopeful at sight of two returning where only one went forth.

Cadfael was down by the time they approached, and Yves, dazzled and excited, had recovered from his sleepiness and braced himself to encounter with a nobleman's assurance whoever bore down on him. He set both plump

38

paws to the pommel of the saddle, and vaulted down into the snow. A long way down for his short stature, but he lit like an acrobat, and stretched erect before Beringar's amused and approving eye.

'Make your bow, Yves, to Hugh Beringar, the deputy sheriff of this shire,' said Cadfael. 'And to Prior Leonard of Bromfield, your host here.' And to Hugh, aside, he said fervently, while the boy made his solemn reverences: 'Ask him nothing, yet, get him within!'

Between them they made a reasonable job of it, quick in response to each other from old habit. Yves was soon led away contentedly with Leonard's bony but benevolent hand on his shoulder, to be warmed and fed and made much of before bed. He was young, he would sleep this night. He was cloister-educated, he would stir in response to the bells for office, and find nothing but reassurance, and sleep again heartily.

'For God's sake,' said Cadfael, heaving a great sigh as soon as the boy was safely out of sight, 'come within, somewhere quiet, where we can talk. I never expected you here in person, seeing the ties you have at home . . .'
Beringar had taken him companionably by the arm, and was hurrying him into the doorway of the prior's lodging, and eyeing him intently along his shoulder as they shook the snow from boots and cloaks on the threshold. 'We had but a first breath of news of our quarry, I never thought it could tear you away, though thanks be, it did!'

'I've left all in very good order behind me,' said Hugh. He had come to meet his friend expecting a glow of good news, and found himself confronted with a gravity that promised little but trouble. 'If you have burdens on your mind here, Cadfael, at least you may be easy about affairs in Shrewsbury. The very day you left us, our son was born, a fine, lusty lad as yellow-haired as his mother, and the pair of them flourishing. And for good measure, the Worcester girl has given her man a son, too, only one day after. The house is full of exultant women, and no one is going to miss me for these few days.'

'Oh, Hugh, the best of news! I'm happy for you both.' It was right and fitting, Cadfael thought, a life emerging in defiance of a death. 'And all went well for her? She had not too hard a time of it?'

'Oh, Aline has the gift! She's too innocent to under-

39

stand that there can be pain in a thing so joyful as birth, so she felt none. Faith, even if I hadn't had this errand to occupy me, I was as near being elbowed out of my own house as makes no matter. Your prior's message came very aptly. I have three men here with me, and twenty-two more I have quartered on Josce de Dinan in Ludlow castle, to be at hand if I need them, and to give him a salutary jolt if he really is in two minds about changing sides. He cannot be in any doubt now that I have my eye on him. And now,' said Hugh, drawing up a chair to the fire in the prior's parlour, 'you owe me a story, I fancy, and for my life I can't tell what to expect of it. Here you come riding in with the boy we've been hunting on your saddle-bow, and yet a face on you as bleak as the sky, when you should be beaming. And not a word to be got out of you until he was safe out of earshot. Where did you find him?'

Cadfael sat back with a small groan of weariness and stiffness after his chill ride. There was no longer any urgent need for action. In the night they would never find the place, especially now that the wind was high and the fresh snow altering the landscape on all sides, blowing hillsides naked, filling in hollows, burying what yesterday had uncovered. He could afford to sit still and feel the warmth of the fire on his legs, and tell what he had to tell at his own pace, since there was nothing to be done about it until daylight.

'In an assart in Clee Forest, in shelter with a decent cottar and his wife, who would not let him take his chance alone through the woods until some trustworthy traveller came by to bear him company. Me they considered fit for the task, and he came with me willingly enough.'

'But he was there alone? A pity,' said Hugh with a wry grimace, 'that you did not find his sister, too, while you were about it.'

'I am only too afraid,' said Cadfael, the warmth of the fire heavy on his eyelids, 'that I have indeed found her.'

The silence lasted a shorter time than it seemed. The significance of that last utterance there was no mistaking.

'Dead?' asked Hugh bluntly.

'And cold.' Cold as ice, encased in ice. The first bitter frost had provided her a glassy coffin, preserving her flesh immaculate and unchanged to accuse her destroyer.

'Tell me,' said Hugh, intent and still.

Cadfael told him. The whole story would have to be told again when Prior Leonard came, for he, too, must help to stand between the boy and too early and too sudden knowledge of his loss. But in the meantime it was a relief to heave the burden from his heart, and know that this was now Hugh's responsibility as much as his own.

'Can you find the place again?'

'By daylight, yes, I'll find it. In darkness, no use trying. It will be a fearful thing . . . We shall have to take axes to hew her out of the ice, unless the thaw comes.' It was a forlorn hope, there was no possible sigh of a thaw.

'That we'll face when we come to it,' said Hugh sombrely. 'Tonight we'd best get the boy's story out of him, and see if we can gather from it how she ever came where you happened on her. And where, in heaven's name, is the nun who fled with her?'

'According to Yves, he left her in Cleeton, safe enough. And the girl—poor fool!—he says went off with a lover. But I took him no further into matters, it was towards the end of the day, and the most urgent thing was to get one, at least, into safety.'

'True enough, and you did well. We'll wait for the prior, and until the boy's fed and warmed and easy. Then between us we'll hope to get out of him all he knows, and more, perhaps, than he realises he knows, without betraying that he's lost a sister. Though he'll have to learn it soon or late,' said Hugh unhappily. 'Who else knows the poor girl's face?'

'But not tonight. Let him sleep soundly tonight. Time enough,' said Cadfael heavily, 'when we've brought her in and made her as comely as may be, before he need see her.'

Supper and security had done much for Yves, and his own natural resilience had done even more. He sat in the prior's parlour before Compline, face to face with Hugh Beringar, and with Prior Leonard and Brother Cadfael in watchful attendance, and told his story with bluntness and brevity.

'She is very *brave*,' he said judicially, giving his sister her due, 'but very obstinate and self-willed. All the way from Worcester I did feel she had something up her sleeve, and was taking advantage of having to run away.

41

We had to go round-about at first, and slowly, because there were bands of soldiers roaming even miles from the town, so it took us a long time to get safely to Cleobury, and there we stayed one night, and that was the night Brother Elyas was there, too, and he came with us as far as Foxwood, and wanted us to come with him into Bromfield for safety, and I wanted that, too, and so did Sister Hilaria. From here we could have got an escort into Shrewsbury, and it would not have been a much longer way. But Ermina would not have it! She must always have her own way, and she *would* go on over the hills to Godstoke. No use my arguing, she never listens, she claims that being the elder makes her the wiser. And if we others had gone with Brother Elyas she would still have gone on over the hills alone, so what could we do but go with her?' He blew out his lips in a disgusted breath.

'Certainly you could not leave her,' agreed Beringar reasonably. 'So you went on, to spend the next night at Cleeton?'

'It's close by Cleeton, a solitary holding. Ermina had a nurse once who married a tenant of that manor, so we knew we could get a bed there. The man's name is John Druel. We got there in the afternoon, and I remembered afterwards that Ermina was talking apart with the son of the house, and then he went away, and we didn't see him again until evening. I never thought of it then, but now I'm sure she sent him with a message. That was what she intended all along. For a man came late in the evening, with horses, and took her away. I heard the stir, and I got up and looked out . . . Two horses there were, and he was just helping her up into the saddle . . .'

'He?' said Hugh. 'You knew him?'

'Not his name, but I do remember him. When my father was alive he used to visit sometimes, if there was hunting, or for Christmas or Easter. Many guests used to come, we always had company. He must be son or nephew to one of my father's friends. I never paid him much attention, nor he never noticed me, I was too young. But I do remember his face, and I think . . . I *think* he has been visiting Ermina now and then in Worcester.'

If he had, they must have been very decorous visits, with a sponsoring sister always in attendance.

'You think she sent him word to come and fetch her?' asked Hugh. 'This was no abduction? She went willingly?'

'She went *gaily!*' Yves asserted indignantly. 'I heard her laughing. Yes, she sent for him, and he came. And that was why she *would go* that way, for he must have a manor close by, and she knew she could whistle him to her. She will have a great dower,' said the baron's heir solemnly, his round, childish cheeks flushing red with outrage. 'And my sister would never endure to have her marriage made for her in the becoming way, if it went against *her* choice. I never knew a rule she would not break, shamelessly . . .'

His chin shook, a weakness instantly and ruthlessly suppressed. All the arrogant pride of all the feudal houses of Anjou and England in this small package, and he loved as much as he hated her, or more, and never, never must he see her mute and violated and stripped to her shift.

Hugh took up the questioning with considerate calm. 'And what did you do?' The jolt back into facts was salutary.

'No one else had heard,' said Yves, rallying, 'unless it was the boy who carried her message, and he had surely been told *not* to hear anything. I was still dressed, there being only one bed, which the woman had, so I rushed out to try and stop them. Older she may be, but *I* am my father's heir! I am the head of our family now.'

'But afoot,' said Hugh, pricking him back to the real and sorry situation, 'you could hardly keep their pace. And they were away before you could hale them back to answer to you.'

'No, I couldn't keep up, but I could follow. It had begun to snow, they left tracks, and I knew they could not be going very far. Far enough to lose me!' he owned, and bit a lip that did not quite know whether to curl up or down. 'I followed as long as I could by their tracks, and it was uphill, and the wind rose, and there was so much snow the tracks were soon covered. I couldn't find the way forward or back. I tried to keep what I thought was the direction they'd taken, but I don't know how much I may have wandered, or where I went. I was quite lost. All night I was in the forest, and the second night Thurstan found me and took me home with him. Brother Cadfael knows. Thurstan said there were outlaws abroad, and I should stay

43

with him until some safe traveller came by. And so I did. And now I don't know,' he said, visibly sinking into his proper years, 'where Ermina went with her lover, or what has become of Sister Hilaria. She would wake to find the two of us gone, and I don't know what she would do. But she was with John and his wife, they surely wouldn't let her come to harm.'

'This man who took your sister away,' pressed Beringar. 'You don't know his name, but you do remember he was acceptable in your father's house. If he has a manor in the hills, within easy reach of Cleeton, no doubt we can trace him. I take it he might, had your father lived, have been a possible suitor for your sister, even in a more approved fashion?'

'Oh, yes,' said the boy seriously, 'I think he well might. There were any number of young men used to come, and Ermina, even when she was only fourteen or fifteen, would ride and hunt with the best of them. They were all men of substance, or heirs to good estates. I never noticed which of them she favoured.' He would have been playing with toy warriors and falling off his first pony then, uninterested in sisters and their admirers. 'This one is very handsome,' he said generously. 'Much fairer than me. And taller than you, sir.' That would not make him a rarity, Beringar's modest length of steel and sinew had been under-estimated by many a man to his cost. 'I think he must be about twenty-five or six. But his name I don't know. There were so many came visiting to us.'

'Now there is one more thing,' said Cadfael, 'in which Yves may be able to help us, if I may keep him for his bed a few minutes more. You know, Yves, you spoke of Brother Elyas, who left you at Foxwood?'

Yves nodded, attentive and wondering.

'Brother Elyas is here in the infirmary. After leaving for home, his errand done, he was attacked by footpads in the night and badly hurt, and the countrymen who found him brought him here to be cared for. I am sure he is on the mend now, but he has not been able to tell us anything about what happened to him. He has no memory of these recent days, only in his sleep he seems to struggle with some half-recalled distress. Waking, his mind is blank, but in sleep he has mentioned you, though not by name. The boy would have gone with me, he said. Now if he

44

claps eyes on you, safe and well, it may be the sight will jog his memory. Will you try it with me?'

Yves rose willingly, if somewhat apprehensively, looking to Beringar for confirmation that he had done all that was required of him here. 'I am sorry he has come to harm. He was kind . . . Yes, whatever I can do for him . . .'

On the way to the sickroom, with no other witness by, he slipped his hand thankfully, like an awed child, into Brother Cadfael's comfortable clasp, and clung tightly.

'You mustn't mind that he is bruised and disfigured. All that will pass, I promise you.'

Brother Elyas was lying mute and still, while a young brother read to him from the life of Saint Remigius. His bruises and distortions were already subsiding, he seemed free from pain, he had taken food during the day, and at the office bell his lips would move soundlessly on the words of the liturgy. But his open eyes dwelt unrecognisingly upon the boy who entered, and wandered away again languidly into the shadowy corners of the room. Yves crept to the bedside on tiptoe, great-eyed.

'Brother Elyas, here is Yves come to see you. You remember Yves? The boy you met at Cleobury, and parted from at Foxwood.'

No, nothing, nothing but the faint tremor of desperate anxiety troubling the patient face. Yves ventured close, and timidly laid his hand over the long, lax hand that lay upon the covers, but it remained chill and unresponsive under his touch.

'I am sorry you have been hurt. We walked together those few miles, I wish we had kept your company all the way . . .'

Brother Elyas stared and quivered, shaking his head helplessly.

'No, let him be,' said Cadfael, sighing. 'If we press him he grows agitated. No matter, he has time. Only let his body revive as it is doing, and memory can wait. It was worth the trying, but he is not ready for us yet. Come, you're dropping with sleep, let's get you safely into your bed.'

They arose at dawn, Cadfael and Hugh and his men, and went out into a world which had again changed its shape in the night, hillocks levelled and hollows filled in, and a spume of fine snow waving like a languid plume from every crest, in the subsiding winds. They took axes with them, and a litter of leather thongs strung between two poles, and a linen cloth to cover her, and they went in dour silence, none of them with anything to say until words were to the point for the grim work in hand. The fall had stopped at the coming of daylight, as it had now ever since that first night when Yves had set off doggedly to trail his errant sister. Iron frost had begun the next night, and that same night some nocturnal beast had ravished and murdered the girl they went out now to seek, for the ice had taken her to itself very shortly after she had been put into an already congealing stream. Of that Cadfael was certain.

They found her, after some questing and probing in new snow, swept the fresh fall from the ice, and looked down upon her, a girl in a mirror, a girl spun from glass.

'Good God!' said Hugh in awe. 'She's younger than the boy!' So slight, so childlike, did the shadowy form appear.

But they were there, perforce, to break her rest and take her away for Christian burial, though it seemed almost a violation to shatter the smoothness of the ice that encased her. They did it with care, well aside from the delicate, imprisoned flesh, and it proved hard work enough. For all the bite of the frost, they were sweating when they hoisted out heavily the girl and her cold coffin, laid her like a piece of statuary in the thongs of the litter, covered her with the linen cloth, and carried her slowly back to Bromfield. Not a drop fell from the ice until they had it stowed privately in the chill, bare mortuary of the priory. Then the glittering edges began to soften and slide, and drip into the channel where the water flowed away from the washing of the dead.

The girl lay remote and pale within her lucid shroud, and yet grew steadily more human and closer to life, to pain and pity and violence, and all the mortal lot of mankind. Cadfael dared not leave the place for long, because the boy Yves was now up and active, and inquisitive about everything, and no one could guess where he would appear next. He was well brought up, and his manners were charming, but with his inbred conviction of privilege

46

and his very proper thirteen-year-old energy, he might
yet prove a hazard.

It was past ten, and High Mass in progress, when the
shell of ice had dwindled so far that the girl began to
emerge, the tips of thin, pale fingers and stretched toes,
her nose, as yet only a minute pearl, and the first curling
strands of hair, a fine lace on either side her forehead. It
was those curls that first caught Cadfael's acute attention. For they were short. He wound a few fine threads on
his finger, and they made but a turn and a half. And they
were no darker than dark gold, and would be even fairer
as they dried. Then he bent to the calm stare of her open
eyes, still thinly veiled with ice. Their colour seemed to
him the soft, dim purple of irises, or the darkest grey of
lavender flowers.

The face emerged as Mass ended. After the air touched
her, bruises began to darken on cheek and mouth. The
tips of her small breasts broke the glaze over them. And
now Cadfael could see clearly the smear that darkened
her flesh and her linen there, on the right side, a reddish
mark like a graze, faintly mottled from shoulder to
breast. He knew the traces of blood. The ice had taken
her before the stilling water could wash the stain away.
Now it might pale as the remaining ice thawed, but he
would know how it had lain, and where to look for the
source.

Well before noon she was freed of her shell, and soften-
ing into his hands, slender and young, her small, shapely
head covered all over with an aureole of short bronze
curls, like an angel in an Annunciation. Cadfael went to
fetch Prior Leonard, and they cared for her together, not
yet to wash her body, not until Hugh Beringar had
viewed it, but to compose her worthily in her everlasting
stillness. To the throat they covered her with a linen
sheet, and made her ready to be seen.

Hugh came, and stood by her silently. Eighteen could
well be her age, so white and slim and tranquil, gone far
beyond them. And beautiful, as reported? Yes, that she
was. But was this the dark, headstrong, spoiled daughter
of the nobility, who had insisted on her own way in despite of the times, the winter, the war and all?

'Look!' said Cadfael, and turned back the linen to show
the crumpled folds of her shift, just as they had emerged

from the ice. The dull, reddish smear speckled her right shoulder, the edge of her shift, and the creases over her right breast.

'Stabbed?' said Hugh, looking up into Cadfael's face.

'There is no wound. See now!' He drew down the linen and showed the flesh beneath. Only a smudge or two showed on her pale skin. He wiped them away, and she shone white without blemish. 'Certainly not stabbed. The night frost that took her closed in very quickly, and preserved these marks, faint as they are. But she did not bleed. Or if she did,' he added bleakly, 'it was not from knife-wounds, and not there. More likely she fought him—him or them, such wolves hunt happiest in packs!—and drew blood. A clawed face, it might be, or a hand or wrist as she tried to force him off. Bear it in mind, Hugh, as I will also.' He covered her again reverently. The alabaster face looked up from veiled eyes into the vault, supremely unmoved, and her head of clipped curls was beginning to shine like a halo as it dried.

'She begins to bruise,' said Hugh, and drew a fingertip over her cheekbone and down to the faint discolorations round her lips. 'But her throat is unmarked. She was not strangled.'

'Smothered, surely, in the act of ravishment.'

They were all three so intent upon the dead girl that they had not heard the footsteps that approached the closed door of the room, and even had they been listening, the footsteps were light enough to be missed, though they came briskly and without conceal. The first they knew of the boy's coming was the white burst of reflected light from the snow, as the door was opened wide to the wall, and Yves marched over the threshold with the innocent boldness of his kind. No creeping ingratiatingly through a narrow chink for him, nothing he did was done by half-measures. The abruptness with which they all whirled upon him, and their frowning consternation gave him sharp pause and mild offence. Both Hugh and Prior Leonard stepped quickly between him and the trestle on which the body lay.

'You should not be here, child,' said the prior, flustered.

'Why should I not, Father? No one has told me I should be at fault. I was looking for Brother Cadfael.'

'Brother Cadfael will come out to you in a little while. Go back to the guest-hall and wait for him there . . .'

48

It was late to ward him off, he had seen, beyond the sheltering shoulders, enough to tell him what lay behind. The linen sheet, quickly drawn up, the unmistakable shape, and one glimpse of short, bright hair where the linen, too hastily drawn, had folded back on itself. His face grew still and wary, his eyes large, and his tongue was silenced.

The prior laid a hand gently on his shoulder and made to turn him back to the doorway. 'Come, you and I will go together. Whatever is to be told, you shall hear later, but leave it now.'

Yves stood his ground, and went on staring.

'No,' said Cadfael unexpectedly, 'let him come.' He came out from behind the trestle, and took a step or two towards the boy. 'Yves, you are a sensible man, no need to pretend to you, after your travels, that violence and danger and cruelty do not exist, and men do not die. We have here a dead body, not known to us. I would have you look at it, if you will, and say if you know this face. You need not fear anything ill to see.'

The boy drew near steadily and with set face, and eyed the shrouded form with nothing worse than awe. Doubtful if it had ever entered his head, thought Cadfael, that this might be his sister, or indeed any woman. He had seen the dilated eyes fix on the short, curling hair; it was a young man Yves expected. Nevertheless, Cadfael would have approached this somewhat differently if he had not been certain already, in his own mind, that this dead girl, whoever she might be, was not Ermina Hugonin. Beyond that he had only a pitiful suspicion. But Yves would know.

He drew down the sheet from her face. The boy's hands, clenched together before him, tightened abruptly. He drew in breath hard, but made no other sound for a long moment. He shook a little, but not much. The wide-eyed stare he raised to Cadfael's questioning face was one of shocked bewilderment, almost of disbelief.

'But how is this possible? I thought . . . I don't understand! She . . .' He gave up, shaking his head violently, and hung over her again in fascinated pity and wonder. 'I do know her, of course I do, but how *can* she be here, and dead? This is Sister Hilaria, who came with us from Worcester.'

49

5

Between them they coaxed and shooed him away across the snowy court. Yves went still in his daze, frowning helplessly over this sudden and inexplicable reappearance in another place of someone he had left safe under a friendly roof some miles away. He was too shaken and puzzled at first to realise fully the meaning of what he had seen, but halfway to the guest-hall it hit him like a blow on the head. He baulked, gulped breath in a great sob, and startled himself, if no one else, by bursting into tears. Prior Leonard would have clucked over him like a dismayed hen, but Cadfael clapped him briskly on the shoulder, and said practically:

'Bear up, my heart, for we're going to need you. We have a malefactor to trace now, and a wrong to avenge, and who but you can lead us straight to the place where you left her? Where else should we start?'

The fit passed as abruptly as it had begun. Yves scrubbed at his smudged cheeks hastily with his sleeve, and looked round alertly enough to see what he could read in Hugh Beringar's face. In Hugh the authority lay. The role of the cloistered was to shelter and counsel and offer prayers, but justice and law were the business of the sheriff. Yves was not a baron's heir for nothing, he knew all about the hierarchies.

50

'That's true, I can take you straight from Foxwood to John Druel's holding, it lies higher than Cleeton village.' He caught eagerly at Hugh's sleeve, wise enough to ask nicely instead of demanding. '*May* I go with you and show the way?'

'You may, if you'll stay close and do all as you're bidden.' Hugh was already committed, Cadfael had seen to that. But far better for the boy to be out in men's company, and active, than to sit fretting here alone. 'We'll find you a pony your size. Run, then, get your cloak and come after us to the stables.'

Yves ran, restored by the prospect of doing something to the purpose. Beringar looked after him thoughtfully. 'Go with him, Father Prior, if you will, see that he has some food with him, for it may be a long day, and no matter how large a dinner he's eaten half an hour ago, he'll be hungry before night.' And to Cadfael he said, as they turned together towards the stables: 'You, I know, will do whatever you fancy doing, and I'm always glad of your company, if your charges, live and dead, can spare you. But you've had some hard riding these last days . . .'

'For an ageing man,' said Cadfael.

'As well I did not say so! I doubt you could outlast me, for all your great burden of years. What of Brother Elyas, though?'

'He needs no more from me, now, than a visit or two each day, to see that nothing's turned back for him and gone amiss. His body is recovering well. And as for the part of his mind that's astray, my being here won't cure it. It will come back of itself one day, or it will cease to be missed. He's well looked after. As *she* was not!' he said sadly.

'How did you know,' asked Hugh, 'that it could not be the child's sister?'

'The cropped hair, first. A month now since they left Worcester, long enough to provide her that halo we have seen. Why should the other girl clip her locks? And then, the colouring. Ermina, so Herward said, is almost black of hair and eye, darker brown than her brother. So is not this lady. And they did say, as I remember, the nun was also young, no more than five and twenty or so. No, I was sure he was safe from that worst threat. Thus far!' said Cadfael soberly. 'Now we have to find her, and make sure

51

he never shall have to uncover another known face and set a name to it. I have the same obligations as you, and I'm coming with you.'

'Go get yourself booted and ready, then,' said Hugh, without surprise, 'and I'll saddle you one of my own remounts. I came well prepared for any tangles you might get me into. I know you of old.'

To Foxwood was a fairly easy ride, being a used highway, but from Foxwood they climbed by even higher ways, and on tracks more broken and steep. The vast flank of Titterstone Clee rose here to a bleak plateau, with the highest ground towering over them on the left hand, in cloud that dropped lower as the afternoon passed its peak. Yves rode close at Hugh's side, intent and important.

'We can leave the village away on our right, the holding lies above here. Over this ridge there's a bowl of fields John has, and a sheep-pen up the hill.'

Hugh reined in suddenly, and sat with head raised, sniffing the air with stretched nostrils. 'Are you getting the same waft I have in my nose? What should a husbandman be burning at this end of the year?'

The faint but ominous stink hung in the air, stirred by a rising wind. One of the men-at-arms at Beringar's back said with certainty: 'Three or four days old, and snowed over, but I smell timber.'

Hugh spurred forward up the climbing track, between bushes banked with snow, and up to the crest where the ground declined into the hollow. In the sheltered bowl trees grew, providing a wind-break for byre and barn and house, and partly screening the holding from view. They could see the stone walls of the sheep-pen on the rising ground beyond, but not until they had wound their way through the first belt of trees did John Druel's tenant-farm reveal itself to their appalled sight. Yves uttered a muted howl of dismay, and reached to clutch at Brother Cadfael's arm.

The corner-posts of blackened buildings stood stark out of the drifts of snow, the timbers of roof and barn, what remained of them, jutted in charred ruin where they had fallen. A desolation in which nothing moved, nothing lived, even the near-by trees shrivelled and brown. The

Druel homestead was emptied of livestock, stores and people, and burned to the ground.

They threaded the forlorn wreckage in grim silence. Hugh's eyes intent on every detail. The iron frost had prevented worse stinks than burning, for in the littered yard they found the hacked bodies of two of the household dogs. Though some two or three fresh falls of snow had covered the traces since the holocaust, it seemed that a party of raiders at least ten or twelve strong had committed this outrage, driving off the sheep and the household cow, emptying the barn, and probably the house, too, of anything portable, stringing the fowls together by the legs, for scattered feathers still blew about the ground and clung to the blackened beams.

Hugh dismounted, and clambered in among the wreckage of the house and barns. His men were quartering all the ground within and without the enclosing wall, probing the drifts.

'They've killed them,' said Yves in a small, hollow voice. 'John and his wife, and Peter, and the shepherd— killed them all, or carried them off, as they carried off Sister Hilaria.'

'Hush!' said Cadfael. 'Never jump to meet the worst until you've looked about you well. You know what they're looking for?' The searchers were turning to exchange looks and shrugs, and drawing together again to the yard. 'Bodies! And they've found none. Only the dogs, poor creatures. They did their proper work, and gave the alarm. Now we'd best hope they gave it in time.'

Hugh came picking his way back from the barn, beating soiled palms together. 'No dead here to find. Either they had warning enough to run for it, or they've been dragged off with the raiders. And I doubt if masterless men living wild would bother with captives. Kill they might, but take prisoners, of this simple kind, that I doubt. But I wonder which way they came? As we did, or by tracks of their own, along the hillside here above? If there were no more than ten of them, they'd keep to their measure, and the village might be too strong to tempt them.'

'There was one sheep slaughtered by the fold,' said his sergeant, back from the hillside. 'There's a traverse comes along the slope there, that might be their path if

53

they wanted to avoid Cleeton and pick off some meat less well defended.'

'Then Druel may have got his family away towards the village.' Hugh pondered, frowning at the drifts that had covered all traces of coming and going of men and beasts. 'If the dogs gave tongue for the sheep, there may have been time. Let's at least go and ask in the village what they know of it. We may yet find them all alive,' he said, clapping Yves reassuringly on the shoulder, 'even if they've lost their home and goods.'

'But not Sister Hilaria,' said Yves, clinging to a quarrel which had become his own, and bitterly felt. 'If they could run away in time, why could they not save Sister Hilaria?'

'That you shall ask them, if by God's grace we do find them. I do not forget Sister Hilaria. Come, we've found all we are going to find here.'

'One small thing,' said Cadfael. 'When you heard the horses, Yves, in the dark, and ran out to try to follow your sister, which way did they lead you from here?'

Yves turned to view the sorry remains of the house from which he had run. 'To the right, there, behind the house. There's a little stream comes down, it was not frozen then—they started up the slope beside it. Not towards the top of the hills, but climbing round the flank.'

'Good! That direction we may try, another day. I'm done, Hugh, we can go.'

They mounted and turned back by the way they had come, out of the desolation and ruin of the hollow, over the ridge between the trees, and down the track towards the village of Cleeton. A hard place, bleak to farm, meagre to crop, but good for sheep, the rangy upland sheep that brought the leanest meat but the longest fleeces. Across the uphill edge of the settlement there was a crude but solid stockade, and someone was on the watch for strangers arriving, for a whistle went before them into the huddle of horses, shrill and piercing. By the time they rode in there were three or four sturdy fellows on hand to receive them. Hugh smiled. Outlaws living wild, unless they had considerable numbers and sufficient arms, might be wise to fight shy of Cleeton.

He gave them good-day and made himself known. Doubtful if men in isolated places hoped much from the king's protection, or the empress's either, but a county sheriff did offer hope of his being on their side in the fight to survive. They brought their reeve, and answered questions eagerly. Yes, they knew of the destruction of John Druel's holding, and yes, John was safe here, sheltered and fed by the village, at least alive if he had lost everything but life. And his wife and son with him, and the shepherd who laboured for him, all saved. A long-legged boy ran eagerly to bring Druel to answer for himself.

At sight of the lean, wiry husbandman approaching. Yves scrambled down from his saddle and ran to meet him, incoherent in his relief. The man came up with an arm about the boy's shoulders.

'My lord, he says you've been up there . . . where my house was. God knows how grateful I am for the kindness here, that won't let us starve when all our goods and gear are gone, but what's to become of us poor souls that work hard to make a living, if it's to be clawed away in a night, and the roof burned over us? It's hard to live solitary in the hills,' he said roundly, 'at best. But outlawry the like of this we never thought to see.'

'Friend,' said Beringar ruefully, 'you may take it I never looked for it, either. Reparation for your losses I cannot offer, but some of what was yours may still be recovered, if we can trace the raiders who took it from you. The boy, here, lodged with you several nights since, and his sister with him . . .'

'And vanished from us in the night,' said John, and gave Yves a disapproving frown.

'That we know, he has told us, and he, at least, had sound reasons, and took his own grave risks. But what we need from you is some account of this attack that fell upon you . . . when?'

'Two nights after the lady and the lad fled us. The night of the fourth of the month, it was, but very late, towards dawn. We woke to hear the dogs going mad, and rushed out thinking there might be wolves, in such hard weather. For the dogs were chained, d'you see?—and wolves they were, but of the two-legged kind! Once out, we could hear the sheep bellowing up the hill and see torches up there. Then they began to come bounding down the slope, knowing the dogs had given the alarm. I don't know how many men, there might have been a dozen or more. We could not stand, we could only run. From the ridge there we saw the barn take fire. The wind was wild, we knew it must all burn out. And here we are, master, bereft, to make a new start from villeinry, if there's a yardland to be had under any lord. But with our lives, thanks be to God!'

'So they came first to your sheep-fold,' said Hugh. 'From which direction along that slope?'

'From the south,' said John at once, 'but not from the road—higher on the hill. They came down at us.'

'And you have no notion who they may be, or from where? You've had no rumour beforehand of outlaws setting up anywhere near?'

No, there had been no warning until then. It had come out of the blue, between midnight of the fourth, and pre-dawn of the fifth.

'One more question,' said Hugh. 'Since you brought off your family with their lives, what became of the nun of Worcester who lodged with you the night of the second, along with this young man and his sister? That they left you that night we know. What of the nun?'

'Why, she was well out of it,' said Druel thankfully. 'I had not her on my heart that night of the burning. She was gone, the afternoon before. Rather late it was for the daylight, but not too far gone. And a safe escort along the way, I reckoned she would do well enough. In a sad, distracted way she'd been, the poor girl, when she found she'd been left alone, but she did not know where to look for her chicks, and neither did we, and what was she to do?'

'Someone came for her?' asked Hugh.

'A Benedictine brother. She knew him, he had walked a part of the way with them before, and urged them to go with him to Bromfield, she said. So he urged then, and when she told him how she was forsaken, he said all the more she should put herself and her trouble into the hands of others, who would search for her charges for her, and keep her safe until they were found. He'd had to make his way here from Foxwood, asking after her,' said John, making allowance for the waning of the day when he had reached them. 'I never saw woman so thankful to have a friend take her in care. She went with him, and I make no doubt she came safe to Bromfield.'

Yves stood dumb. 'She came,' said Hugh drily, rather

56

to himself than to any other. Safe? Yes, take it as large as words will hold, yes, she came safe. Sinless, conscientious, brave, who at this moment was safer than Sister Hilaria, an innocent gone straight to God?

'A strange thing followed, though,' said Druel, 'for the next day, while we were here telling our tale, and the good folk making room for us in their homes, like Christians as they are, there came a young man afoot, up from the road by the proper way, and asked after just such a party as we had housed. Had any here news, he said, of a young nun of Worcester, in company with two young gentlefolk, brother and sister, making towards Shrewsbury. We were full of our own troubles, but we told him all we knew, and how they were all gone from us before ever this evil befell. And he listened and went away. Up to the wreck of my holding, first, but after that I cannot tell where.'

'A stranger to all here?' asked Hugh, looking round the circle that had gathered, for by then the women had come forth, and hung attentive on the outskirts.

'Never seen before,' said the reeve emphatically.

'What manner of man, then?'

'Why, by his dress husbandman or shepherd like any of us here, a brown homespun man. Not so much as thirty years old, nearer five or six and twenty. Bigger than your lordship, but built like you, light and long. And dark, a black-rimmed eye on him with a yellow glint, like a hawk. And black hair under his hood.'

The women had drawn closer in silence, quiet-eyed and prick-eared. Their interest in the stranger was all the plainer because not one of them voiced it, or volunteered any detail concerning him. Whoever he was, he had made an impression upon the women of Cleeton, and they did not mean to miss anything they could glean about him, or surrender anything they had already gleaned.

'Dark-skinned,' said Druel, 'and beaked like a hawk, too. A very comely man.' Yes, so the attentive eyes of the women said. 'There was something a thought slow about his speech, now I come to recall . . .'

Hugh took him up alertly on that. 'As though he were not at home in the common English?'

John had not thought of that for himself; he considered

57

it stolidly. 'It might be that. Or as if he had a small stumble of the tongue, like.'

Well, if English was not his proper tongue, what was? Welsh? Easily possible here along the borders, but what would a Welshman be doing asking after the fugitives from Worcester? Angevin, then? Ah, that was another matter.

'If ever you should hear or see more of him,' said Hugh, 'send me word into Ludlow or Bromfield, and you shall not be losers. And for you, friend, let's own honestly there's little chance of recovering all or most of your losses, but some of your stock we may yet win back for you, if we can trace these outlaws to their lair. We'll do our best to that end, be sure.'

He wheeled his horse, and led the way towards the downward track, the others following, but he did not hurry, for one of the young women had drawn off in that direction, and was eyeing him meaningly over her shoulder. As Hugh came by she closed alongside, and laid a hand to his stirrup-leather. She knew what she was about, she had moved far enough to be out of earshot of the village.

'My lord . . .' She looked up at him with sharp blue eyes, and spoke in a purposeful undertone. 'One more thing I can tell you about the dark man, that no one else saw. I said no word, for fear they would close up against him if they knew. He was a very well-looking man, I trusted him, even if he was not what he seemed . . .'

'In what particular?' asked Hugh, just as quietly.

'He kept his cloak close about him, my lord, and in the cold that was no marvel. But when he went away I followed a little, and I saw how the folds hung at his left side. Country lad or no, he wore a sword.'

'So they went from here together,' said Yves, as they rode down towards the highroad, where they might make haste if they were to use the remainder of the daylight. He had been very silent, struggling with revelations that seemed only to make the pattern of events more complex and entangled. 'He came back to look for us all, and found only Sister Hilaria. It was evening already, they would be caught in the darkness and the snow. And these same rob-

58

bers and murderers who have ruined poor John must have attacked them, and left them both for dead.'

'So it would seem,' said Hugh sombrely. 'We have a plague among us that needs burning out before it spreads. But what are we to make of this simple countryman who wore a sword under his cloak?'

'And asking after us!' Yves recalled, marvelling. 'But I know no one like that.'

'What like was the young lord who took away your sister?'

'Not black, nor like a hawk, rather fair-skinned, and fair in the hair, too. And besides, even if he came seeking the two of us she'd left behind, he would not come up from the highroad, not according to the way we set off when I followed them. And he would not come dressed as a peasant, either. Nor alone.'

All of which was shrewd sense. There were, of course, other possibilities. The men of Gloucester, elated by their gains, might well be sending agents in disguise into these regions, probing for any weak spots, and such envoys, thought Cadfael, might have been told to pursue, at the same time, the search for Laurence d'Angers' nephew and niece, strayed in the Worcester panic.

'Let it lie by a while,' said Beringar, half-grim and half-appreciative, as if he looked forward to interesting encounters. 'We shall certainly hear more of Cleeton's dark stranger, if we just bide quiet and bear his image in mind.'

They were within two miles of Ludlow before the expected snow began with the dusk. They drew close cloak and capuchon, and rode sturdily with heads down, but so close to home that they were in no danger of losing the road. Hugh parted from them under the walls of Ludlow, to ride in to his company there, leaving two of his men to escort Cadfael and the boy the short way on to Bromfield. Even Yves had lost his tongue by then, a little drunk with fresh air and exercise, and already growing hungry, for all he had eaten his hunk of bread and strip of hard bacon long before. He sat braced and stolid in the saddle, hunched under his hood, but emerged from it with a face like a rosy apple as soon as they lighted down in the great court at the priory. Vespers was long over. Prior Leonard was hovering, watchful and uneasy, for the return of his fledgling, and ventured out into the thick haze of snow to reclaim him and bring him in to supper.

It was after Compline when Beringar rode in, let his tired mount be led away to the stables, and came to find Cadfael, who was sitting by the bed where Brother Elyas already slept his secret, remote and troubled sleep. At sight of Hugh's face, full of hard tidings, Cadfael laid a finger to his lip, and rose to steal away from the bedside into the anteroom, where they could talk without disturbing the sleeper.

'Our friend above Cleeton,' said Hugh, sitting back with a great sigh against the panelled wall, 'is not the only one who has fallen victim, Cadfael. We have the devil among us, no question. Ludlow's in a hum tonight. It seems one of Dinan's archers has an old father at a hamlet south of Henley, a free tenant holding from Mortimer, and today the lad went off to visit, to see how the old man was making out in this hard weather. A holding not two miles from Ludlow, though solitary. He found the place as we found Druel's homestead. Not burned, though— smoke or flames would have been seen, and brought Dinan out with all his force like a swarm of bees disturbed. But swept clear of life, goods, gear and all. And there the folk did not escape. Butchered, every one, except for one poor idiot wretch the archer found wandering from house to house, foraging for any crumbs left to live on.'

Brother Cadfael gaped at him in appalled wonder. 'That they should dare, so near a strong town!'

'Trying out their claws, in despite of a well-found garrison. And the one man left alive, who hid in the woods until the raiders left, may be uncertain in his wits, but he saw it all, and has given an account that makes excellent sense, and for my part, I think him a good witness. And he says there were about twenty men, and they had daggers, axes and swords among them. Three, he says, were mounted. They came about midnight, and in a few hours had driven off all the stock and departed into the night. And he has small notion of how many days he has been solitary and starving there, but such things as the changes of weather he understands very well, and he says, and will not be shifted, that this took place on the

60

night of the first hard frost, when all the brooks stopped flowing.'

'I take your meaning,' said Cadfael, and gnawed his knuckles in fierce thought. 'The same two-legged wolves? The same night, surely. The first hard frost! About midnight this slaughter and pillage by Henley . . . As if they set out deliberately to blacken Dinan's face!'

'Or mine,' said Hugh grimly.

'Or King Stephen's! Well, so they moved off with their spoils maybe two hours after midnight. They would not move fast, driving cattle and carrying food and grain. Not long before dawn they ransacked and burned John Druel's holding, high on Clee. And in between—would you not say, Hugh?—in between they happened on Brother Elyas and Sister Hilaria, and after their fashion let loose in a little exuberant sport, leaving both dead or dying. Could there be two such bands out on their grisly business on the same night? A wild night, a blizzard night, that might well keep even thieves and vagabonds close to home. There are here men who know these parts like their own palms, Hugh, and neither snow nor frost can cage them.'

'Two such bands?' said Hugh, darkly pondering. 'No, that's out of the reckoning. And consider the line they took that night. The night's ventures began here under our noses—that's the furthest range of their foray. They returned eastward, crossing the highway—for somewhere there your Brother Elyas was found—and before dawn they were rounding the high shoulder of Titterstone Clee, where they burned out Druel's holding. It may not even have been in their plan, simply a frolic by men drunk with success. But it was on their way home, for they'd want to be snug and unseen by dawn. Agreed?'

'Agreed. And are you thinking, Hugh, what I am thinking? Yves rushes out to recall his sister from her folly, and strikes off from that holding uphill, perhaps not on the same level, but surely in the same direction your outlaws took on their way home, two nights later. Somewhere in those uplands lies the manor to which his sister fled with her lover. Does it not look as though he may have taken her to a house far too close neighbour to the devil to be a safe place either for him or for her?'

'I have already made my dispositions,' Hugh assured

him with grim satisfaction, 'with that in mind. There's a great swathe of upland there, some of it forested, some of it rock, and bleak as death, too barren even for sheep. The workable manors there go no higher than Druel's homestead, and even there nest in the sheltered places. Tomorrow at first light I'm going out with Dinan to follow that same line the boy took, and see if I can find what he lost himself seeking, the manor where the girl was taken. First, if we can, let's get her safe out of it. Then we may go after this challenger who spits in the face of law, with no hostages at stake.'

'But leave the boy here!' said Cadfael, more peremptorily than he had intended.

Hugh looked down at him with a wry and burdened smile. 'We shall be away before ever he opens his eyes. Do you think I dare risk confronting him with another and dearer corpse, with your fierce eye on me? No, if luck's with us we'll bring him his sister, either intact or a wife irreclaimable, and they shall fight it out between them, he, she and the lover! If luck turns her back on us—well, then you may be needed. But once the girl's well out of it, this burden is mine, and you may take care of your patient and sit quietly at home.'

Cadfael watched the night through with Brother Elyas, and got nothing more for his pains than he had known already. The barrier remained immovable. When a dutiful brother came to relieve him, he went to his bed, and slept as soon as he lay down. He had the gift. There was no profit in lying awake fretting for what would, in any case, have to be faced on awaking, and he had long ago sloughed off the unprofitable. It took too much out of a man, of what would be needed hereafter.

He awoke only when he was roused by Prior Leonard, which was in the early afternoon, a couple of hours at least after he had intended to be up and doing. By which time Hugh was back from his foray into the hills, and tramped in weary and bleak of countenance to share a late dinner, and report the fruits of his labours.

'There is a manor known as Callowleas, a quarter-circle round the flank of Clee from Druel's place, and much on the same level.' Hugh paused to frown over his own choice of words. 'There was such a manor! It has been

62

wiped out, drained, filleted like a fish. What we found was Druel's homestead over again, but to another degree. This was a thriving manor, and now it's a snowy waste, a number of bodies buried or frozen there, nothing living left to speak. We've brought back the first of the dead into Ludlow, and left men breaking out others from the drifts. No telling how many they'll find. By the covering of snow, I should judge this raid took place even *before* the frost set in.'

'Do you tell me?' Cadfael sat staring, appalled. 'Then before the raids of which we already know, and before our little nun was killed, and Brother Elyas reduced to this haunted condition he lies in now. Now you have your finger on a fixed place, is there a name and a lord to go with it? Dinan will know all these tenants who hold from him, and it must be his writ, the old Lacy writ, that runs there.'

'It is. The manor of Callowleas is held from him by a young man who came into his father's honour only two years ago. Of suitable fortune, person, and age, yes. His name is Evrard Boterel. Not a great family, but respected. By many tokens, he may well be the man.'

'And this place lies in the right direction? The way the girl fled with her lover?' It was a grim reflection, but Hugh shook his head emphatically at despondency.

'Ah, but wait! Nothing's certain yet, Yves could not name the man. But even if it is so—as I believe it must be—no need yet to bury the girl. For Dinan pointed out that Boterel also holds the manor of Ledwyche, down in the valley of the Dogditch brook, and there's a good downhill track continues on that way from Callowleas, into forest, and thick forest at that. A little over three miles between the two holdings. We followed it a short way, though I own I had little hope of finding any traces, even if some of the household had escaped the slaughter that way. We had better fortune than I expected, or maybe deserved. Look, this is what I found!'

He drew it out from the breast of his cotte, and held it up over his fist, a net of fine gold filigree threads on a band of embroidered ribbon, made to pass round the head when the hair was netted, and tie over the brow. The bow in which it had been tied had been dragged askew, but not undone, for the band had torn apart a little aside from it.

'Caught in thick woodland, well down the path. They were in haste, whoever rode that way, they cut through a dense thicket to come the quickest way down the slope, there were broken twigs hanging to bear witness. I say they, but I fancy one horse only, with two riders. A low branch caught and dragged this from her head. And since that gives us every hope that the wearer got away safely from that terror, we may very well show this to Yves, and say how it was found. If he knows it for hers, then I'm bound for Ledwyche, to see if luck's still on our side.'

There was no hesitation. The moment Yves set eyes on the handful of gold cobweb, his eyes opened wide and grew luminous with hope and eagerness.

'That is my sister's!' he said, shining. 'It was too fine for the journey, but I know she had it with her. For *him* she might wear it! Where did you find it?'

6

This time they took Yves with them, partly because, though he might have accepted Hugh's fiat gracefully if refused, he would have been restless and miserable all the time of waiting, and partly because, in addition to being the only one who could positively identify Ermina's suitor when found, he was indeed the man of his blood here, the head of his household, and had every right to partake in the search for his lost sister, now they knew she should be well alive.

'But, this is the same way we came down from Thurstan's assart,' he said, after they had turned off the highroad by the bridge over the Corve. 'Must we continue so?'

'We must, for some while. Well past the place where you and I would as soon not be,' said Cadfael simply, divining his unease. 'But we need not turn our eyes away. There is nothing evil there. Neither earth nor water nor air have any part in man's ill-doing.' And with an attentive but cautious eye on the boy's grave face, he said: 'You may grieve, but you must not begrudge that she is gone. Her welcome is assured.'

'She was, of all of us, the only best,' said Yves, abruptly eloquent. 'You don't know! Never out of temper, always patient and kind and very brave. She was much more beautiful than Ermina!'

He was thirteen, but taught and gifted, perhaps, somewhat beyond his years, and he had gone afoot in Sister Hilaria's gallant and gentle company many days, close and observant. And if he had glimpsed for the first time a mature kind of love, surely it had been a most innocent and auspicious kind, even now after the apparent mutilation of loss. Yves had come to no harm. In the past two days he seemed to have grown in stature, and taken several long strides away from his infancy.

He did not avert his eyes when they came to the brook, but he was silent, and so remained until after they had crossed the second brook also; but from that point they veered to the right, and came into open woodland, and the new vistas revived his interest in the world about him, and brightened his eyes again. The brief winter sunlight, which had again drawn down slender icicles from eaves and branches, was already past but the light was clear and the air still, and the patterns of black and white and dusky greens had their own sombre beauty.

They crossed the Hopton brook, still motionless as before, half a mile lower down its course than when they had come to Godstroke together. 'But we must have been very near,' said Yves, marvelling that he might have passed almost within touch of his sister that day, and never known it.

'Still a mile or so to go.'

'I hope she may be there!'

'So do we all,' said Hugh.

They came to the manor of Ledwyche over a slight ridge and emerged from woodland to look down an equally gentle slope toward the Ledwyche brook, into which all the others drained before it flowed on, mile after mile, southward to join the River Teme. Beyond the watered valley the ground rose again, and there, directly before them in the distance, hung the vast, bleak outline of Titterstone Clee, its top shrouded in low cloud. But in between the valley lay sheltered on all sides from the worst winds. Trees had been cleared from round the manor, except for windbreaks left for protection to crops and stock in the most open places. From their ridge they looked down at an impressive array of buildings, the manor-house itself built long and steep-roofed over a squat undercroft, the entire visible sweep of the stockade lined within with barn and byre and store. A considerable holding, and surely a temptation to the hungry and covetous, in these lawless times, but perhaps too strongly manned to be easy prey.

It seemed, however, that the holder was not quite easy about his property, for as they drew nearer they could see that on the narrow timber bridge that crossed the brook beyond the manor, men were working busily, erecting a barrier of logs, and above the old, dark wood of the stockade, and especially along the eastward side, glared the white, new wood of recent building. The lord of the manor was heightening his fences.

'They are here, surely,' said Hugh, staring. 'Here lives a man who has taken warning, and does not mean to be caught by surprise a second time.'

They rode down with rising hopes to the open gate in the stockade, which here to the west was still only breast-high. Nevertheless, even on this side an archer rose in the gate to challenge them, and his bow was strung, and if he had not an arrow braced, he had a quiver on his shoulder.

He was a shrewd fellow, so quick to measure the good equipment of the men-at-arms at Hugh's back that he had changed his wary front for a smile before ever Hugh could recite his name and titles.

'My lord, you're very welcome. The lord sheriff's deputy could not come better. If our lord had known you were so near he would have sent to you. For he could not well come himself . . . But ride in, my lord, ride in, and my boy here will run for the steward.'

The boy was already in full flight across the trampled snow within the pale. By the time they had ridden across the stone stairway that led up to the great door of the hall, the steward was scurrying out to receive them, a stout elderly man, russet of beard and bald of head.

'I am seeking Evrard Boterel,' said Hugh, descending with a flurry of snow at his heel. 'He's within?'

'He is, my lord, but not yet in full health. He has been in a sharp fever, but it mends gradually. I'll bring you to him.'

He went before, stumping up the steep stairs, and Hugh followed him close, with Brother Cadfael and Yves on his heels. Within the great hall, at this hour of this winter day, and with hardly a soul using it and hardly a torch to light it, thick gloom hung heavy, warmed only grudgingly by the damped fire on the stones of the central hearth. All the manor's menfolk were working on the defenses. A middle-aged matron jingled her keys along the passage behind the screens, a couple of maids whispered and peered from the kitchen.

The steward brought them with a flourish into a small room at the upper end of the hall, where a man lay back languidly in a great, cushioned chair, with wine and a smoky oil-lamp on a table at his side. One small window was unshuttered, but the light it provided was growing dim, and the yellow flame from the wick of the lamp cast deceptive shadows, and gave them only a dusky view of the face that turned towards them as the door was opened.

'My lord, here are the sheriff's officers come south to Ludlow.' The steward had softened his bluff voice to the coaxing tone he might have used to a child, or a very sick man. 'The lord Hugh Beringar comes to see you. We shall have help if we should need it, you can put your mind at rest.'

A long and muscular but slightly shaky hand was put out to move the lamp, so that it might show host and visitors to each other more clearly. A low-pitched voice said, over somewhat quick and shallow breath: 'My lord, you're heartily welcome. God knows we seem to have need of you in these parts.' And to the steward he said: 'Bring more lights, and some refreshment.' He leaned forward in the chair, gathering himself with an effort. 'You find me in some disarray, I am sorry for it. They tell me I have been in fever some days. I am out of that now, but it has left me weaker than I care to be.'

'So I see, and I am sorry,' said Hugh. 'I brought a force south here, I must tell you, upon other business, but by chance it has taken me to your manor above at Callowleas. I have seen, sir, what has been done to you there. I am glad that you, and some, at least, of your people escaped alive from that massacre, and I intend to make it my business to find and root out whatever nest of vultures brought that upon you. I see you have been busy strengthening your own defenses.'

'As best we can.'

A woman brought candles, disposed them silently in

68

scones on the walls, and withdrew. The sudden brightness brought them all vividly close, eyes startled wide. Yves, who had stood rooted and stiff by Cadfael's side, a lordling ready to confront his enemy, suddenly clutched at Cadfael's sleeve and softened in uncertainty.

The man in the great chair looked no more than twenty-four or twenty-five. He had heaved himself forward, and the cushions had slid down at his back. He presented to the light a face pale and hollow-cheeked, the eyes large and dark, and sunken into bruised hollows, glittering still with the hectic brilliance of fever. His thick fair hair was rumpled and on end from the pillows that had propped him. But no question, this was a very handsome and engaging person, and when in health a tall and athletic one. He was clothed and booted, plainly he had been out during the day among his men, ill-advisedly, for his boots were wet and dark with melted snow. He was bending his brows now and peering attentively at his three visitors, and when his gaze reached the boy, it halted and hung there. He was not sure. He shook his head a little, peered again, and pondered, frowning.

'You know the boy?' asked Hugh mildly. 'He is Yves Hugonin, here seeking a lost sister. If you can help us, we shall be greatly relieved, both he and I. For I think you did not retreat from Callowleas alone. Caught in a tree along the woodland track that bears this way, we found this.' He drew out the thimbleful of gilt thread that expanded to a filigree globe in the palm of his hand. 'Do you know it?'

'Only too well!' said Evrard Boterel harshly, and closed for an instant, large, full eyelids over too-bright eyes. He opened them again to look directly at Yves. 'You are the young brother? Forgive me that I could not be sure of you. I have not seen you but once, I think, since you were a child. Yes, this is hers.'

'You brought her here with you,' said Hugh, not questioning, stating. 'Safe out of that attack.'

'Yes—safe! Yes, I brought here here.' There was a fine dew of sweat on Evrard's broad brow, but his eyes were wide open and clear.

'We have been in search of her and her companions,' said Hugh, 'ever since the sub-prior of Worcester came to

69

Shrewsbury asking after them, since all trace of them had been lost after their flight. If she is here, send for her.'

'She is not here,' said Evrard heavily. 'Nor do I know where she is. All these days between, either I or men of mine have been hunting for her.' He set his long hands to the arms of his chair, and hauled himself shakily to his feet. 'I will tell you!' he said.

He stalked about the room as he told them, a gaunt young man, filled with restless energy, but enfeebled by his days of sickness.

'I was a frequent and welcome guest in her father's house. This boy will know that is truth. She grew up in beauty, and I loved her. I did and do love her! Since she was orphaned I have ridden three times to Worcester to see her, and borne myself as I must to be admitted there, and never did I have any evil design on her, but intended to ask for her hand when I might. For her proper guardian now is her uncle, and he is in the Holy Land. All we could do was wait for his return. When I heard of the sack of Worcester, all my prayer was that she should be escaped well out of it. I never thought of any gain to me, nor that she might be fled this way, until she sent her boy up from Cleeton . . .'

'On which day was that?' demanded Hugh, cutting in sharply.

'On the second day of this month. Come by night, she said, and fetch me away, for I am here waiting for you. Never a word of any others along with her. I knew only what she told me, and I went as she asked, with a horse for her, and brought her away to Callowleas. She had taken my by surprise,' he said jerking up his head in defensive challenge, 'but I wished of all things to wed her, and so did she me. And I brought her there, and used her with all honour, and with her consent I sent out to bring a priest to marry us. But the next night, before ever he reached us, we were all undone.'

'I have seen the ruin they left,' said Hugh. 'From which direction did they come? In what numbers?'

'Too many for us! They were into the bailey and into the house before ever we knew what was happening. I cannot tell whether they came round the flank of the hill, or over the crest at us, for they broke in round half our stockade, ringing us from above and from the east. God knows I may have been too taken up with Ermina to set as strict a watch as I should have done, but there had been no warning, never a word until then of any such banditry in the land. It fell like lightning-stroke. Their numbers I can hardly guess, but surely as many as thirty, and well-armed. We were but half that, and caught easy and half-sleeping after supper. We did what we could—I came by some hurts . . .' Cadfael had already observed how he held one arm and shoulder hunched and still, the left, where a right-handed opponent would lunge for his heart. 'I had Ermina to save. I dared not attempt more. I took her and rode. The downhill way was still possible. They did not follow us. They were busy.' His mouth twisted in a painful grimace. 'We came here safely.'

'And then? How comes it that you have lost her again?'

'You cannot charge me more bitterly than I have accused myself,' said Evrard wearily. 'I am ashamed to face the boy here, and own how I let her slip through my hands. It is little excuse to say, however truly, that I had bled too much, and fell into my bed too weak to move. My leech may say what he can for me, I will not plead. But by the next day this prod here in my shoulder had taken bad ways, and the fever set in. By evening, when I had my wits for a while, and asked for her, they told me she had been frantic with fears for her brother, left behind at the house from which I took her. Now that she knew there were such cutthroats abroad in these parts, she could not rest until she knew him safe, and so she took horse in the middle of the day, and left word she would ride to Cleeton to enquire after him. And she did not return.'

'And you did not follow her!' accused Yves, stiff as a lance and quivering by Cadfael's side. 'You let her go alone, and stayed nursing your grazes!'

'Neither the one nor the other,' said Boterel, but gently and ruefully. 'I did not *let* her go, for I did not know she was gone. And I did, when I learned of it—as my people here will tell you—I did get up from my bed and go out to hunt for her. It was the cold of that night, I think, and the rubbing of my clothes and the motion of riding, that fetched me down for so long. Sorry I am, I swooned and fell out of the saddle, and those I had with me carried me home the miles I'd ridden. I never reached Cleeton.'

71

'As well for you,' said Hugh drily, 'for that night the very house she was seeking was gutted and burned, and the family driven out.'

'So I have now been told. You do not think I have left things so, and never stirred to try and find her? But she was not there when the holding was attacked. If you have been there, and spoken with those who sheltered her, you know so much. She never got there. I have had men out hunting for her all this time, even though I myself was a useless wretch laid here shivering and raving. And now that I have my legs under me again, I shall go on searching. Until I find her!' he said vehemently, and shut his mouth with a snap of strong teeth.

There was nothing more for them here, nothing to be gained and little to be blamed it seemed. The girl had set in motion the whole disastrous course, doubly headstrong in decamping with her lover in the first place, and afterwards, because he was stricken down, in setting off alone to try and amend what she had done so sadly amiss.

'If you hear any word of her,' said Hugh, 'send to tell me at Bromfield, where I am lodged, or in Ludlow, where you will find my men.'

'I shall, my lord, without fail.' Evrard fell back again among his untidy pillows, and flinched at a twinge of pain, shifting his shoulder tenderly to ease it.

'Before we go,' said Brother Cadfael, 'can I not dress your wound again for you? For I see that it gives you trouble, and I fancy you have still a raw surface there that sticks to your dressing, and may do further damage. You have a physician here tending you?'

The young man's hollow eyes opened wide at this kindly interest. 'My leech, I call him, I know. He's none, but he has some skill, from experience. I think he has looked after me pretty well. You are wise in such matters, brother?'

'Like your own man, from long practice. I have often dealt with wounds that have taken bad courses. What has he used on you?' He was curious about other men's prescriptions, and there was clean linen bandaging and a clay ointment jar laid aside on a shelf by the wall. Cadfael lifted the lid and sniffed at the greenish salve within. 'Centaury, I think, and the yellow mild nettle, both good. He knows his herbs. I doubt if you could do better. But since he is not here, and you are in discomfort, may I assay?'

Evrard lay back submissively and let himself be handled. Cadfael unlaced the ties of the young man's cotte, and drew the left shoulder gently out from the wide sleeve, until the shirt could also be drawn down, and his arm freed.

'You have been out and active today, this binding is rubbed into creases, and dried hard, no wonder it hurts you. You should lie still a day or two yet, and let it rest.' It was his physician's voice, practical, confident, even a little severe. His patient listened meekly, and let himself be unwound from his wrappings, which enveloped both shoulder and upper arm. The last folds were stained in a long slash that ran from above the heart down to the underside of the arm, with a thin, dark line of blood that ebbed out on either side into pale, dried fluid. Here Cadfael went delicately, steadying the flesh against every turn of the linen. The folds creaked stiffly free.

A long slash that could have killed him, but instead had been deflected outwards, to slice down into the flesh of his arm. Not deep nor dangerous, though he might well have bled copiously until it was staunched, and since he had ridden hard that same night, no wonder he had lost blood enough to enfeeble him. It was healing now from either end, and healing clean, but certainly, by exertion or some contagion of dirt entering, it had been ugly and festering, and even now, in the centre of the wound, the flesh showed pink, soft and angry. Cadfael cleansed it with a morsel of the linen, and applied a new plaster coated with the herbal salve. The pallid young face stared up at him all the while with unblinking, bruised eyes, wondering and mute.

'You have no other wounds?' asked Cadfael, winding a fresh bandage about his dressing. 'Well, rest this one a day or two longer, and rest your own uneasy mind with it, for we are all on the same quest. Take a little air in the middle of the day, if the sun comes, but keep from cold and give your body time. There, now your sleeve, so . . . But it would be wise to have these boots off, wrap yourself in your gown, and make yourself content.'

The hollow eyes followed his withdrawal, marvelling.

He found his voice to follow them with thanks only as they were leaving.

'You have a gifted touch, brother. I feel myself much eased. God be with you!'

They went out to their horses and the gradually fading light. Yves was dumb. He had come to challenge, and remained to feel sympathy, though almost against his will. He was new to wounds and pain and sickness, until the shock of Worcester he had lived indulged, sheltered, a child. And for his sister's sake he was deep in bitter disappointment and anxiety, and wanted no promptings from anyone.

'He has what he claims,' said Brother Cadfael simply, when they were cresting the ridge and heading down into the trees. 'A thrust meant for his heart, rubbed raw again later, and poisoned by some foulness that got into the wound. He has been in fever, sure enough, and fretted gouts from his flesh. Everything speaks him true.'

'And we are no nearer finding the girl,' said Hugh.

The nightly clouds were gathering, the sky drooping over their heads, an ominous wind stirring. They made all the haste they could to get back into Bromfield before the snow began.

7

After Vespers that night the wind rose violently, the vague wisps of snow that drifted aimlessly on the air changed to thin, lashing whips, driving horizontally against the walls and piling new layers of white against every windward surface. By the time supper was over, and Brother Cadfael scurried across the great court to the infirmary to look at his patient, the world outside was an opaque, shifting, blinding mass of flakes, growing ever thicker. This was to be a blizzard night. The wolves might well be abroad again. They knew their ground exceedingly well, and weather that might daunt the innocent had no terrors for them.

Brother Elyas had been allowed out of his bed for the first time, and was reclining propped by his pillow, bony and shrunken in his voluminous habit. His head wounds had healed over, his body mended of itself, but the constitution of his mind had not the same strength. With mute submission he did whatever he was bidden, with low and listless voice he gave thanks humbly for all that was done for him, but with sunken eyes and painfully knotted brows he stared beyond the walls of his cell, as if half-seeing and half-deluding himself that he saw that part of him that had been reft away and never returned. Only in sleep, and particularly when falling asleep or awaking out

75

of sleep, was he agitated and shaken, as if between waking life and the gentler semblance of death the veil that hid his lost memory from him thinned but did not quite part.

Yves had followed Cadfael across the court, restless and anxious. He was hovering outside the door of the sickroom when Cadfael came out.

'Should you not be in your bed, Yves? Such a long, hard day as you've had!'

'I don't want to sleep yet,' pleaded the boy querulously. 'I'm not tired. Let me sit with him for you until after Compline. I'd rather have something to do.' And indeed it might be the best thing for him, to be doing something for someone else, and feeding a draught of herbs to Brother Elyas might spill a drop of comfort to soothe his own troubles and disappointments. 'He still hasn't said anything to help us? He doesn't remember us?'

'Not yet. There is a name he calls sometimes in his sleep, but none of our acquaintance.' He called for her as for a thing hopelessly lost, an irreparable grief but not an anxiety, she being beyond pain or danger. 'Hunydd. In his deepest sleep he calls for Hunydd.'

'A strange name,' said Yves, wondering. 'Is it a man or a woman?'

'A woman's name—a Welshwoman. I think, though I do not know, that she was his wife. And dearly loved, too dearly to leave him in peace if she is only a few months dead. Prior Leonard said of him, not long in the cloister. He may well have tried to escape from what was hard to bear alone, and found it no easier among any number of brethren.'

Yves was looking up at him with a man's eyes, steady and grave. Even sorrows as yet well out of his range he could go far towards understanding. Cadfael shook him amiably by the shoulder. 'There, yes, sit by him if you will. After Compline I'll bring someone to take your place. And should you need me, I'll not be far away.'

Elyas dozed, opened his eyes, and dozed again. Yves sat still and silent beside the bed, attentive to every change in the gaunt but strong and comely face, and pleased and ready when the invalid asked for a drink, or needed an arm to help him turn and settle comfortably. In the wakeful moments the boy tried tentatively to reach a mind surely not quite closed against him, talking shyly of the winter weather, and the common order of the day within these walls. The hollow eyes watched him as though from a great distance, but attentively.

'Strange,' said Elyas suddenly, his voice low and creaky with disuse. 'I feel that I should know you. Yet you are not a brother of the house.'

'You have known me,' said Yves, eager and hopeful. 'For a short time we were together, do you remember? We came from Cleobury together, as far as Foxwood. My name is Yves Hugonin.'

No, the name meant nothing. Only the face, it seemed, touched some chord in his disrupted memory. 'There was snow threatening,' he said. 'I had a reliquary to deliver here, they tell me I brought it safely. They tell me! All I know is what they tell me.'

'But you will remember,' said Yves earnestly. 'It will come clear to you again. You may trust what they tell you, no one would deceive you. Shall I tell you more things? True things, that I know?'

The wondering, doubting face watched him, and made no motion of rejection. Yves leaned close, and began to talk solemnly and eagerly about what was past.

'You were coming from Pershore, but roundabout, to avoid the trouble in Worcester. And we had run from Worcester, and wanted to reach Shrewsbury. At Cleobury we were all lodged overnight, and you would have had us come here to Bromfield with you, as the nearest place of safety, and I wanted to go with you, but my sister would not, she would go on over the hills. We parted at Foxwood.' The face on the pillow was not responsive, but seemed to wait with a faint, patient hope. The wind shook the stout shutter covering the window, and filtered infinitely tiny particles of snow into the room, to vanish instantly. The candle flickered. The whine of the gale outside was a piercingly desolate sound.

'But you are here,' said Elyas abruptly, 'far from Shrewsbury still. And alone! How is that, that you should be alone?'

'We were separated.' Yves was not quite easy, but if the sick man was beginning to ask questions thus intelligently, the threads of his torn recollections might knit again and present him a whole picture. Better to know both the bad and the good, since there was no guilt in it for him, he was the blameless victim, and surely knowledge should be healing. 'Some kind country people sheltered me, and Brother Cadfael brought me here. But my sister . . . We are seeking her. She left us of her own will!' He could not resist that cry, but would not accuse her further. 'I am sure we shall find her safe and well,' he said manfully.

'But there was a third,' said Brother Elyas, so softly, so inwardly, that it seemed he spoke to himself. 'There was a nun . . .' And now he was not looking at Yves, but staring great-eyed into the vault above him, his mouth worked agitatedly.

'Sister Hilaria,' said Yves, quivering in response.

'A nun of our order . . .' Elyas set both hands to the sides of his bed, and sat up strongly. Something had kindled in the deeps of his haunted eyes, a yellow, crazed light too vivid to be merely a reflection from the candle's flame. 'Sister Hilaria . . .' he said, and now at last he had found a name that meant something to him, but something so terrible that Yves reached both hands to take him by the shoulders, and urge him to lie down again.

'You mustn't fret—she is not lost, she is here, most reverently tended and coffined. It is forbidden to wish her back, she is with God.' Surely they must have told him, but maybe he had not understood. Death could not be hidden away. He would grieve, naturally, but that is permitted. But you may not begrudge it that she has left us, Brother Cadfael had said.

Brother Elyas uttered a dreadful, anguished sound, yet so quiet that the howl of the wind at the shutter almost drowned it. He clenched both hands into large, bony fists, and struck them against his breast.

'Dead! Dead? In her youth, in her beauty—trusting me! Dead! Oh, stones of this house, fall and cover me, unhappy! Bury me out of the sight of men . . .'

Barely half of it was clear, the words crowded so thick on his tongue, choking him, and Yves in his alarm and dismay was hardly capable of listening, he cared only to allay this storm he had innocently provoked. He stretched an arm across Elyas' breast, and tried to soothe him back to his pillow, his young, whole strength pitted against this demented vigour.

'Oh, hush, hush, you musn't vex yourself so. Lie down, you're too weak to rise . . . Oh, don't, you frighten me! Lie down!'

Brother Elyas sat rigidly upright, staring through the wall, gripping both hands against his heart, whispering what might have been prayers, or self-reproaches, or feverish, garbled recollections of times past. Against that private obsession all the force Yves could exert had no influence. Elyas was no longer even aware of him. If he spoke to any, it was to God, or to some creature invisible.

Yves turned and fled for help, closing the door behind him. Through the infirmary he ran full tilt, and out into the piled, whirling, howling snow of the court, across to the cloister and the warming-room, where surely they would be at this hour. He fell once, and plucked himself shivering out of a drift, halting to clear his eyes. The whole night was a rain of goosefeathers, but cold, cold, and the wind that flung them in his face cut like a knife. He stumbled and slithered to the door of the church, and there halted, hearing the chanting within. It was later than he had thought. Compline had already begun.

He had been too well schooled in the courtesies and proper observancies, he could not for any cause burst in upon the office and bawl for help. He hung still for a few moments to get his breath and shake the snow from his hair and lashes. Compline was not long, surely he could go back and battle with his disordered charge until the office was over. Then there would be help in plenty. He had only to keep Brother Elyas quiet for a quarter of an hour.

He turned, half-blinded as soon as he left cover, and battled his way back through the drifts, labouring hard with his short, sturdy legs, and lowering his head like a little fighting bull against the wind.

The outer door of the infirmary stood open wide, but he was all too afraid that he had left it so in his haste. He blundered along the passage within, fending himself off from the walls with both hands as he shook off the snow that clung to his face. The door of the sickroom was also wide open. That brought him up with a jolt that jarred him to the heels.

The room was empty, the coverings of the bed hung low

to the floor. Brother Elyas' sandals, laid neatly side by side under the head of the bed, were gone. And so was Brother Elyas, just as he had risen from his sick-bed, clothed, habited but without cloak or covering, out into the night of the ninth of December, into such a blizzard as had raged the night he came by his all but mortal injuries, and Sister Hilaria by her death. The only name that had reached him in his solitary place.

Yves charged back along the passage to the doorway, and out into the storm. And there were tracks, though he had not seen them when he entered, because he had not expected them to be there, nor would they last long. They were filling fast, but they showed, large feet tramping down the steps and across the court, not towards the church, no—straight for the gatehouse. And Brother Porter had leave to attend Compline.

They were still chanting in the church, and Elyas could not have got far. Yves ran to grab his cloak from the porch of the guest-hall, and bolted like a startled hare, in convulsive leaps, toward the gatehouse. The tracks were filling fast, they lingered only as shallowing pits in the whiteness, picked out by the shadows cast from the few burning torches. But they reached and quitted the gate. The world without was nothing but a boiling whiteness, and the depth of the fall made walking hard labour for his short legs, but he plodded on relentlessly. The tracks turned right. So did Yves.

Some way along the road, waking blindly, with no sense of direction left to him in a snowfall that looked the same wherever he turned his face, but where the ground below him was still dimpled faintly with the furrows and pits of passage, he glimpsed in a momentary emptiness cleared by the gale's caprice, a black shadow flitting before him. He fixed his eyes upon it, and plunged determinedly after.

It took him a long time to overtake his quarry. It was incredible how fast Elyas went, striding, thrusting, ploughing his way, so that now a torn furrow showed where he had passed. In sandals, bare-headed, a sick man—only some terrible force of passion and despair could give him such strength. Moreover, which frightened Yves more than ever, he seemed to know where he was going, or else to be drawn to some desperate meeting-place without his own knowledge or will. The line he sheered through the drifts looked arrow-straight.

Nevertheless, Yves did overtake him at last, struggling closer with every step, until he was able to stretch out his hand and catch at the wide sleeve of the black habit. The arm swung steadily, as though Elyas remained totally unaware of the weight dragging at him. Almost he plucked himself clear, but Yves clung with both hands, and heaving himself in front of the striding figure, wound his arms about its middle and held on, blocking the way forward with all his weight, and blinking up through the blinding snow into a face as chill and immovable as a death-mask.

'Brother Elyas, come back with me! You must come back—you'll die out here!'

Brother Elyas moved on inexorably, forcing his incubus before him, hampered but undeterred. Yves maintained his hold, and went with him, but hanging back hard, and pleading insistently: 'You're ill, you should be in your bed. Come back with me! Where is it you want to go? Turn back now, let me take you home . . .'

But perhaps he was not going anywhere, only trying to get away from somewhere, or from someone, from himself, from whatever it was that had come back to him like lightning-stroke, and driven him mad. Yves pleaded breathlessly and insistently, but in vain. He could not turn him or persuade him. There was nothing left but to go with him. He took a firm grip on the black sleeve, and set himself to keep pace with his charge. If they could find any cottage, or meet with any late traveller he could ask for shelter or help. Surely Brother Elyas must weaken and fail at last, and let himself be prevailed upon to accept any aid that offered. But who would be out on such a night? Who but a poor madman and his sorry keeper! Well, he had offered to take care of Brother Elyas, and he would not let go of him, and if he could not protect him from his own frenzy, he could at least share the penalty. And strangely, in a little while they were moving together as one, and Brother Elyas, though his face remained fixed and his purpose secret, laid an arm about Yves' shoulders and drew him close against his side, and small, instinctive motions of mutual kindness arose between them, to ease the labour and the cold and the loneliness.

Yves had no longer any idea of where they were, though he knew that long ago they had left the road. He thought they had crossed a bridge, and that could not have been anything but the River Corve. Somewhere on that upland slope, then. A poor chance of finding a cottage here, even if the snow gave over and let them see their way.

But it seemed that Brother Elyas knew his way, or was guided to the place where he could not choose but go, for some awful, penitential purpose of which only he knew. A thicket of thorny bushes, heaped with snow, snatched at their garments, sheltering a shallow hollow in the slope. Yves stumbled against a hard, dark surface, and grazed his knuckles on rough wood. A low but sturdy hut, built to give shelter to shepherds in the lambing, and store fodder and litter. The door was held by a heavy bar, but Brother Elyas drew it clear and thrust the door open. They burst through into blessed darkness, Elyas stooping his head low beneath the lintel. The door, clapped to against the wind, fitted snugly, and suddenly they were in blindness, stillness and comparative silence. After the blizzard without, this was almost warmth, and the smell of old but dry hay, stirred by their feet, promised bed and blankets together. Yves shook off snow, and his heart lifted hopefully. Here Brother Elyas might survive the night. And before dawn, before he awakes, thought the boy, I can slip out and bar the door on him, while I go to find someone to help me, or carry a message for me. I've held on to him thus far, I won't lose him now.

Brother Elyas had moved away from him. He heard the rustling whisper of the hay as a man's weight was flung down into it. The howl of the wind outside ebbed into a desolate moaning. Yves crept forward with hand extended, and touched a stooped shoulder, caked with snow. The pilgrim had reached his strange shrine, and was on his knees. Yves shook the snow from the folds of the black habit, and felt Elyas shuddering beneath his hand, as though he contained by force what should have been deep and bitter sobbing. Now that they were in utter darkness the thread that bound them seemed to have drawn them closer together. The kneeling man was whispering almost soundlessly, and though all words were lost, the desperation of their import was plain.

Yves felt his way into the pile of hay beside him, and with an arm about the tense shoulders tried to draw Elyas down to lie at rest, but for a long while the pressure was resisted. At last the lean body softened and sank forward with a muted, wordless groan, whether in consent to the boy's urging or in the collapse of exhaustion there was no telling. He lay stretched on his face, his forehead on his arms, and Yves raked up the hay on either side to fold him in with at least a measure of warmth, and lay down beside him.

After a while he knew by the long, deep breathing that Elyas slept.

Yves lay holding him, pressed close to his side, determined not to sleep. He was cold and weary, and in great need of thought, but his mind was numbed and unwilling. He did not want to remember the words Brother Elyas had spoken, much less try to make out their meaning, for whatever it might be, it was terrible. All he could do now for this broken man, for whom he felt so obstinate and strange an affection, having taken the responsibility for him, was to make certain that he could not escape again to wander and be lost, and to go out and seek help for him in the morning. To which end he must stay awake.

For all that, he may have been very close to dozing when he was startled into wakefulness again by a voice beside him, not whispering now, only muffled by the cradling arms.

'Sister . . . my sister . . . Forgive me my weakness, my mortal sin—I, who have been your death!' And after a long pause he said: 'Hunydd—she was like you, even so warm and confiding in my arms . . . After six months starving, suddenly such hunger—I could not bear the burning, body and soul!'

Yves lay still, clasping him, unable to move, unable to stop listening.

'No, do not forgive! How dare I ask? Let the earth close on me and put me out of mind . . . Craven, inconstant—unworthy.'

A longer silence yet. Brother Elyas was still asleep, and out of his sleep he gave voice to his torments, uncovered now, mercilessly remembered. He slept and writhed. Never before had Yves felt himself enlarged to

83

contain either such horror, or such fierce and protective pity.

'She clung to me . . . she had no fear at all, being with me! Merciful God, I am a man, full of blood, with a man's body, a man's desires!' cried Brother Elyas in a muted howl of pain. 'And she is dead, who trusted in me . . .'

8

Brother Cadfael came back from Compline to see Elyas settled for the night, and brought a young brother with him to relieve Yves of his watch. They found the door standing open, the bed wildly disturbed, and the room empty.

There might, of course, have been explanations less dire than the obvious one, but Cadfael made straight for the outer door again at a purposeful run, and looked for the signs he had not looked for when entering. The court had been criss-crossed with new tracks at the end of Compline, and even these the continuing snow was rapidly obliterating, but there were still traces of someone who had set a straight course for the gatehouse. Mere dimples in the whiteness, but discernible. And the boy gone, too! What could have erupted there in the sickroom to spur Elyas into such unreasonable and perilous action, after his long apathy and submission? Certainly if he had taken it into his disordered head to do something drastic a half-grown lad would not have been able to stop him, and more than likely pride would not let Yves abandon a creature for whom he had assumed, however briefly, the responsibility. He was getting to know Yves fairly well by now.

'You run to the guest-hall,' he ordered the young

85

brother briskly, 'tell Hugh Beringar what's amiss, and make sure they are not within there. I'll go to Prior Leonard, and we'll have the whole household searched.'

Leonard took the news with concern and distress, and had every brother scouring the enclave at once, even to the grange court and the barns. Hugh Beringar came forth booted and cloaked, in resigned expectation of the worst, and was short with any who got in his way. With both the secular and the cloistral law directing, the search did not take long, and was fruitless.

'My fault entirely,' Cadfael owned bitterly. 'I entrusted the poor wretch to a boy hardly less wretched. I should have had more sense. Though how or why this can have arisen between them is more than I can see. But I should not have taken the least risk with either of them. And now my foolishness has lost them both, the most forlorn pair this house held, who should have been guarded at every step.'

Hugh was already busy disposing the men he had here at hand. 'One to Ludlow, as far as the gate, where either they'll have passed, or you may have them kept safely if they arrive hereafter. And you go with him, but to the castle, have out ten men, and bring them down to the gate, where I'll come. Wake up Dinan, too, let him sweat, the boy's son to a man he must have known, and nephew to one he may well want to have dealing with soon. I won't risk men by sending them out in this beyond a mile or so, or in less than pairs, but our pair can't have got far.' He turned on Cadfael just as vehemently, and clouted him hard, between the shoulders. 'And you, my heart, stop talking such arrogant foolery! The man seemed quiet and biddable, and the boy needed using, and could be trusted to the hilt, as you very well know. If they've miscarried, it's none of your blame. Don't arrogate to yourself God's own role of apportioning blame and praise, even when the blame lands on your own shoulders. That's a kind of arrogance, too. Now come on, and we'll see if we can't bring home the two of them out of this cold purgatory. But I tell you what I shall be telling my fellows at Ludlow—move out no more than an hour from home, keep touch, and turn back on the hour, as near as you can judge. I'm not losing more men into the snow this night. At dawn, if

86

we've caught nothing before, we'll take up the search in earnest.'

With those orders they went forth into the blizzard, hunting in pairs, and obscurely comforted, in Cadfael's case at least, by the reflection that it was a pair they were hunting. One man alone can give up and subside into the cold and die, far more easily than two together, who will both brace and provoke each other, wrangle and support, give each other warmth and challenge each other's endurance. In extremes, not to be alone is the greatest aid to survival.

He had taken Hugh's impatient reproof to heart, too, and it gave him reassurance no less. It was all too easy to turn honest anxiety over someone loved into an exaltation of a man's own part and duty as protector, a manner of usurpation of the station of God. To accuse oneself of falling short of infallibility is to arrogate to oneself the godhead thus implied. Well, thought Cadfael, willing to learn, a shade specious, perhaps, but I may need that very argument myself some day. Bear it in mind!

Blundering blindly ahead with a burly young novice beside him, northwards across the Corve, Cadfael groped through a chill white mist, and knew that they were all wasting their time. They might probe the drifts as they would, but the weather had the laugh of them, covering everything in the same blank pall.

They all drew in again resignedly to Bromfield when they judged the time to be spent and the work impossible. The porter had set fresh pine torches in the shelter of the arched gateway to provide a beacon glow homeward, for fear some of the searchers should themselves go astray and be lost, and from time to time he set the bell ringing as an added guide. The hunters came back snow-caked and weary, and empty-handed. Cadfael went to Matins and Lauds before seeking his bed. The order of observances must not be utterly disrupted, even to go out in defence of innocent lives. Nothing could now be done before dawn. Not by men. But God, after all, knew where the lost might be found, and it would do no harm to put in a word in that quarter, and admit the inadequacy of human effort.

He arose at the bell for Prime, and went down with the rest in the winter darkness to the cold church. The snow

87

had ceased at the first approach of morning, as it had done for several days, and the reflected light from all that depth of whiteness brought a pure and ghostly pallor even before dawn. After the office Cadfael ploughed his way alone down towards the gatehouse. The world around him was a waste of white broken by shadowy dark shapes of walls and buildings, but the porter had kept his torches burning hopefully under the archway, and they shed a full, reddish light over the stonework, and into the outer world beyond. To replenish them he had had to open the wicket in the gate and pass through, and as Cadfael approached he was in the act of re-entering, pausing in the shelter to stamp off snow before he came within, and closed the wicket again behind him.

Thus it happened that he was facing inwards while Cadfael was facing out, and only Cadfael saw what he saw. The wicket was lofty, to admit mounted men, and Brother Porter was short and slight, and stooping to shake his skirts clear. Behind him, and not many paces behind, two faces suddenly glowed out of the dimness into the flickering light of the torches, and shone clear before Cadfael's eyes. Their suddenness and their beauty took his breath away for a moment, as though a miracle had caused them to appear out of the very air. No heavenly visitors, however, these, but most vividly and vitally of this world.

The girl's hood had fallen back on her neck, the red light flowed over a great disordered coil of dark hair, a wide, clear forehead, arched, imperious black brows, large dark eyes too brilliant to be black, by reflections in them the darkest and reddest of browns. She had, for all her coarse country clothes, a carriage of the head and a lance-like directness of gaze that queens might have copied. The lines that swooped so graciously over her cheekbones and down to full, strongly folded lips and resolute chin made so suave a moulding that Cadfael's finger-ends, once accomplished in such caresses, stroked down from brow to throat in imagination, and quivered to old memories.

The other face hung beyond and above her left shoulder, almost cheek to brow with her. She was tall, but the man behind her was taller, he was stooped protectively and watchfully to bring his face close to hers. A long, spare, wide-browed face with a fine scimitar of a nose and a supple bow of a mouth and the dilated, fearless golden eyes of a hawk. His head was bared, and capped closely with blue-black hair, coiling vigorously at his temples and sweeping back thick and lustrous over a lofty skull. Cadfael had visions of that face terminating in a short, pointed beard, and with fine-drawn moustaches over the long, fastidious lips. With just such faces had he seen, in his time, proud, mailed Syrians wheeling their line of charge outside Antioch. This face had the same dark colouring and sculptured shape, like cast bronze, but this face was shaven clean in the Norman fashion, the rich hair cropped, the head framed by rough, dun-coloured homespun, a local peasant's wear.

Well, they happen, the lightning-strokes of God, the gifted or misfortunates who are born into a world where they nowhere belong, the saints and scholars who come to manhood unrecognised, guarding the swine in the forest pastures among the beech-mast, the warrior princes villein-born and youngest in a starving clan, set to scare the crows away from the furrow. Just as hollow slave-rearlings are cradled in the palaces of kings, and come to rule, however ineptly, over men a thousand times their worth.

But this one would not be lost. It needed only that flashing glimpse of the black-lashed golden eyes to make it certain they would burn their way before him to wherever he set out to go.

And all in the brief moment while the porter was ridding himself of the snow he had collected on his skirts. For the next moment he had stepped within, and closed the wicket behind him, just in time to cut off, short of the gates, the dual vision of youth that was surely advancing to ask for entry.

Brother Cadfael closed his eyes, opened them hopefully, and closed them again upon dazzled recollection that might almost have been delusion. In the between-light of dawn, in the grip of a hard winter, and complicated by the pleasurable, warming glow of torchlight, what dreams may not come!

He had taken but three more laboured paces through the fall, and the porter had barely reached the door of his lodge, when the bell pealed at the gate.

The porter turned, startled. He had been preoccupied first with reaching up to the sconces in which his torches were set, and then hurrying back into shelter, and he had seen nothing stirring in the lingering darkness without. Only after his back was turned had the two—if they were real indeed!—stepped within range of the light. He hoisted resigned shoulders, and waded back to open the small grid that would show him who stood without. What he saw astonished him still more, it seemed, but it spurred him into instant action. The great latch listed, and the lofty wicket swung open.

And there she stood, tall, meek and still confronting them, in a too-large gown of faded brown homespun, a coarse short cloak, and ragged-edged capuchon flung back from her head, the sheaf of dark hair tumbling to her shoulders. The sting of cold air had brought out a rosy flush on her cheekbones, in a skin otherwise creamy-white and smooth as ivory.

"May I enter and take shelter here a while?" she said in the mildest of voices and humblest of manners, but with that confidence and calm about her that could not be quenched. 'Through weather and mishap and the distresses of war I am here along. I think you have been looking for me. My name is Ermina Hugonin.'

While the porter was conducting her excitedly into his lodge, and hurrying to inform Prior Leonard and Hugh Beringar of the sudden appearance of the missing lady at their gates. Brother Cadfael lost no time in slipping out into the roadway and casting a shrewd eye on the empty countryside in all directions. Empty it was, to all appearance. There were corners, copses, bushes, any of which could quickly conceal the departure of a young and swift-moving man, and either her companion had chosen to vanish among these, or the falcon had indeed taken wing and flown. As for tracks in the snow, a few early-rising goodmen with sheep to dig out or beasts to feed had already gone to and fro past the gate house, and among their traces who was to pick out one man's foot? She had spoken truth, if a somewhat deceptive truth; she entered here alone. But two had approached the gate, though only one rang to ask admittance.

Now why should such a man, bringing a lost girl to

safety, avoid showing his face within? And why, pondered Cadfael, should not the one man who was aware of the evasion make it known openly to all? On the other hand, until he knew of a good reason one way or the other, why should he? First hear and consider what the lady had to say.

He went back very thoughtfully to the lodge, where the porter had hurried to prod his fire into life and seat her beside it. She sat self-contained and silent, her wet shoes and skirts beginning to steam gently in the warmth.

'You are also a brother of this house?' she asked, raising dark eyes to study him.

'No, I am a monk of Shrewsbury. I came here to tend a brother who has been lying sick here.' He wondered if any word of Brother Elyas' misfortunes had reached her, but she gave no sign of knowing anything of a wounded monk, and he forbore from mentioning a name. Let her tell her own story once for all, before Hugh and the prior as witnesses, then he might know where he himself stood. 'You know how diligently you have been sought since you fled from Worcester? Hugh Beringar, who is deputy sheriff of the shire, is here in Bromfield, partly on that very quest.'

'I heard it,' she said, 'from the forester who has sheltered me. I know from them, too, that my brother has been here, while I have been hunting for him. And only now that I find my way here myself do I learn that he is again lost, and half the night men have been out searching for him. All this countryside knows of it. I fear you have made a poor exchange,' she said with sudden, flashing bitterness, 'gaining me and losing Yves. For I am the one who has cost you all so much trouble and time.'

'Your brother was safe and in excellent health,' said Cadfael firmly, 'as late as Compline last night. There is no need to suppose that we shall fail of finding him again, for he cannot have gone far. The sheriff's men in Ludlow will have had their orders overnight, and be out by now. And so will Hugh Beringar, as soon as he has seen you safe and well, and heard whatever you can tell him.'

Hugh was at the door by then, and the brothers had hastily cleared a path through the drifts to bring the girl almost dryshod up to the guest-hall. Prior Leonard himself led her in to warmth and food and a comfortable seat

91

by the fire. He was distressed that there was no woman guest to provide her a change of clothing.

'That shall be seen to,' said Beringar shortly. 'Josce de Dinan has a household full of women, I'll get from them whatever is needed. But you had better get out of those wet skirts, madam, if it must needs be into habit and sandals. You have nothing with you but what you wear?'

'I gave what I had in exchange for what I wear,' she said with composure, 'and for the hospitality that was given me without thought of reward. But some money I still have about me. I can pay for a gown.'

They left her to strip beside the fire, and provided her the habit and shoes of a novice. When she opened the door to them again, and bade them in, it was with the grace of a countess welcoming guests. She had let down and combed her mass of dark hair, it was drying into curls on her shoulders, and swung like heavy, lustrous curtains either side her face. Wrapped in the black habit, and girdled close about the waist, she returned to her chair and braced herself, facing them squarely, the most beautiful novice Bromfield had ever housed. She had spread her wet clothes to dry on a bench beside the fire.

'My lord,' she said, 'and Father Prior, to say this briefly, I have been the cause of great trouble and cost to you and many others, and I am sensible of it. It was not intended, but I did it. Now that I am come to make what amends I may, I hear that my brother, who was here in safety, and whom I hoped to join here, has gone forth overnight and vanished again. I cannot but lay this, with the rest, to my own charge, and I am sorry. If there is anything I can do to help in the search for him . . .'

'There is but one thing you can do to help us all,' said Hugh firmly, 'and that one anxiety, at least, off our hands. You can remain here, not setting a foot outside these walls, until we find and bring your brother to join you. Let us at least be sure that *you* are safe, and cannot be lost again.'

'I could wish better, but what you order, I will do. For this while,' she added, and jutted her lip at him.

'Then there are things I need to know from you, now, shortly, and the rest can wait. You are but a part of my business here. The king's peace is also my business, and you, I think, have good reason to know that the king's peace is being flouted in these parts. We know from Yves how you left him and Sister Hilaria at Cleeton, and sent word to Evrard Boterel to come and fetch you away to his manor of Callowleas. We have seen what is left of Callowleas, and we have been to Ledwyche looking for you, and heard from Boterel that you reached there with him safely, but rode out while he lay in fever from his wounds got in the fighting, and went to look for the companions you had left behind. What had befallen Callowleas could well befall others, no wonder you were in desperate anxiety.'

She sat gnawing her underlip and staring at him with unwavering eyes, her brows drawn close. 'Since Evrard has told you all this, I need only confirm it. He is recovered, I trust? Yes, I did fear for them. There was good cause.'

'What happened to you? Boterel has already told us that you did not return, and from the time he recovered his wits and found you were gone, he has been searching for you constantly. It was folly to set out alone.'

Surprisingly, her lips contorted in a wry smile. She had already admitted to folly. 'Yes, I am sure he has been hunting high and low for me. We may set his mind at rest now. No, I did not reach Cleeton. I don't know these ways, and I was benighted, and then the snow came . . . In the dark I lost myself utterly, and had a fall, and the horse bolted. I was lucky to be found and taken in by a forester and his wife, lifelong I shall be grateful to them. I told them about Yves, and how I feared for him, and the forester said he would send up to Cleeton and find out what had happened, and so he did. He brought word how poor John's holding was ravaged, the night after Callowleas, and how Yves was lost even before—the same night I committed my greatest fault and folly.' Her head reared proudly and her back stiffened as she declared her regret, and with fiery stare dared anyone else here present either to echo her self-condemnation, or attempt to deprecate it. 'Thank be to God, John and his family escaped alive. And as for their losses, I take them as my debts, and they shall be repaid. But one relief they brought me from Cleeton,' she said, quickening into warmth and affection, 'for they told me Sister Hilaria was gone, well before the raiders came, for that good brother of Pershore

93

came back, in his anxiety over us, and he brought her away safely.'

The dead silence passed unnoticed, she was so glad of that one consolation. One innocent escaped from the landslide her light-hearted escapade had set in motion.

'All this time, while I stayed with them, we have been sending about for news of Yves, and for how could I make any move until I knew how he fared? And only yesterday morning we heard at last that he was here, safe. So I came.'

'Only in time,' owned Hugh, 'to find him lost again just as you are found. Well, I trust he need not be lost for long, and if I leave you without ceremony, it is to look for him.'

Cadfael asked mildly: 'You found your own way here, alone?'

She turned her head sharply, and gave him the wide, challenging gaze of her dark eyes, her face still calm and wary.

'Robert showed me the way—the forester's son.'

'My business,' said Hugh, 'is also with these outlaws who have set up house somewhere in the hills, and hunted you out of Callowleas and Druel out of his holding. I mean to have out enough men to smoke out every yard of those uplands. But first we'll find the two we've lost.' He rose briskly, and with a meaningful gesture of his dark head and lift of an urgent eyebrow drew Cadfael away with him out of the room.

'For all I can see, the girl knows nothing of what happened to Sister Hilaria, and nothing of Brother Elyas. I have my men and as many of Dinan's mustering to take up this hunt, and small time to break unpleasant news gently. Stay here with her, Cadfael, make sure she doesn't elude us again—and tell her! She'll have to know. The more truths we can put together, the nearer we shall be to clearing out this next of devils once for all, and going home for Christmas to Aline and my new son.'

She was hungry, and had a healthy appetite, Cadfael judged, at any time. It was plenteous activity that kept her slender as a young hind. She ate with pleasure, though her face remaining guarded, thoughtful and withdrawn. Cadfael let her alone until she sat back with a sigh of physical content. Her brows were still drawn close, and her eyes looked rather inward than outward. Then, quite suddenly, she was looking at him, and with sharp attention.

'It was you who found Yves and brought him here? So Father Prior said.'

'By chance it was,' said Cadfael.

'Not only chance. You went to look for him.' That commended him; her face warmed. 'Where was it? Was he very cold and wretched?'

'He was in all particulars a young gentleman very much in command of himself. And he had found, as you did, that simple country people can be hospitable and kind without thought of reward.'

'And since then both you and he have been looking for me! While I was looking for him! Oh, God!' she said softly and with dismayed reverence. 'All this I began. And so mistakenly! I did not know even myself. I am not now the same woman.'

'You no longer wish to marry Evrard Boterel?' asked Cadfael placidly.

'No,' she said as simply. 'That is over. I thought I loved him. I did think so! But that was children's play, and this bitter winter is real, and those birds of prey in that eyrie up there are real, and death is real, and very close at every step, and I have brought my brother into danger by mere folly, and now I know that my brother is more to me by far than ever was Evrard. But never say I said so,' she flared, 'when he comes back. He is vain enough already. It was he told you what I had done?'

'It was. And how he tried to follow you, and lost himself, and was sheltered in the forest assart where I found him.'

'And he blamed me?' she said.

'In his shoes, would not you?'

'It seems to me so long ago,' she said, wondering, 'and I have changed so much. How is it that I could do so much harm, and mean none? At least I was thankful when they told me that the good brother from Pershore—how I wish I had listened to him!—had come back to look for us, and taken Sister Hilaria away with him. Were they still here when you came from Shrewsbury? Did she go on, or turn back to Worcester?'

She had arrived at what was for her a simple question

before he was ready, and the flat silence fell like a stone. She was very quick. The few seconds it took him to marshal words lasted too long. She had stiffened erect, and was staring at him steadily with apprehensive eyes.

'What is it I do not know?'

There was no way but forward, and plainly. 'What will give you no comfort in the hearing, and no joy in the telling,' said Brother Cadfael simply. 'On the night when your upland wolves sacked Druel's house, they had already done as much to a lonely hamlet nearer here, barely two miles from Ludlow. Between the two, on their way back to their lair, it seems that they encountered, by cruel ill-luck, the two after whom you ask. It was already evening when they left Druel's holding, and the night was wild, with high winds and blinding snow. It may be they went astray. It may be they tried to take shelter somewhere through the worst. They fell in the way of thieves and murderers.'

Her face was marble. Her hands gripped desperately at the arms of her chair, the knuckles bone-white. In a mere thread of a whisper she asked: 'Dead?'

'Brother Elyas was brought back here barely alive. Your brother was watching with him last night when they both went out into the snow, who can guess why? Sister Hilaria we found dead.'

There was no sound from her for a long moment, no tear, no exclamation, no protest. She sat containing whatever grief and guilt and hopeless anger possessed her, and would show none of it to the world. After a while she asked in a low and level voice: 'Where is she?'

'She is here, in the church, coffined and awaiting burial. In this iron frost we cannot break the ground, and it may be the sisters at Worcester will want to have her taken back to them when that is possible. Until then Father Prior will find her a tomb in the church.'

'Tell me,' said Ermina with bleak but quiet urgency, 'all that befell her. Better to know the whole of it than to guess.'

In simple and plain words he told her the manner of that death. At the end of it she stirred out of her long stillness, and asked: 'Will you take me to her? I should like to see her again.'

Without a word and without hesitation he rose, and led

the way. His readiness she accepted thankfully; he knew that he had gained with her. She would not be hemmed in, or sheltered from what was her due. In the chapel where Sister Hilaria lay in her new coffin, made in the brothers' own workshop and lined with lead, it was almost as cold as out in the frost, and the body had not suffered any flawing of its serene beauty. She was not yet covered. Ermina stood motionless by the trestles a long time, and then herself laid the white linen face-cloth back over the delicate face.

'I loved her very much,' she said, 'and I have destroyed her. This is my work.'

'It is nothing of the kind,' said Cadfael firmly. 'You must not take to yourself more than your due. What you yourself did, that you may rue, and confess, and do penance for, to your soul's content, but you may not lift another man's sins from his shoulders, or usurp God's right to be the only judge. A man did this, ravisher and murderer, and he, and only he, must answer for it. Whatever action of any other creature may have thrown our sister in his way, *he* had command of the hands that killed and outraged her, he and no other. It's of him her blood will be required.'

For the first time she shook, and when she would have spoken she had not her voice under control, and was forced to wait and wrestle for clear speech.

'But if I had not set my heart on that foolish marriage, if I had consented to go with Brother Elyas straight here to Bromfield, she would be living now . . .'

'Do we know that? Might not you, too, have fallen into such hands? Child, if men had not done as they did, any time these five centuries, of course things would have gone on differently, but need they have been better? There is no profit in ifs. We go on from where we stand, we answer for our own evil, and leave to God our good.'

Ermina wept suddenly and irresistibly, but would not be seen to weep. She swept away from him to kneel trembling at the altar, and remained there a long time. He did not follow her, but waited patiently until she chose to rejoin him. When she came back her face was drained but calm. She looked very tired, and very young and vulnerable.

'Come back to the fire,' said Cadfael. 'You'll take cold here.'

She went with him docilely, glad to settle beside the hearth again. The shivering left her, she lay back and half-closed her eyes, but when he made a move as if to leave her she looked up quickly. 'Brother Cadfael, when they sent from Worcester to ask for news of us, was there word said of our uncle d'Angers being in England?'

'There was. Not only in England but in Gloucester, with the empress.' That was what she had meant, though she had been feeling her way towards it cautiously. 'Openly and fairly he asked leave to come into the king's territories himself to look for you, and leave was refused. The sheriff promised a search by his own men, but would not admit any of the empress's party.'

'And should any such be found here and taken—in the search for us—what would happen to him?'

'He would be held prisoner of war. It is the sheriff's duty to deny to the king's enemies the service of any fighting man who falls into his hands, you must not wonder at it. A knight lost to the empress is a knight's gain to the king.' He saw how doubtfully and anxiously she eyed him, and smiled. 'It is the sheriff's duty. It is not mine. Among men of honour and decent Christian life I see no enemies, on either side. Mine is a different discipline. With any man who comes only to rescue and fetch away children to their proper guardian, I have no quarrel.'

She frowned momentarily at the word children, and then laughed, with angry honesty, at the very instinct that showed her still a child. 'Then you would not betray such a man even to your friend?'

Cadfael sat down opposite her and settled himself comfortably, for it seemed she had matters on her mind, and wished to unburden herself. 'I have told you, I take no side here, and Hugh Beringar would not expect me to go always his way in every particular. He does his work and I do mine. But I must tell you that he has already some knowledge of a presence in these parts, a stranger, who came to Cleeton enquiring for all you three who left Worcester together. A countryman by his dress, they said, young, tall and dark, eyed and beaked like a hawk, black-haired and dark-skinned.' She was listening intently, her underlip caught between her teeth, and at

98

every detail the colour flamed and faded in her cheeks. 'And one that wore a sword under his cloak,' said Cadfael.

She sat very still, making up her mind. The face at her shoulder in the torchlight of the gatehouse hung vividly in Cadfael's imagination, and surely even more urgently in hers. For a moment he thought she would prevaricate, shrug off the image, declare her guide to be no more than she had said, a forester's son. But then she leaned forward and began to speak with vehement eagerness.

'I will tell you! I will tell you, and not even exact any promise, for I know I need not. You will not give him up. What I said was true, that I was taken in and helped by the forester and his wife. But the second day that I was there with them, there came a youth asking for news of such a company as I had, before I shattered it. Dressed as I was when you first saw me today, still he knew me for what I was, and so did I him, for nothing could show him less than noble. He spoke French freely, but English a little slowly. He told me that my uncle had returned, and was in Gloucester with the empress, and had sent him secretly to find us and bring us safe to him. His errand is that, and nothing more, but here he goes with danger all about him, knowing he may fall into the sheriff's hands.'

'He has eluded them so far,' said Cadfael mildly. 'He may very well go on slipping through our fingers to the end, and hale you away with him to Gloucester.'

'But not without Yves. I will not go without my brother, he knows that. I did not want to come here, but he so wished it. Let me know, he said, that you at least are in safety, and leave the hunt to me. And I have done and I will do what he bids me. But I could not bear it if through his care for us he fell into the king's hands, and was left to rot in a prison.'

'Never go looking for disaster,' said Cadfael cheerfully. 'Expect the best, and walk so discreetly as to invite it, and then leave all to God. You have not given this paladin a name.' No, but he had a face, and a memorable face, too.

She was bouyantly young. Grief was fiercely felt, but so was hope, so was joy, so was the adulation of heroes. The very thought of her champion had lifted her out of the shadows of guilt and death, she glowed as she spoke of him. 'They call him Olivier de Bretagne—it is a name they gave him in his own land, because of his parentage. For he

99

was born in Syria, and his mother was of that country, and his father a Frankish knight of the Crusade, from England. He leaned to his father's faith, and made his way to Jerusalem to join his father's people, and there he took service with my uncle, six years ago now. He is his favourite squire. Now he has come home with him, and who else would be trusted with this search?'

'And with his small experience here and halting English,' said Cadfael appreciatively, 'he was not afraid to venture into these stormy regions, among his Lord's enemies?'

'He is not afraid of anything! He is bravery itself! Oh, Brother Cadfael, you do not know how fine he is! If you could only once see him, you must become his friend!'

Cadfael did not say that he had seen him, that requisite first time, briefly, like the blazing recollection of a dream. He was thinking, with nostalgic fondness, that some other lonely soul wearing the Cross had found, somewhere in that burning land of sun and sea and sand, a woman to his liking, who must have liked him no less, if she had borne him such a son. The east was full of glorious bastards. That one of them should come home to his father's land, baptised into his father's faith, was no marvel! No need to look beyond the admirable fruit.

'You have that promise you did not ask,' said Brother Cadfael. 'Oliver is safe with me. I will do nothing to uncover him. In your need or his, I will stand your friend.'

9

Yves started awake out of an involuntary doze, instantly aware of movement and sound, though both seemed so distant and faint that they might have been no more than the fading shreds of a dream. Under his arm Brother Elyas lay in exhausted sleep, sunk far too deep for dreaming, and briefly at peace. His breathing was quiet and steady. The boy felt rather than heard by its rhythm how strongly Elyas had survived the night that might well have killed him, tenacious even of a life that tormented him.

Yet something, Yves was sure, he had heard, some human sound. Not the wind, for that had dropped, and as he sat very still, listening with ears stretched, he was sensible of absolute silence. There is nothing more silent than deep snow, until men break the spell. And there it came again, small and distant but no illusion, the faint murmuring of voices, a mere snatch, gone in an instant. And again, some strained moments later, the tiny jingle of metal, a horse's harness clashing. Yves got to his feet stiffly, careful not to disturb the sleeper, and fumbled his way to the door. It was still only the deep twilight that comes before the promise of dawn, but the waste of snow before him cast up an eerie pallor. The night was well advanced, and already there were men abroad. Men with

101

horses! Yves left the door of the hut closed but unbarred, and struggled out into the drifts in haste lest the promise of help should pass before he could intercept it.

Somewhere down the slope, out of sight beyond a thicket of snow-heaped bushes and a clump of trees bowed down and turned white like the heads of tired old men, someone laughed, and again a bridle rang. The travellers, as he had hoped, were coming from the direction of Ludlow and Bromfield. Fearful that they might pass by, and never notice the hut at all, Yves plunged downhill, stumbling and wading, found a ridge which the wind had partially stripped and broke into an eager run. Skirting the bushes, he began to thread the copse, fending his way through the darkness of the close-set trees with hands outstretched. The voices were drawing nearer, loud, unsubdued voices, still wordless, but a most welcome sound. Someone raised a snatch of song, someone broke in with a loud remark, and there was more laughter. Yves was somewhat disconcerted to hear it, even indignant. If these were a party searching for the wanderers, they did not sound too anxious about their errand. But even if he was mistaken in thinking them Hugh Beringar's men, what did that matter? They were men, at any rate, and they could help him.

Nearing the far edge of the copse, and with eyes now growing more accustomed to the eerie twilight, he caught glimpses of movement between the trees. He burst out into the open with their line strung before him, more of them than he had thought, ten or a dozen at least. Three horses, and four pack-ponies, well-loaded, blew forth pale clouds of frosty breath. Even in the dimness he knew the shapes of sword and axe and bow. These men went heavily armed through the ending of the night, but not in the disciplined order of Hugh Beringar's men-at-arms, rather raggedly and merrily, and soiled with smoke. Faintly but unmistakably, the stink of burning wafted from them, and the pack-ponies were loaded high with grain-sacks, wineskins, pots, bundled clothing, the carcases of two slaughtered sheep.

His heart misgave him. Hastily he made to draw back into cover, but he had been seen, and one of the men afoot loosed a mock hunting-call, and darted into the trees to cut off his retreat. Another took up the cry, and there were the pair of them, with spread arms and broad grins, between him and return. A moment more, and half a dozen were all round him. He tried to slip between them and make off in the opposite direction from the hut, instinctively aware that whatever happened he must not betray the presence close by of Brother Elyas. But a long arm reached for him almost lazily, took him by the liripipe of his capuchon and a fistful of his hair, and hauled him painfully out to the open ride.

'Well, well!' crowed his captor, turning him about by the grip on his hair. 'What's such a small nightbird doing abroad at this hour?'

Yves struggled, but was quick to sense that he achieved nothing. Dignity forbade that he should wriggle or beg. He grew still under the large hand that held him, and said with creditable steadiness: 'Let me go! You're hurting me. I'm doing no harm.'

'Unwary nightbirds get their necks wrung,' said one, and went through the motions of wringing, with lean and dirty hands. 'Especially if they peck.'

The mounted man who led the column had halted and was looking back. A high, peremptory voice demanded: 'What game have you caught there? Bring him, let me see. I want no spies bearing tales back to the town.'

They laid hands willingly on Yves and hauled him forward to where the tallest of the three horses stood. The horse, being mainly white, was plainly visible, the man on his back loomed only as a great shadow against the sky. When he shifted a little in the saddle to stare down at the captive, some stray gleam of lambent light flowed over the links of chain mail, and flickered out like spent lightning. Afoot, he might not be a very tall man, but the breadth of his shoulders and breast, and the lion's mane of thick hair that covered his head and flowed down on to his chest in a bushy beard made him look immense. He sat his horse as if they made one powerful body between them. He was all the more frightening because his face was but a shadow, and there was nothing to be read in it.

'Hale him close,' he ordered impatiently. 'Here to my knee. Let me see him.'

Yves felt his head yanked back by the hair, to lift his face to view. He stiffened his back and his lips, and stared up in silence.

'Who are you, boy? What's your name?' It was no common country voice, but one accustomed to lordship and to being obeyed.

'They call me Jehan,' lied Yves, and did his best to avoid having his own manner of speech so easily recognised.

'What are you doing here at this hour? Are you here alone?'

'Yes, my lord. My father folds his sheep up yonder.' He pointed firmly in the opposite direction from the hut where Elyas, he hoped, still lay asleep. 'Yesterday some of them strayed, we came out early looking for them. Father went t'other way there, and sent me this. I'm no spy, what should I be spying on? We're only bothered for the sheep.'

'So! A shepherd, eh? And a very pretty little shepherd, too,' said the voice above him drily. 'In good broadcloth that cost enough when it was new. Now take breath, and tell me again: who are you?'

'My lord, I've told you true! I'm only Jehan, the shepherd's lad from Whitbache . . .' It was the only manor he could remember to the west and on the near side of Corve. He had no idea why it should raise a bellow of rough laughter from all the listening crew, and his blood chilled at hearing the short, harsh bark of mirth that came from the man above him. His own fright angered him. He set his jaw and glared up into the shadowy face. 'You have no right to question me when I am about lawful business and do no wrong. Tell your man to loose hold of me.'

Instead, the voice, interested but unmoved, said shortly: 'Hand me up that toy he wears at his belt. Let me see what our shepherds are sporting against wolves this year.'

Rough handling had plucked aside the fullness of Yves' cloak, and left his belt exposed to view, the little dagger dangling. Willing hands unbuckled it and handed it up.

'So they favour silver,' said their lord musingly, 'and precious pebbles set in their hilts. Very fine!' He looked up, aware of the first lightening of sky to eastward. 'Time's too short for starting his tongue wagging here, and my feet grow cold. Bring him! Alive! Amuse yourselves if you must, but stop short of damaging him. He may be valuable.'

He turned at once and spurred forward, his two mounted companions bearing him company. Yves was left to the mercies of the underlings. There was never a moment when he had the remotest chance of breaking away. They valued him, or their lord's orders, so highly that at every turn three of them had a grip on him. They took his own belt, and strapped it round him just above the elbows, to deny him the use of his arms, and though it had a foot to spare about his waist, to close it thus they drew it painfully tight. They found a short cord to tie his wrists before him, palms together, and a long rope to attach him, by a running noose round his neck, to the pack-saddle of the hindmost pony. If he lagged, the noose would tighten. If he hurried he could raise his bound hands high enough to grasp the rope and slaken it enough to breathe, but he could not raise them high enough to get hold of the noose itself and keep it slack. He was shrewd enough to realise that if he fell they would stop to pick him up. They had been told to deliver him wherever their lord was bound, alive and repairable. But short of killing, they were pleased to avail themselves of the permission they had been given to use him for their amusement.

He tried to shrug a fold of his cloak into the noose when they slung it over his head, and someone laughed aloud and clouted him on the ear and dragged the obstruction loose. It was at that moment that Yves remembered that under the collar of that same cloak lay hidden the ring broach that fastened it. It was very old, a Saxon piece with a formidable pin, the only weapon he had about him now, and they had not discovered it.

'Now, little bird, fly!' said his first captor, wheezing with laughter. 'But bear in mind you're flown on a creance. No making off into the sky for you.' And he strode away to set the column moving again after its master. Between sleep, fright and anger, Yves stood shivering and in a daze so long that the first jerk on his tether half-choked him. He had to gasp and scurry and clutch at his leash to recover, and a wave of raucous laughter washed back over him in recompense.

But after that he soon found that their jest could be made as amusing or as tame as he chose. For they had to move so modestly with their booty that he had no real difficulty in keeping up. Their loads were heavy and un-

wieldy, his was very light, and once fully awake, very
agile. For the first few minutes he took care to give them
some occasion for laughter, falling behind and then rushing to preserve his neck. These repeated recoveries
brought him well acquainted with the pony to which he
was tied and its load, which was two great sacks of grain,
slung in balance, and two equally vast goatskins, surely of
wine, behind the grain, with an erection of bundled cloth
and slung pots on top. When he scuttled up close he was
moving with his cheek almost against the hair of the goatskin on his side. It bulged and undulated with the liquid
within. Moreover, when he came thus close he was at the
very end of this ponderous procession, and hidden by the
lofty load from those who went before. And the way,
though clearly they knew it too well to be much aggrieved
at its drifts, still put delays enough in their path, they
soon forgot to look behind.

Under the lurching load, Yves stretched up his bound
hands as far as they would go, and felt under the collar of
his cloak for the brooch. No one could see him here, he
shrank close to the pony's patient, labouring quarter.
Fumbling fingers found the edge of the metal, and felt for
the ring of the pin, to draw it forth. His arms, bound cru-
elly tight, ached with tension, and his finger-ends were
growing numb. Doggedly he kept his hold, and began to
coax the brooch loose, terrified that he might drop it,
from pure strain, when it came out from the folds of cloth.
If he could free it and retain his hold with arms lowered,
until the use and the blood returned to his hands, he knew
he could manipulate it thereafter.

The point of the pin sprang loose, and the round brooch
almost slipped from his hold. He closed both hands upon it
in desperation, and the point pierced his finger. He bore
the prick gratefully, drew his hands down still impaled,
let the blood flow freely down his aching arms and into his
hands, and the thin ooze from the wound slide unregarded
down his finger until he could feel power there again. He
had the precious thing, sharp as a dagger. He took some
minutes before he dared try to make use of it, nursing it
between his locked palms, flexing his fingertips against it
until they felt nimble and supple as ever.

The full goatskin wallowed beside his cheek, the morning twilight hid him. The leather, though rubbed bare of

106

hair in places, and soft and portly with age, was tough, but the pin of the brooch was strong, and protruded the length of his little finger beyond the ring. It took him some moments to work it through the hide at the lowest part of the swaying bag, the yielding folds slithered away from him so vexingly, but he leaned a shoulder hard against it to hold it still, and the pin slid through.

A satisfying spurt of dark red followed as he drew the pin out again, and he looked down in hope, even in elation, to see the sudden red splash like blood in the whiteness of the snow beneath his feet. After the first gush the hole contracted again, but the weight of the wine kept it open, and trickled a thin drip along the way, and he thought it would do. It would not sink into the snow and be lost, for the frost was hard enough to seal it as it fell. And that way, dripping so meagrely, the load would last a long way. He hoped, long enough. But in case it should become too fine to be followed, from time to time he punched the skin, and found he could force out a brief jet, a tiny pool of wine to confirm what had gone before.

The dawn, grey and still and turning now to white mist that cut off all distances, was well upon them. A cold dawn, in which a few starved birds wheeled hopelessly. They had timed their return to the lair to be safe within before full light. If they were now near, Yves thought the depletion in the leaky wineskin might pass for a natural loss. They had been climbing for a long time. Lofty, bleak and inhospitable, the uplands of Titterstone Clee received them. Even in thick mist they knew where they were going, and knew when they drew near; they had begun to prod the pack-beasts and hurry the line along, scenting refuge, food and rest.

Yves took thought for his precious brooch, and managed to thread it inside the hem of his short tunic, out of sight. That freed his bound hands to grasp the rope that had begun to tighten uncomfortably round his neck when he tired, and haul himself along by it. It could not be far now. They had smelled their nest.

From barren, misty desert, without features within the short distance, the eye could see, but always climbing, suddenly they were moving between close, low-growing trees, with rising rocks just discernible behind. Then it seemed that they emerged again upon an open summit, and there before them rose a high stockade, with a narrow gate in it, and over it showed a dark, squat, broad tower. There were men on watch, the gate opened as they approached.

Within, there were low, rough lean-to buildings all round the stockade, and men in plenty moving about between them. Below the tower a long hall extended. Yves heard cattle lowing and sheep calling plaintively. All was timber, all was new, raw and crude, but solid and formidably manned. No wonder they moved at ease in the night, insolently aware of their numbers, and of the strength of their secret fortress.

Before they entered the gate Yves had the wit to draw back the length of his leash, well away from the punctured wine-skin, and blunder in droopingly, like one exhausted and cowed. Since sighting the stockade he had let the leaky skin alone, so that it dripped only a meagre droplet by the time they halted in the snowy bailey. A leaky skin was no great marvel, and the pair to it, at least, was sound. And he had luck, for his first captor made haste to undo him and haul him away by the scuff of the neck, before anyone had noticed the thin red drip, and cursed at half a wineskin lost on the journey.

Yves went where he was dragged, scrambling meekly up the steps into the hall and through the seething warmth and smokiness and stunning noise within. Torches burned along the walls, well primed out from the timber, a great fire blazed on a stone-laid hearth in the midst, and twenty voices at least plaited a lattice of noise through the haze, loud, merry and secure. Of furniture there was little, a few hewn benches, great tables on trestles or rough logs. Men teemed, and many turned to stare and grin at the passage of this small prisoner.

At the far end of the hall there was a low dias, and here there were candles in tall sconces, hangings of tapestry, and carved chairs round a table spread with food and drinking horns and pitchers of ale, where three men sat. Yves felt himself hoisted unceremoniously by a fistful of his garments at the neck, heaved bodily to the dias, and flung down on his knees at the feet of the man who sat at the end of the table. Almost he fell flat on his face, but fended himself off with his still bound hands, and hung for a moment knocked clean out of breath.

'My lord, here's your shepherd as you ordered, safe and sound. We're unloading the goods, and all's well. Not a soul stirring on the way.'

Yves gathered himself sturdily and got to his feet. He took time to draw a deep breath and steady the shaking of his knees before he looked up into the face of the chief of these nightbirds.

Mounted and looming in the twilight, the man had seemed immense. Easy now in his great chair, he was seen to be no more than common tall, but very powerfully built, wide-shouldered, deep-chested. After a savage fashion he was very comely. Now with the candlelight to show him clearly he was more like a lion than ever, for the thick mane of curling hair and the glossy, untrimmed beard were tawny, and the large eyes, narrowed but sharp as a cat's beneath heavy lids, were of the same colouring. His lips, left naked among all that profusion of dull gold, were full and curled and proud. He eyed Yves in silence from head to foot, while Yves stared as doughtily back at him, and kept his mouth shut rather out of discretion than fright. There could be worse moments to come. At least now they were back from another successful raid, laden with booty, eating and drinking and in high content with themselves. And the lion seemed in good humour. If his slow smile was mocking, it was at least a smile.

'Loose him,' he said.

The belt was unbuckled from Yves' cramped arms, the cord untied from his wrists. He stood rubbing the blood back into aching arms, kept his eyes warily on the lion's face, and waited. A number of the henchmen in the hall had drawn in at his back, grinning, to watch.

'You've betten out your tongue on the way?' asked the bearded man amiably.

'No, my lord. I can speak when I have something to say.'

'You might be well advised to think of something to say now, at once. Something nearer truth than you told me under the copse there.'

Yves could not see that boldness was going to do him any harm here, or the discretion of fear very much good. He said bluntly: 'I am hungry, my lord. You would hardly find a truer word than that. And I take it as between gentlemen that you feed your guests.'

The lion threw back his tawny head and loosed a shout of laughter that was echoed down the hall. 'And I take that to be a confession. Gentle, are you? Now tell me more, and you shall eat. No more hunting for lost sheep. Who are you?'

He meant to know. And for all his present easy mood, if he was baulked he would not mind by what means he got what he wanted. Yves spent a few seconds too long considering what he had better say, and got an earnest of what might follow obduracy. A long arm reached out, gripped him by the forearm, and with a casual twist dropped him wincing to his knees. The other hand clenched in his hair and forced his head back to stare into a face still calmly smiling.

'When I ask, wise men answer. Who are you?'

'Let me up and I'll tell you,' said Yves through his teeth.

'Tell, brat, and I may let you up. I may even feed you. A strutting little cockerel of the nobility you may be, but many a cock has got his neck wrung for crowing too loud.'

Yves shifted a little to ease his pain, drew deep breath to have his voice steady, and got out his name. There was no time for the stupidity of heroism, not even for obstinate insistence on his dignity.

'My name if Yves Hugonin. My family is noble.'

The hands released him. The bearded man leaned back in his chair at ease. His face had not changed, he had not been at all angry; anger had little part in his proceedings, which were entirely cold. Predatory beasts feel no animosity against their prey, and no compunction, either.

'A Hugonin, eh? And what were you doing, Yves Hugonin, where we found you, alone in the early morning of such a winter day?'

'I was trying to find my way to Ludlow,' said Yves. He rose from his knees and shook his disordered hair back from his face. Not a word must be said of anyone but himself; he picked his way delicately between truth and falsehood. 'I was at school with the monks in Worcester. When the town was attacked they sent me away to escape the fighting and slaughter there. I was with some other people, trying to reach any safe town, but in the storms we were separated. Country people have fed and sheltered me, and I was making my way to Ludlow as best I could.'

He hoped it sounded convincing. He did not want to have to invent details. He still recalled with misgivings the shout of laughter it had provoked when he mentioned the manor of Whitbache, and claimed residence there, and wondered uneasily why.

'Where did you spend last night, then? Not in the open!'

'In a hut in the fields. I thought I should get to Ludlow before night, but the snow came on, and I lost my way. When the wind dropped and it stopped snowing,' he said, talking to evade further probing, 'I set out again. And then I heard you, and thought you might set me right.'

The bearded man considered, eyeing him with the disturbing smile that contained merriment without warmth. 'And here you are, with a stout roof over your head, a good fire at your back, and food and drink for you if you behave yourself seemly. There's a price, of course, to pay for your bed and board. Hugonin! And Worcester . . . Are you son to that Geoffrey Hugonin who died a few years back? The most of his lands, I recall, lay in that shire.'

'I'm his son and heir, if ever I come to it.'

'Ah! There should be no difficulty, then, in paying for your entertainment.' The narrowed eyes gleamed satisfaction. 'Who stands guardian to your lordship now? And why did he let you go stravaging off into the winter so poorly provided, and alone?'

'He was only newly arrived in England from the Holy Land, he knew nothing of it. If you send now, you may hear of him in Gloucester, he is of the empress's party.' The lion shrugged that off indifferently. In the civil war he belonged to neither side, and cared nothing which side others chose. He had set up his own party, and acknowledged no other. But certainly he would extort ransom as cheerfully from one as from the other. 'His name is Laurence d'Angers,' said Yves, 'my mother's brother.' That name was known and welcomed with satisfaction. 'He will pay handsomely to have me back,' said Yves.

'So sure?' The bearded man laughed. 'Uncles are not always so anxious to ransom nephews who will one day come into great estates. Some have been known to prefer to leave them unredeemed, to be hustled out of the world

111

as unprofitable, and come into the inheritance themselves.'

'He would not come into my inheritance,' said Yves. 'I have a sister, and *she* is not here in this extreme.' It pierced him with sudden renewed dismay that he did not know where she was at this moment, and her situation might be just as dire as his own, but he kept his voice steady and his countenance wooden. 'And my uncle is an honourable man,' he said stiffly. 'He will ransom me and never grudge it. So he gets me back alive and undamaged,' he added emphatically.

'Complete to every hair,' said the lion, laughing, 'if the price is right.' He gestured to the fellow who stood at Yves' shoulder. 'I put him in your charge. Feed him, let him warm himself by the fire, but if you let him slip through your fingers, your own neck pays for it. When he has eaten, lock him away safe in the tower. He'll be worth far more than all the plunder we've brought from Whitbache.'

Brother Elyas awoke from the dreamless peace of sleep to the agonising dream of waking life. It was daylight, lines of pale morning slid between the boards of the hut, cold and white. He was alone. But there had been someone else, that he remembered. There had been a boy, a boy who had kept him company sturdily, and lain by him in the hay, a warmth by his side. Now there was no one, Brother Elyas missed him. In the snow they had clung together in mutual kindness, trying to alleviate more than the cold and the cruelty of the wind. Whatever became of him, he must find the boy, and make sure that no harm should come to him. Children hava a right to life, a right so many of their elders have forfeited by follies, by failures, by sins. He was outcast, but the boy was innocent and pure, and must not be surrendered to danger and death.

Elyas rose, and went to open the door. Under the eaves, where the wind had driven the snow away, leaving only a thin layer, the small footmarks showed clearly, only the powdering of a late squall clouding them. They turned right, down the slope, and there in the deeper snow a short, vigorous body had ploughed a jagged furrow, round the bank of bushes, down into the coppice of trees.

Elyas followed where the boy had led. Beyond the belt of trees there was a beaten track that crossed on an almost level course, climbing gently towards the east. Horses had passed this way, and men afoot with them, enough men to carve out a flattened road. They had come from the west. Had they taken boy away with them toward the east? There would be no tracing one child's passage here, but surely he had run and struggled down the slope to join them.

In his dream, which neither cold nor pain could penetrate, and only the memory of the boy could influence, Brother Elyas turned towards the east, and set out along the track the unknown company had taken. The furrow they had ploughed through barren level, even fall and drift was simple to follow, the weaving route was surely older than all the pathways here, made to render the climb equable and easy. It wound along the hillside in a long curve. Elyas had gone some three hundred paces when he saw beneath him the first splash of dark red in the white.

Someone had shed blood. Only a little blood, but a dotted line of ruby beads continued from it, and in a few moments he found another blossom of blood at his feet. The sun was rising now, pale through the mist, which lifted with the day. The red gleamed, frozen on the surface of the snow. Not even the brief noon sun would thaw it away, though the wind might spread blown snow over it. Brother Elyas followed, drop by drop along the way where someone had bled. Blood can requite blood. If someone had taken and hurt the boy, then a man already fingered by despair and death might still die to some purpose.

Immune from any further onslaughts of cold, pain and fear, on sandalled feet through frozen drifts, Brother Elyas went in search of Yves.

10

Brother Cadfael came out from High Mass with Prior
Leonard, into the brief and grudging sunshine of the middle hours of the day, and the sudden glitter reflected from
the banked piles of snow. A number of the priorty tenants
had mustered to help in the search for the missing pair,
while the light was favourable and no snow falling. Prior
Leonard pointed out one of them, a big bluff fellow in his
prime, with red hair just salted with grey, and the
weatherbeaten face and far-gazing blue eyes of the
hillman.

'That is Reyner Dutton, who brought Brother Elyas in
to us in the first place. I feel shame to think what he must
he feeling, now the poor man has slipped through our fingers after all.'

'No blame is all to you,' said Cadfael glumly. 'The fault
was mine, if there's any question of blame.' He studied
Reyner's solid person thoughtfully. 'You know, Leonard,
I have been wondering about this flight. Which of us has
not! It seems Elyas, once something set him off, went
about it with great determination. This was no simple
clambering out of bed and wandering at large. Barely a
quarter of an hour, and they were well away. And plainly
the boy could not turn or dissuade him, but he would go
wherever it was he was going. He had an end in view. It

114

need not be a reasonable end, but it meant something to him. How if he had suddenly recalled the attack that all but killed him, and set off to return to that place where it happened? That was the last he knew, before memory and almost life were taken from him. He might feel driven to resume there, in this twilight state of his mind.'

Prior Leonard conceded, though doubtfully: 'It might be so. Or may he not have recalled his own errand from Pershore, and started back to his duty there. It might take a man so, his wits being still so shaken up in him.'

'It comes to me now,' said Cadfael earnestly, 'that I have never been to the spot where Elyas was attacked, though I suppose it must be not far from where our sister was killed. And that again has been fretting me.' But he forbore from spelling out what he found peculiar about it, for Leonard had been a man of the cloister from puberty, serenely content and blissfully innocent, and there was no need to trouble him by reflecting aloud that the night of Hilaria's death had been a blizzard as intense as the night just past, that even lust has its preference for a modicum of shelter, and of shelter he had seen none close to her icy grave. A bed of snow and ice, and a coverlet of howling wind, do not constitute the most conducive of circumstances for rape. 'I was meaning to go out with the rest,' he said, 'as soon as I have taken a bite to eat. How if I should borrow Reyner to bring me to the place where he found Brother Elyas? As well begin there as anywhere.'

'That you could,' agreed the prior, 'if you are sure the girl will bide quietly here, and not try to take some action of her own.'

'She'll bide,' said Cadfael confidently, 'and give you no trouble.' And so she would, but not for his asking. She would wait here obediently because one Oliver, a paragon, had ordered her to do so. 'Come, and we'll ask your man if he'll be my guide.'

The prior drew his tenant out of the group before it moved off from the gatehouse, and made them acquainted. Clearly Reyner had a warm relationship with his lord, and was ready to fall in cheerfully with whatever course Leonard suggested.

'I'll take you there, brother, gladly. The poor man, to be out again in this, when it's almost been the death of him once. And he making such a good recovery. A madness must have come on him, to want out on such a night.'

'Had you not better take two of our mules?' wondered the prior. 'The place may not be far, but how far beyond may it not take you, if you should find a trace to follow? And your horse has been worked hard since coming here, Cadfael. Our beasts are fresh and hardy.'

It was not an offer to be refused. Mounted or afoot, travelling would be slow, but better mounted. Cadfael went to snatch a hasty dinner, and returned to help Reyner saddle the mules. They set forth eastward along a road by this time well trampled. The best of the day would last them perhaps four hours, and after that they must be prepared for a possible return of the snow, as well as fading light. They left Ludlow distant on their right hand, and went on along the beaten road. The sky hung heavy and grey before them, though a feeble sun still shone upon this stretch of their way.

'Surely it was not on the very highroad you found him?' said Cadfael, as Reyner made no move to turn aside.

'Very close, brother, a little to the north of it. We'd come down the slope below the lacy woods, and all but fell over him lying naked there in the snow. I tell you,' said Reyner forcibly, 'I'll take it very ill if we lose him now, after such an escape, and him as near death when we picked him up as ever man was and lived to tell it. To filch a good man back from the grave, and cheat those devils who did their worst to thrust him under, that did my heart good. Well, please God we'll haul him back from the edge a second time. I hear you had a lad went with him,' said Reyner, turning his far-sighted blue eyes on Cadfael. 'One that was lost beforetime, and now to seek again. I call it handsome, in one so young, to stick like a burr where he could not persuade. We'll be after the pair of them, every hale man who tills or keeps stock around these parts. We are near, brother. Here we leave the road and bear left.'

But not far. A shallow bowl only a few minutes from the road, lined with bushes and two squat hawthorn trees on the upper side, to the north.

'Just here he lay,' said Reyner.

It had been well worth coming, for this posed glaring problems. It fitted the marauding pattern of that night, yes. The outlaws had come from their early raid south of the road, and crossed, it seemed, somewhere here, to climb to some track well known to them, by which they could return unnoticed into the winderness of Titterstone Clee. Here they could well have happened on Brother Elyas, and killed him more for sport than for his gown and linen, though not despising the small pickings of the supposed corpse. Granted all that, but then, where was Sister Hilaria?

Cadfael turned to look northwards, into the gentle upland across which he had ridden with Yves before him. The brook where he had found Sister Hilaria lay somewhere up there, well away from the road. North and east from here, he judged, at least a mile.

'Come up the fields with me, Reyner. There is a place I want to view again.'

The mules climbed easily, the wind having scoured away some of last night's fall. Cadfael set his course by memory, but it did not fall far astray. One thin little brook clashed under the hooves, in the suave hollows the snow lay cushioned over bushes and low trees. They were long out of sight of the road, waves of snowy ground cutting them off, as they continued to climb. They hit the tributary of the Ledwyche brook somewhat downstream, had there been any stream flowing, from the place where Sister Hiliria had been laid, and retraced its gently rising course until they came to the unmistakable spot where the coffin-shaped hole had been hacked in the ice. Even the previous night's snow, though it smoothed off the razor-sharp outlines, kept the remembrance alive. This was the place where her murderers had thrown and abandoned her.

More than a mile from where Brother Elyas had been battered and left for dead!

Not here, thought Cadfael, looking round at a hillside as bare and bleak, almost, as the bald, craggy head of Clee. It did not happen here. She was brought here afterwards. But why? These outlaws otherwise had left all their victims where they fell, and cared nothing to hide them. And if she had been brought here, from where? No one would choose to carry a dead body very far. Somewhere nearby there must be some kind of shelter.

'They'll be running sheep, rather than cattle, up here,' he said, scanning the slopes above them.

'So they do, but they'll have got the most of them folded now. It's ten years since we had a spell such as this.'

'Then there'll be a hut or two, somewhere about, for the shepherds' use. Would you know where the nearest may be?'

'A piece back along the traverse here toward Bromfield, the half of a mile it might be.' That must be along the selfsame track Cadfael had ridden with Yves on his saddle-bow, going home to Bromfield from Thurstan's assart in the forest. He could not recall seeing such a hut that day, but evening had been setting in by then.

'We'll go that way,' he said, and turned his mule back along the path.

A good half-mile it certainly was before Reyner pointed left, to a shallow bowl below the track. The roof of the hut was almost completely screened by the mounds of snow that covered it. Only a straight black shadow under the eaves betrayed its presence from above. They descended the gentle slope to come round to the southern side, where the door was, and found it thrust open, and saw by the sill of the previous night's snow along the threshold that it had not stood thus longer than a matter of hours, for within there was no snow, except for the infinitely fine powder blown between the boards.

Cadfael halted on the brink. In two places, close together, a foot had trampled flat the ridge of snow which had built against the door while it remained closed. A line of icicles fringed the eaves, and successive noons had warmed them enough to drip for a brief while each day, and freeze again before the approach of evening, for the roof was open to the south, and sheltered from the north by the rise of the land. A slow drip fell as Cadfael gazed, and a line of fine black perforations punctured the whiteness of the layer of snow below the eaves, where the wind during the night had already thinned it. At the corner of the hut the drips had bored a small pit, revealing the ripe, rounded brownness of something that was not turf nor soil. Cadfael stirred more snow away with the toe of his boot.

Frost is a great preserver. All the sunshine of all the noons had not produced thaw enough to do more than pierce the crest of this pile of horse-droppings with one tiny shaft. The next snow would cover it again, and the frost seal it. But the hole the drip had bored in it went too deep to be the result of this one day's grudging sun. No knowing exactly how many days had passed since a horse had stood here, but Cadfael judged it might be as many as five or six. Tethered? The wood of the hut was rough-hewn, and there were props under the low, projecting eaves to which a bridle could easily be hitched.

He might never have noticed the hair, pale almost to white as it was, if a sudden rising breeze had not caused it to flutter, somewhat above the level of his eyes, from the rough timber of the corner. Had it been motionless it would have passed for one with the snow plastered and frozen there. It was the wind that had shaken the weight from its waving strands, and given it play to catch his eye. He detached it carefully from the splinters that held it, and smoothed out in his hand a tress of coarse, springy hair the colour of fading primroses. The horse tethered here had rubbed shoulder and mane against the corner of the hut, and left a token behind.

And this must be the nearest roof to the brook where he had found her. And given a horse to carry it, it would be no great labour to transport the body of a murdered girl that distance. But that might be going too fast. Better see what else the place had to tell, before he jumped to such doubtful conclusions.

He stowed away the scrap of horse-hair carefully in the breast of his habit, and went into the hut. The slight tempering of the bitter air without closed round him grate-fully, and the dry, faint scent of the piled hay tickled his nostrils. Behind him, Reyner watched in attentive silence.

Someone had done well with his hay harvest in the past season, and had still a plentiful store here. A bed and bedding provided together, a stout roof overhead—yes, any-one benighted would be thankful to hit on such a refuge. Someone had made use of it in the night just past, the great pile of hay was pressed down by the weight of a long body. So it might have been during other nights. So it might have been by two bodies. Yes, this could well be the place he was looking for. Yet even this place was at least half a mile from the spot where Brother Elyas had been left for dead, and his murderers had been making

119

their way home, not scouring half a mile of deserted countryside.

'Are you thinking,' wondered Reyner, watching him, 'that it may be the pair we're seeking who were in here last night? For someone was, and there are two breadths of foot have trampled the snow on the doorsill here.'

'It could be so,' said Cadfael abstractedly. 'Let's hope so, for whoever was here went forth live and able this morning, it seems, and has left tracks we'll follow in a moment. If we've found all there is to be found here.'

'What more can there be, and they gone?' But Reyner watched Cadfael's concentration with respect, and was willing to use his own eyes. He came within, looked all round him sharply, and stirred the great pile of hay with a vigorous foot. 'Not bad lying, if they got this far. They may have taken no real harm, after all.' His disturbance of the pile had loosed a wave of scent and a tickling haze of dust, and uncovered a corner of black cloth, well buried under the load. He stooped and tugged at it, and a long black garment emerged, unrolling in his hand, creased and dusty. He held it up, astonished. 'What's here? Who would throw away a good cloak?'

Cadfael took it from him and spread it out to see. A plain travelling cloak, in the coarse black cloth of the Benedictines. A man's cloak, a monk's cloak. The cloak of Brother Elyas?

He dropped it without a word, and plunged both arms into the pile, scooping a way down to the floor like a terrier after a rat. More black cloth there, rolled up and thrust deed, deep, to be hidden from all eyes. He brought up the roll and shook it out, and a crumpled ball of white fell clear. He snatched it back and smoothed it in his hands, the austere linen wimple of a nun, soiled now and crushed. And the black, held up to view, was a slender habit tied with its own girdle, and a short cloak of the same cloth. And all thrust away into hiding, where no chance shepherd would ever think to delve until all that hay was used.

Cadfael spread out the habit and felt at the right shoulder, sleeve and breast, and the traces, all but invisible in the shrouding black, confided to his touch what his eyes could not distinguish. On the right breast a patch the size of a man's hand was stiff and caked, crusted threads

120

crumbled away as he handled it. The folds of shoulder and sleeve bore streaks and specks of the same corruption.

'Blood?' said Reyner, watching and marvelling.

Cadfael did not answer that. He was grimly rolling up his habit and cloak together, the wimple tucked inside, and hoisting the bundle under his arm. 'Come, let's see where they went, who slept the night here.'

There was no question where the hut's last occupants had gone. From the thin layer of snow before the door, where the prints of large feet and small ones showed clearly, two tracks led downhill and merged, first with the broken slurring of people forging through a moderate fall, then ploughing a furrow to the knee and the hip through fluctuating drifts, down towards the bank of bushes and the coppice of burdened trees below. They followed, leading the mules and keeping to the narrow way carved out by those they pursued. It rounded the bushes, but cleft and passage through the belt of trees, where the branches had held off much of the fall. They emerged upon a level, where the tracks of a number of men and horses crossed them, coming from the west and moving east. Cadfael stared eastward, marking the course of the tracks till they faded from sight in distance, bearing downward here toward the drainage valley of the brooks, and surely preserving the same direct line and rising again beyond, pointing straight at the wilderness of Titterstone Clee.

'Did we cross such tracks, coming up from the road? For you see the line they take. We came from below, we end above. We must have crossed.'

'We were not looking for such, then,' said Reyner sensibly. 'And the wind may have blotted them out here and there.'

'True, so it may.' He had been bent on reaching the empty coffin in the ice, he had not been paying attention to the ground. 'Well, let's see what we have here. Whoever they were, they halted, they came circling, here where the tracks from the above come forth from the trees.'

'A horse turned and stood, here,' said Reyner, probing ahead. 'Then he wheeled and went on. So did they all. Let's follow a short way.'

The first scarlet flower of blood sprang up from their

feet within three hundred paces. A chain of ruby beads wavered on for as far again, and there was a second starry bloom, and beyond, the chain continuing, thin and clear. The frozen snow held its dyes well. They were at the peak of the day, the brief clarity would soon be gone, but while it was at its height it showed them the frowning outline of the Clee straight before them, the goal of this ancient pathway. Distant, savage and lonely, a fit place for wolves.

'Friend,' said Cadfael, halting with his eyes on that ominous skyline, 'I think you and I part company here. By all that I can see, these are last night's tracks, and they mean several horses and many men, and something aboard that dripped blood. Slaughtered sheep, perhaps? Or wounded men? The band we have to root out come from up there, and if they were not out about their grisly business last night, these tracks lie. There's a holding somewhere binding up its wounds and laying out its dead at the very least grieving for its goods and gear. Turn back, Reyner, follow these traces back to where they burned and stole last night, and go take the word to Hugh Beringar, to save what can be saved. Into Ludlow, if Hugh Beringar is not yet back—Josce de Dinan has as much to lose as any.'

'And you, brother?' demanded Reyner doubtfully.

'I'm going ahead, to follow them the way they took. Whether they've borne our pair away with them or not, this is our best chance to find where they've made their nest. Oh, never fret!' he said, seeing his companion frown and hesitate to leave him. 'I'll mind my going, I'm no beginner at this. But here, take these back with you, and leave them with Prior Leonard until I come.' He drew out the strand of primrose mane, mindful of its importance, and made it secure in the middle of the roll of clothing. 'Tell him I'll be with him before night.'

He had gone no more than a quarter of a mile when he crossed the tracks of Reyner's mule and his own, climbing to the brook. Loose, powdery snow had already been blown over the path there, but if he had been keeping his eyes open he must have seen that a number of travellers had passed that way, though he would not necessarily

122

have read any sinister meaning into that, for the snow-spume had covered the dotted line of red.

From that point on the track dipped gently to cross the Ledwyche brook and the Dogditch brook, its tributary from the north-east threading its way between holdings on either side without ever sighting them, and at once began to climb again steadily. An old, old road, maintaining its level as easily as possible over undulating country, until it was forced to climb more steeply, as every approach must, to mount to that inhospitable summit, a bleak, blistering mile of rock, starved turf, broken escarpment and treacherous, shivering moss.

The face of Clee thus approached presented surfaces of sheef cliff striated with the brief glare of sunlight. There the path certainly could not go, yet it still aimed like an arrow for the wall of rock. Soon it must veer either to the right or left, to circle the hill as it climbed, and remembering the ravaging of John Druel's holding, Cadfael judged that it must bear to the right. That way they had certainly returned home on that night, leaving the village of Cleeton well below, too strongly manned to be a quick or an easy prey so late towards dawn.

Some minutes later his guess was borne out, for the path inclined to the right, and began to follow the course of a small brook, muted now by ice, that flowed down out of the mass, until it dwindled in the high reaches, and ended in a hollow of frozen moss, which the track carefully skirted. The rocky bulk of the hill loomed on his left hand now, but often hidden from view by the folds of ground near to him, even by rare stands of stunted trees. Circling always, he climbed, until he saw below him in its bowl the desolate remains of Druel's house and byres. The next curve of the spiral took him higher, and the ruin passed from his sight.

In the rocky hillside on his left hand appeared a sudden cleft, so narrow that he might have missed it if the frail string of red drops had not turned into it. The valley within was deep and dark, and cut off at once much of the light and all the force of the wind. Herbage grew here, glad of the shelter, and had built up soil enough to support swart, strong trees. He could not be far from the summit, and he must have made more than half the circuit of the hill by this time. Whatever was at the end of this rough approach must back upon the sheer cliffs of the south-western face, and it might well be that it could be reached by no other way, except by birds.

In that thin and lofty air sounds carried far. Deep into the ravine, Cadfael had alreay halted to consider his next move when the distant metallic chinking came down to him in a regular rhythm. Somewhere above him a smith was at work. Then, faintly, but clearly, he heard cattle lowing.

If this was their gateway, it might be strongly watched, and if he was within earshot of the stronghold, it could not be far. He dismounted, led his mule well into the trees, and there tethered him. There was no longer any question in his mind that he had found his way to the outlaw company who had killed and pillaged across this countryside to the very gates of Ludlow. Who else would have built in this hidden and formidable place?

Where he could not venture in the open he might still penetrate with caution. He threaded a silent way up through the trees, and between their dark tops saw the grey pallor of the sky. Into that pallor a squat dark shape projected the top of a wooden tower. He was drawing near to the source of the brook which had carved out so deep a cleft, and before him, viewed through the trees, a plateau of rock and snow opened. He saw the long, staked line of a high stockade, the crests of roofs within, the long ridge of the hall, with the tower at its end. Not a high tower, built solid and low to withstand the winds, but tall enough to have the master's view of all that surrounded it. For the outline of wall and tower stood stark on the sky. They had no need to guard their rear, except from falcons. Behind the castle the cliffs fell sheer. From a distance, Cadfael reflected, not even the tower would be visible as separate from the dark rock from which it rose.

He stood for a while memorising what he saw and heard, for Hugh would need every detail he could get. The enclosing wall was high, topped with pointed stakes set close, and by the heads he saw appear and vanish again above the serrated crest, there were watch-platforms at frequent intervals, if not a guard-walk the whole way round. Voices floated clearly from within the pale, wordless but insistent, many voices shouting, laughing, even singing. The armourer continued his busy hammering, cattle bellowed, sheep bleated, and the hum of much busy coming and going made a confident music. They were quite unafraid, within there, they felt themselves equal to anything the hampered, divided law of the land could do against them. Whoever commanded there must have gathered to him the lawless, restless, masterless men of two or three shires, happy at seeing England torn in two, and its open wounds inviting their teeth.

Cloud was settling low overhead. Cadfael turned and made his way back to his mule, and with heightened care led him, still in the shelter of the trees, down to the opening of the ravine, and waited and listened for a while before mounting and riding. He went back the way he had come, and never encountered a living soul until he was well down towards the lowlands. There he could very well have branched left and descended to the highroad from Cleobury, but he did not do it, preferring to retrace his course all along the road the reivers used. He needed to know it well, for the night's snow, if it came as was now customary, might grievously disguise it.

It was dark by the time he came out on to the road within a mile of Bromfield, and made his way thankfully and wearily home.

Hugh Beringar did not come back until Compline, and rode in tired, hungry, and for all the cold, sweating from his exertions. Cadfael went to join him over his late supper, as soon as he came from the church.

'You found the place, then? Reyner brought you word where last night's devilry fell?' He was answered by the grimness of Hugh's face.

'And told me what you were about at the other end of it. I hardly thought to find you home before me—faith, or at all, undamaged! Need you always be the one to put your hand straight into the hornet's nest?'

'Where was it they burned and slew, last night?'

'At Whitbache. Barely two miles north of Ludlow, and they strode in and out again as freely as in their own bailey.' It fitted well. Their way home from Whitbache would run below the hut to the old road, just as Cadfael had witnessed it. 'I was back in Ludlow when your man came, I fetched Dinan out to come with me. Every house pillaged, every soul hewn down. Two women escaped by

125

running away into the woods, and carried their babes with them, all that ails them is cold and horror, but the rest—one may live to tell it, and two young lads, but all hurt. And the rest, dead. They're Dinan's people, he'll see them cared for. And have blood for their blood, given half a chance.'

'Both you and he may have your chance,' said Cadfael. 'Reyner Dutton found what he was seeking, and so did I.'

Hugh's head, inclined wearily back against the wall, jerked erect again sharply, and his eyes regained their brightness. 'You found the den these wolves are using? Tell!'

Cadfael told the whole store in detail. The clearer the picture they could draw now of the problem confronting them, the better the chance of dealing with it with little loss. For it was not going to be easy.

'As far as I can see, there is but that one road to them. Behind the fortress the ground still rises somewhat, to the rim of the cliff. Whether their stockade continues round the rear of the bailey I could not see. With that drop at their backs they may have felt it unnecessary. I daresay the rocks could be climbed, in a better time of year, but in this ice and snow no one would dare attempt it. And being the men they are, I fancy they have store of stones and boulders ready in case any should venture.'

'And the place is indeed so strong? I marvel how they've contrived so much building in secrecy.'

'A place so remote and harsh, who goes there? A few holdings clinging to the lower slopes, but what is there to draw an honest man above? Not even good grazing. And, Hugh, they have an army within there, the scourings of God knows how wide a swathe of middle England, labour in plenty. And Clee Forest at their feet, and stone all about them, the only crop that summit bears. You know and I know how fast a castle can be reared, given the timber and the need.'

'But runaway villeins turned robber, and petty thieves fleeing from the towns, and such fry, do not build on such a scale, but make themselves hovels in the woods,' said Hugh. 'Someone of more weight has the rule there. I wonder who! I do wonder!'

'Tomorrow, if God please,' said Cadfael, 'we may find out.'

'*We?*' Briefly and distractedly Hugh smiled at him. 'I thought you had done with arms, brother! You think our two are within there?'

'So the tracks would seem to show. It is not certain that those who slept in the hut through the night, and ran down to meet the horsemen, were Yves and Elyas, but man and boy they were, and do you know of any other such couple gone astray in the night? Yes, I do think they have fallen into the hands of these rogues. Armed or unarmed, Hugh, I am coming with you to get them out.'

Hugh regarded him steadily, and said outright what was on his mind. 'Would they bother to burden themselves with Elyas? The boy, yes, his very clothes mark him out as worthy prey. But a penniless monk, wandering in his wits? Once already they've battered him all but to death. You can think they would hesitate the second time?'

'If they had discarded him,' said Cadfael firmly, I should have found the body lying. I did not find it. There is no way, Hugh, of knowing what is truth, but to go out and exact it from those who know.'

'That we will do,' said Hugh. 'At first light tomorrow I go to the town, to order out on the king's business every man Josce de Dinan can muster, along with my own men. He owes allegiance, and he will pay it. He has no more use for anarchy in his own baileywick than has King Stephen himself.'

'A pity,' said Cadfael, 'that we cannot take them at first dawn, but that would lose us a day. And we need the daylight more than they do, they knowing their ground so much better.' His mind was away planning the assault, which was no business now of his, nor had been for many years, but the old enthusiasm still burned up at the scent of action. He caught Hugh's smiling eye, and was ashamed. 'Pardon, I forget myself, unregenerate as I am.' He turned back to what was his concern, the matter of troubled souls. 'There is more to show you, though it has no immediate link with this devils' castle.'

He had brought the roll of black clothing with him. He unrolled it upon the trestles, drawing aside the creased white wimple and the strand of creamy mane. 'These I found in the hay, in that hut, buried well from sight, if Reyner had not kicked the pile apart. See for yourself what lay in that hiding place. And this—this from without, snagged in the rough wood at the corner of the hut, and a pile of horse-droppings left at the spot.'

He told that tale with the same exactness, needing another mind at work upon these discoveries. Hugh watched and listened with frowning attention, quickened utterly from his weariness and alert to every implication.

'Hers *and* his?' he said at the end of it. 'Then they were there together.'

'So I read it, also.'

'Yet he was found some distance from this hut. Naked, stripped of his habit—but his cloak left behind where they sheltered. And if you are right, then Elyas set off wildly back to this very place. By what compulsion? How drawn?'

'This,' said Cadfael, 'I cannot yet read. But I doubt not it can be read, with God's help.'

'And hidden—well hidden, you say. They might have lain unnoticed well into the spring, and been an unreadable riddle when they did reappear. Cadfael, have these wolves hidden any part of their worst deeds? I think not. What they break, they let lie where it falls.'

'Devils do so,' said Cadfael, 'being without shame.'

'But perhaps not without fear? Yet there is no sense in it, take it all in all. I cannot see where this leads. I am none too happy,' owned Hugh ruefully, 'when I try.'

'Nor I,' said Cadfael. 'But I can wait. There will be sense in it, when we know more.' And he added sturdily: 'And it may not be so dismaying as we think for I do not believe that evil and good can be so dismally plaited together that they cannot be disentangled.'

Neither of them had heard the door of the room open or close, the small anteroom of the guest-hall where Hugh's supper had been laid. But when Cadfael went out with his bundle of clothing under his arm, she was there, outside in the stone passage, the tall, dark girl with her sleepless, proud, anxious eyes huge in her pale face, and her black hair a great, swaying cloud round her shoulders, and he knew by the strained urgency of her face that she had come in innocence, hearing voices, and looked within, and drawn back in awe of what she saw. She had shrunk into the shadows, waiting and hoping for him. She was shivering when he took her firmly by the arm and led her away in haste to where the remnants of the day's fire still burned sullenly in the hall, banked to continue live until morning. But for the surly glow, it was in darkness there. He felt her draw breath and relax a little, being thus hidden. He leaned to stab at the fire, not too roughly, and get an answering red and gratifying warmth out of it.

'Sit down here and warm yourself, child. There, sit back and fear nothing. This same morning, on my life, Yves was live and vigorous, and tomorrow we shall bring him back, if man can do it.'

The hand with which she had gripped his sleeve released him slowly. She let her head rest back against the wall, and spread her feet to the fire. She had on the peasant gown in which she had entered at the gate, and her feet were bare.

'Girl dear, why are you not long ago asleep? Can you not leave anything to us, and beyond us to God?'

'It was God let her die,' said Ermina, and shuddered. 'They are hers—I know, I saw! The wimple and the gown, they are Hilaria's. What was God doing when she was befouled and murdered?'

'God was taking note of all,' said Cadfael, 'and making place beside him for a little saint without spot. Would you wish her back from thence?'

He sat down beside her, not touching, very considerate of her grief and remorse. Who had more to answer for? And who needed more gental usage and guidance, in respect of her self-destroying rage?

'They *are* hers, are they not? I could not sleep, I came to see if anyone had news, and I heard your voices there. I was not listening, I only opened the door, and saw.'

'You did no harm,' he said mildly. 'And I will tell you all I know, as you deserve. Only I warn you again, you may not take to yourself the guilt of the evil another has done. Your own, yes, that you may. But this death, at whosoever's door it lights, comes not near you. Now, will you hear?'

'Yes,' she said, at once docile and uncompromising in the dark. 'But if I may not arrogate blame, I am noble, and I will demand vengeance.'

'That also belongs to God, so we are taught.'

'It is also a duty of my blood, for so I was taught.'

It was every bit as legitimate a discipline as his own, and she was just as dedicated. He was not even sure, sitting beside her and feeling her passionate commitment, that he did not share her aim. If there was a severance, yet they did not go so far apart. What they had in common, he reasoned, was a thirst for justice, which she, bred into another estate, called vengeance. Cadfael said nothing. A devotion so fierce might burn long enough to carry all before it, or it might soften and concede some degree of its ferocity. Let her find her own way, after eighteen her spirit might abate its fury as it saddened and became reconciled to the human condition.

'Will you show me?' she said almost humbly. 'I would like to handle her habit. I know you have it there.' Yes, almost humbly, she was feeling her way to some end of her own. Humility in her would always be a means to an end. But of her whole-hearted affection for the lost friend there could be no doubt at all.

'It is here,' said Cadfael, and unrolled the bundle on the bench between them, putting aside the cloak that belonged to Brother Elyas. The wisp of creamy mane drifted out of the folds and lay at her foot, stirring like a living thing in the draught along the floor. She picked it up and sat gazing down at it from under drawn brows for some moments, before she looked up questioningly at Cadfael.

'And this?'

'A horse stood tethered under the eaves of that hut for some time, and left his droppings in the snow, and this rubbed off from his mane against the rough boards.'

'That night?' she said.

'Who can be sure? But the droppings were well buried, not new. It could have been that night.'

'The place where you found her,' said Ermina, 'was not close?'

'Not so close that a man would willingly carry a body there, even to hide that circumstances of his guilt—unless he had a horse to bear the burden.'

'Yes,' she said, 'that was my thought, also.' She put the pale strands from her gently, and took the habit into her hands. He watched her drape it over her knees, and run her hands softly over the folds. Her fingers found the stiffened places, halted over the patch on the right breast, traced the folded creases that ran from it, and returned to the source.

'This is blood?' she questioned, wondering. 'But she did not bleed. You told me how she died.'

'That is true. This blood cannot be hers. But blood it is. There were faint traces on her body, where there was no wound.'

'Faint traces!' said Ermina, lifting to his face one flash of her dark eyes. She spread her palm upon the patch that stiffened the breast of the gown, opening her fingers wide to span the clotted stain that was more than a faint trace. A stain from without, then, not from within. 'His blood? The man who killed her? Well done, if she drew blood from him! And yet . . . I would have clawed out his eyes, but she? So slight and so gentle . . .'

Suddenly she was still, quite still, brooding with the habit raised in both hands to her breast, as it would hang if she put it on, and the red glow from the fire gilding her face and kindling reflected fires in her eyes. When she stirred again, it was to rise calmly and shake out the creases, and that done, she folded the garment meticulously, smoothing out the edges to make all neat.

'May I keep this in my charge? Until,' she said with considered emphasis, 'it is needed to confront her murderer?'

11

In the early morning light Hugh Beringar rode from Bromfield for Ludlow, to muster his forces for the march, and Brother Cadfael pulled on his boots, kilted his habit for riding, took his cloak, and went with him. Besides his function as guide, he had loaded his scrip with dressings and ointments for fresh wounds, of which there might be plenty before this day ended.

He saw nothing of Ermina before they departed, and was glad to believe that she must still be fast asleep, and at peace. There was a tension and withdrawal about her that made him uneasy, for no good reason that he could see. It was not simple fear for her brother that weighed on her heart, nor the grief and guilt she had already confessed and was determined to purge by penitence. That braced, armed stillness with which she had taken her leave the previous night, clasping Sister Hilaria's habit, stayed in his mind as much resembling the virgin knight's bathed and accoutred vigil before his first battle.

Blessed be Olivier de Bretagne, who had somehow found a way to master her, ousting an immature fantasy of love from her heart, and at whose command she would even remain still and inactive, and leave the burden of the day to others, wholly against her nature. But why, then, should he think of her as armed, alert and about to do battle?

Meantime they had their own battle to fight and win.

At Ludlow Josce de Dinan marched out from the castle the force Hugh demanded of him, and came himself at their head, a big, burly, full-fleshed man of middle age, ruddy of face and well-mounted. Hugh had asked in particular for archers, and got them. In these border shires there were plenty of men skilled with the short bow, and Cadfael estimated that from the rim of the trees at the head of the gully to the stockade should be just within their range. From the shelter of the branches they could provide cover for an advance, by picking off any defenders who mounted the guard-walk within. A pity that the trees spanned barely a quarter of the open plateau, where the ravine still gave them protection from the bleakest winds, and even there they shrank to dwarf size at the crest. That open arena troubled Cadfael. There would be archers within as well as without, and loopholes to allow them a clear field without exposing them to shafts from the attackers. He had no delusions about the quality of the enemy's dispositions. Whoever had erected that fortress in that lofty place knew what he was about, and by the carefree bustle within he had mustered a formidable garrison.

The march was easier than they had expected. The night's snow had begun later and ended earlier than for some days, and without the worst winds, and Cadfael had the path well in mind. The air, still as frosty, was starkly clear here on the lower ground, but thin, bright mist cut off all summits. That might well be to their advantage when they drew close to their goal, affording at least a veil over their movements.

'Such a morning,' judged Cadfael, 'if they have been out at all in the night, they would make sure of being home and invisible early. Given a remission like this, country people will be out betimes. These night-owls have no objection to leaving their traces where they strike, but so far they've avoided being seen, except by their victims. Those who blunder into their way by chance they kill, unless they have a value living. But with one fat plucking only a night ago, maybe they won't have stirred abroad.

If that's so, they'll be home and wakeful, and less drunk than after a fat foray, which is a pity.'

He rode ahead, with Hugh on one side, and Josce de Dinan a careless pace to the rear on the other. Dinan was too big a man, in every sense, to strain to keep his horse's nose level with that of Hugh's mount, or resent serving under a younger and less experienced man. He had no need to stress his own worth. Cadfael took to him. He had never before seen this supposedly dubious ally, but he thought him a man to be valued, and lost only with grief.

'They may have outposts at the approaches,' said Hugh.

Cadfael considered, and doubted it. 'Towards the foot or even halfway up, their man would be too distant to give fair warning, and too isolated for his own safety. And the best defence of the gully is that it looks so narrow and blind it must usually pass unnoticed. I was following a plain trail. I shall not miss the place. And in between, all is open. I think they rely on secrecy, and if that's penetrated, on their strength.'

The world before them lay bleak and unpeopled, the great hump of land ahead, turbaned in cloud, was a steely blue shadow. Cadfael viewed the sculptured land, narrowed his eyes, and steered his remembered course. In places the night's fall had smoothed out yesterday's tracks, but here and there they still showed faintly as dimpled hollows in the new surface. When they drew near to the stony bulk before them he slowed his pace, and went with raised head, trying to pierce the haze that hid the crest of the cliffs. He could see no square dark ridge reared above the bulk of the rock, though the outline of the rock itself showed very faintly through the veil. If he could not see the tower, there was hope that no watcher from the tower could see this approaching force, even though they moved openly and in considerable numbers. Better get them past this stage as quickly as possible, and round the first curve of the spiral pathway.

When the long gradual climb brought them out on the bleak waste of the summit, and the fissure in the rocky ground opened on their left, Hugh halted his company and sent scouts ahead. But there was no movement, no sign of life but the wheeling of a few birds in the sky above. The cleft was so narrow that it seemed likely it must close after a few paces, and could hardly be expected to lead anywhere.

'It widens, within,' said Cadfael, 'and goes on opening steadily towards the source of the stream, like most upland brooks. There are trees most of the way, though they're dwarfed above.'

They entered the defile, and deployed their numbers among the trees on either side. The mist was lifting by the time Hugh stood within the highest screen of trees, looking out over the open bowl of sparse grass and rock and snow to the stockade. The first step out of cover by any man, and the alarm would be given at once. From this thin fringe of trees onward there was no cover at all. And the distance, Cadfael saw with concern, was greater than he had thought, great enough to decimate the ranks of any attacking host, if there were competent bowmen and a proper watch within the walls.

Josce de Dinan eyed the length of the stockade and the bulk of the tower within. 'You'll not give them formal call to surrender? I see no need, and good reason against it.'

So did Hugh. Why give away the weapon of surprise, if indeed they had managed to spread their archers and men-at-arms round the meagre crescent of cover without being observed. If they could get even halfway to the walls before the archers sprang into concerted action along the guard-walk, they could save lives.

'No. These men have done pillage, violence and murder without mercy, I need give them nothing. Let's dispose our forces to the best advantage, and then have at them before they're 'ware.'

His bowmen he distributed all round the crescent. His men afoot in three groups were spaced along the rim, and his handful of mounted men in two groups between, to converge on the gate and break their way in, to make a way for the following footmen.

There was a stillness when all was ready, before Hugh, from his place as spear-head of one mounted party, spurred forward and raised his arm for the onset. He from the left and Dinan from the right burst out from cover and charged for the gate, the footmen pouring after them. The bowmen in the edge of the trees loosed one volley together, and then drew and shot at will, watching for any head that appeared above the stockade. Cadfael, left behind with the archers, marvelled that the attack could begin almost in silence but for the thudding of hooves, and even that muffled by the snow. The next moment there was uproar within the walls, a frantic scrambling of men to the loopholes, and then an answering hail of arrows. But that first charge had almost succeeded, for the gate had been unbarred, and by the time the guards had clapped it to, Hugh and Dinan and five or six more were under the wall, hidden from the defenders within, and heaving with all their might to burst into the bailey.

Within, men swarmed to hold the gate closed and bar it securely, and the din of shouted orders and confused movements washed back and forth like storm-water in a foundering ship. The stout gate was ajar, quivering, and the running foot soldiers flung themselves into the human ram to hurl it wide and break into the bailey.

From high above their heads a great voice suddenly bellowed like thunder. 'Hold, you below! King's men or whatever you be, stand, and look up here! Look, I say! Put up and quit my gates, or take this infant carrion with you!'

All heads within and without the gate came up with a jerk to stare at the top of the tower, and on both sides archers froze with bows drawn, and lance and sword were lowered. Between two of the crude timber merlons of the parapet Yves stood balanced, held by a great hand gripping his clothes in the small of the back, and over the merlon beside him leaned a raging, bristling head, tawny gold, long hair and beard streaming in a capricious wind that could hardly be felt below. A mailed hand held a naked dagger at the boy's throat.

'You see him?' roared the lion, glaring down with eyes firegold with fury. 'You want him? Living? Then draw off! Haul off out of range, out of sight, or I cut his throat now and throw him down.'

Hugh stood holding the sword he had drawn to probe through the yielding chink of the gate, and stared up with a white, fixed face. Yves was stiff as a beam of wood, looking neither down nor up, but straight before him at empty sky. He never made a sound.

'I do not know you, sir,' said Hugh, carefully and low, 'but I am the king's man here, and I say to you, you have now no refuge, here or anywhere. Harm him, and I will be your death. Be advised. Come down, yield yourself and all these your men and trust to find some mercy that way, for otherwise there is none.'

'And I say to you, king's man, take your rabble out of my sight, now, without argument, or you may have this piglet, bled ready for eating. Now, I say! Turn and go! Shall I show you?' The point of the dagger pricked, in the clear air they saw the little bubble of blood that grew, and burst, and slid down in a fine thread.

Hugh clapped his sword into the scabbard without another word, mounted and wheeled his horse, and waved all his men back from the stockade, back into the trees, back out of sight. Behind him he heard vast laughter that still resembled the hungry roar of a hunting lion.

Archers and all had shrunk far back to be invisible, watching that threat. They drew together in stunned silence, down among the trees. This was deadlock indeed. They knew they dared not advance, and that resplendent wild beast in the tower knew just as surely that they would not depart.

'But I know him, if you do not,' said Josce de Dinan. 'A by-blow of the Lacy clan by a younger son of the house. His brother the right side the sheets, after the father married, is a tenant of mine. This one served in France some years, for Normandy against Anjou. They call him Alain le Gaucher, because he's left-handed.'

Even those who had seen the man now for the first time needed no reminders. It was the left hand that had held the dagger against the boy's throat, and turned the point quite coldly to pierce the skin.

Yves felt himself hoisted by the small of his back, in the fist that gripped the fullness of his clothes and bruised his spine with hard knuckles, and dumped hard upon his feet on the timbers of the roof. The jarring shock ran up from his heels to his head, and shook his eyes wide open. He had been so intent upon uttering no sound that he had bitten his tongue, the blood ran warm within his lower lip. He swallowed it, and braced his quaking feet into the planks under him. The thin thread of blood trickling down his neck from the prick of the dagger hardly troubled him, and was already drying.

He had never yet been so frightened, as he had never been so rough-handled, suddenly plucked erect by the neck, hauled up confusing staircases in the dark, windowless bulk of the tower, finally dragged up a last vertical ladder and through a heavy trap to the dazzle of daylight on the roof. The lion's voice had roared in his ears, the lion's own fist had hoisted him to the parapet, with a furious lunge that might well have hurled him over. By instinct he had held his tongue, and made no sound. Now, suddenly released, he felt his knees give way under him, and stiffened them indignantly. He still had not uttered word or cry. He held that thought to him like an accolade, and stood doggedly waiting for the pounding of his heart to ease. It was an achievement that he stood erect at all.

Alain le Gaucher stood with hands spread along the merlons, grimly watching the besiegers draw off into the gully. The three of his men who had followed him aloft here stood waiting for his orders. So did Yves, bracing himself not to quail when the thick, powerful body swung round on him, and the fiery eyes hung on him with calculating intensity.

'So the brat has his value still, if not in money! Good reason to hold him fast, we may have to make further use of him to the same end. Oh, they'll not go far out of sight, I know—not yet, not until they've tried every roundabout way they can find, and been baulked at every attempt by a small knife at a small piglet's throat. Now we know they'll dance to our tune. Imp, you may yet be worth an army to us.'

Yves found no comfort in that. They would not even seek a ransom for him, his value as a hostage being far higher, now that their fortress was known. They could not hide it again, and enjoy the secrecy of their night exploits by wiping out every witness, as before. But for some while, at least, they could go on repeating the threat to kill their prisoner, perhaps even bargain with his life for freedom to march out unchallenged and resume their activities elsewhere. But no, Hugh Beringar would not so tamely give up, nor would he leave a hostage in such hands a moment longer than he must. He would find some way, short of frontal assault, of breaking into this lair. Yves did his best to believe that, and kept his face expressionless and his mouth shut.

'You, Guarin, stay here with him. You shall be relieved of the watch before dark, and he'll give you no trouble. Short of clambering over the parapet and dashing his brains out below, what can he do? And I fancy he's not yet so mad with fear as to choose that way. Who knows, he may even come to like the life with us—eh, chicken?' He jabbed a hard finger into Yves' ribs and laughed. 'Have your dagger ready. If they come out of hiding, if you see any man of them making roundabout to come at us, challenge on the instant, and repeat the threat. And if they persist,' he said, with a sudden snap of large teeth like a trap closing, 'bleed him! If it comes to worse yet, I'll take the knife myself. Me they'll believe!'

The man called Guarin nodded and grinned, and loosened his dagger in its sheath, suggestively.

'The rest of you, down, and we'll make better dispositions. I want a watch on every foot of our boundaries. They'll be probing busily before they give up from the cold. There's no sheriff born is going to camp in the open up here in such a winter. Not for longer than a night.'

There was a ring set into the trap, by which to lift it. He set his own great hand to it, and heaved it out as easily as lifting a ladle, and dropped it with a hollow thud upon the boards. Below, it could be secured by bolts, the metal rang as it fell.

'We'll shut you up here, for safety's sake. Never fret, you shall have your food brought, and quit your watch by twilight, but with this chick fresh from the egg I take no chances. He's too effective a tool to risk.' He clouted Yves on the shoulder in passing, as forthrightly as he had stroked the knife across his throat, and plunged through the trap, swinging down the tall ladder to the next floor. His men followed him briskly. Guarin hauled the trap into place, and they both heard the bolts slide into their sockets below, and the last man clambering down the ladder.

The two of them were left in their rough timber eyrie, staring at each other. There was frozen snow under their feet, and frost in the air they breathed. Yves licked dried blood from his lip, and looked about him for the most favourable ground. The tower had been built high enough to command as wide a view as possible, without allowing its own outline to stare too obviously above the line of the rock. The wall surrounding it rose breast-high to him before the merlons began, he could lean between them and look out every way, but to the rear, above the sheer cliffs, he could see only the rim of the escarpment, and beyond, the distant land below. The space up here was too wide and open to be comfortable, wind and weather could make it a bitter ordeal, though this day was better than any that had gone before.

Within his vision nothing now stirred, except for the fierce bustle inside the bailey, where every watch-point was being manned, and every loophole supplied with an archer. The king's men had gone to earth like foxes. Yves selected the snow-free corner of his ground, backing into the wind, and sat down on the boards there with his back hunched against the timbers and his arms hugging his knees. Every contact nursed a shred of warmth. He was going to need all he could get. But so was Guarin.

Not one of the worst of them, this Guarin. Yves had taken the measure of many of those close about their chieftain, by this time, he knew those who took pleasure in hurting, in defiling, in making other human creatures writhe and abase themselves. And there were more than enough of them, but this Guarin was none. The boy had even learned how some of them had come into this service, and could pick out worst from best. Some were footpads, murderers, thieves from choice, born to prey on their own kind. Some were petty tricksters from the towns, who had fled from justice and taken refuge where even their small skills could be used. Some were runaway villeins who had committed some angry revolt against tyranny, and put themselves on the wrong side of the law. Several were of better birth, younger sons and landless knights who considered themselves soldiers of fortune in this company. Some were even men disabled in honest service, and cast off when they were of no further profit; but these were few, and trapped, they did not belong in this garrison, but had blundered into it by ill-fortune, and could not get loose.

Guarin was a big, slow-witted, easy-going soul, without cruelty. He had no objection, as far as Yves could see, to robbing and sacking and burning, provided others did the killing. He would go with the crowd and behave himself conformably, but he would rather not let blood himself if it could be avoided. But for all that, he would carry out his orders. It was the only way he knew of ensuring a share with the rest, all the food he needed, and all the drink, a roof above him, and a fire. If his lord told him point-blank to kill, he would kill and never hesitate.

The day enlarged over the two of them, and brightened. The murderous weather, if it had not yet softened, held a kind of promise. It was past noon when someone thumped merrily at the trap, hauled back the bolts below, and rose out of the dark, wood-scented pit of the tower with a bag of bread and meat and a pitcher of hot, spiced ale for the watchman. There was enough for two, and Guarin spared a portion for his prisoner. They were lavish with their provender. They had the provisions from at least four local holdings to feed them.

The food and drink helped for a while, but as the day wore away the cold came down again and bit hard. Guarin stamped about the boards to keep himself warm, constantly patrolling in order to keep watch in every direction, and paid no attention to his prisoner except for a hard stare now and again to remind him that he was helpless, and had better not attempt anything on his own behalf. Yves fell into an uneasy doze for a while, and awoke so cold and stiff that he found it necessary to get up and stamp his feet and clap his arms vigorously to get his blood flowing again. His guard laughed at that, and let him dance and exercise as he liked. What harm could he do?

The light was beginning to fail. Yves fell to pacing the tower a few steps behind his watchman, peering out at every embrasure upon a world still peopled only by his enemies. On the precipice side, in particular, he craned perilously to see below, but still had only the barren cliff-edge and the distance before him. That entire side of the square tower looked out upon the sky. But at the eastern corner, while Guarin's back was turned, Yves found a rough join in the timbers by which he could gain a foothold and hoist himself up to achieve a better view. Below him the rim of rock levelled out, and by straining perilously round towards the void he could see at last that the stockade did not continue all round the castle, but terminated where it met the cliff-edge. Here at the corner the drop was not quite sheer, he could see the first jagged folds over the edge, every ledge with its smooth burden of

141

untrodden snow. All that motionless, empty whiteness everywhere, as though the friends on whom he relied had deserted him.

But the whiteness was not quite motionless, nor the rocky landscape quite empty. Yves blinked in disbelief, seeing the outline of one hanging drift move, and show for an instant the shape of a raised head, a shadowy visage lifted briefly to judge the next stage of a solitary and perilous climb. The next moment there was nothing to be seen there, at the extreme edge of the stockade and some ten yards down the broken face, but a mound of snow. Yves stared, straining anxious, elated eyes, but there was no more movement.

A shout behind him caused him to slither down frantically from his perch, even before Guarin's hand plucked him down and shook him heartily. 'What are you about? Fool, there's no way down there for you.' He laughed at the thought, but blessedly did not look where the boy had been looking. 'As well get your throat slit as break your bones at the bottom of that fall.'

He kept his grip on the boy's shoulder, and marched him along before him, as if he really believed his prisoner might yet slip through his fingers and cost him dear. Yves went where he was hustled, and thought it wise to whine a little about his usage, to keep the man amused and distracted.

For now he was sure he had not been deceived. There was a man down there among the rocks, a man who had covered his dark garments with a white linen sheet to move invisibly in the snow, a man who had clambered at his peril, surely not up the whole cliff-face, but laboriously round the rim from the trees, just below vision, to make his way out across the rock face beyond the stockade, and into the bailey where no one watched, where it was thought impenetrable. And in so disciplined a fashion, slow-moving even in this icy coldness, able to freeze into ice himself, and be part of the rocks and the winter. And now he was waiting for the dark, before venturing the last perilous passage.

Yves trotted submissively where the hand gripping his shoulder drove him, and hugged to his heart the blazing conviction that he was not abandoned, that heroes exerted themselves on his behalf, that heroism was also required of him before all was won, and that he must not fall short.

Darkness had closed in, and Guarin was the one complaining, before his relief came clattering up the ladder, shot back the bolts, and heaved up the trap to emerge on the roof.

This one was decidedly not among the least offensive, a bristle-bearded, pock-marked, flat-nosed cutpurse with a malicious fist, and dirty nails that liked pinching. Yves had some few bruises from him already, and gnawed a dubious lip at seeing him burst up out of the depths. He knew no name for him. Possibly he had never had a name, only some epithet by which he might be known, short of proper parentage or Christian baptism.

Guarin was none too fond of him, either, he grunted vexation at such a late relief, when he had been promised it before dark. They snarled at each other before parting, which left Yves time to shrink into his sheltered corner out of sight and mind. There might be a bleak interval. But there was someone out there in the enclosing night, not so far away, coming to his aid.

Guarin grumbled and clumped his way down the long ladder, and Yves heard the bolts shot home. They had their orders. He was left isolated here with this unpredictable cutthroat, who would stop only short of his lord's ban. He dared not kill or maim. Short of either, no doubt he would take it for granted he had free leave to hurt.

Yves sat back against the solid timber wall, shrunken into his corner with back to the wind. It was made clear to him at once that his new guard felt no goodwill towards him, blaming him for the discomfort of being perched up here in the frosty night, instead of below by the fire.

'Pest of a brat,' he snarled, and kicked savagely at the boy's ankles in passing, 'we should have cut your throat there on the road where we first met you. If the king's men had found you dead they'd have had no call to hunt for you living, and we should have been snug and merry here still.' All of which, Yves had to own as he drew in his feet and sat hunched in his corner, was probably true enough. He made himself as small as he could, and held his tongue, but silence did nothing to placate his custodian, rather it seemed to infuriate him.

'If I had my way, you should dangle from of these merlons for the kites. And never think you'll escape it in the end. Whatever bargain they strike over you, it can be broken once we're clear away. What's to stop you being promised in return for passage, and delivered up carrion? Devil take you, answer me!' He kicked out again viciously, driving his toe deliberately at the boy's groin. The stab was not quite evaded, as Yves rolled hastily away, and cost him a gasp of pain and rage.

'What's to stop it?' he flashed, goaded. 'Only that your lord still keeps some dregs of his breeding, and puts some small value on his word. And you'd best do his bidding to the letter, for this moment he has far more use for me than he has for you. He could swing *you* from a merlon with a light heart and nothing to lose.'

He knew he had been a fool, but he was sick of trying to be wise against his nature. He saw the great fist coming for his hair, and dived below it and sprang clear. On this limited ground he might be cornered in the end, but he was lighter and faster than his tormentor, and at least movement was warmer than keeping still. The man came after him, shrewd enough to do his cursing low-voiced, for any bellowing up here was liable to fetch someone up to enquire the cause. He muttered his obscenities as he charged, both thick arms flailing for a hold. 'What, you naked chick, use such insolence to me, would you? Big talk from a thrapple I could wring one-handed? If your neck's safe, is that warrant for your skin? Or a few teeth down your saucy throat?'

In the act of slipping beneath a grasping arm, Yves saw beyond his enemy's shoulder the heavy trap in the floor beginning to rise. They had been too intent on each other to hear the bolts being withdrawn, even if it had not been done with unusual care and quietness. The head that emerged, though seen only by this late twilight, which below must be already full darkness, was none that Yves knew, and came forth so steadily and silently that his heart leaped with desperate hope. How do you recognize at first sight someone who cannot possibly be a member of an outlaw gang of thieves and murderers? If the guard turned fully about now, he would be looking straight at the newcomer, who was just setting foot to the boards and rising erect. This raving, fumbling wretch must not

144

turn! And if Yves eluded him now he would turn, to follow and punish.

Yves slipped in the frozen snow, or seemed to slip, and the threshing fist had him by the breast of his cotte and slammed him back against the parapet. The fellow to it gripped his hair and forced his head up, as the creature spat copiously in his face, and laughed in triumph. Wrenching aside as best he could from the infamy, and unable to raise a hand to wipe the slime away, Yves saw the invading stranger straighten to his full height, without haste or sound, and lower the trap back into place, eyes fixed all the while on the writhing pair pinned to the wall before him. He did not quit the sensible precaution to rush to the rescue. It was the greatest of praise, and Yves felt his heart swell with gratitude and admiration. For he had just been shown that his act had been understood and appreciated, that he was not a mere victim, but a partner in this secret and splendid war.

He saw the first rapid, silent stride taken towards him, and then his head was buffeted violently aside by a great blow on the cheek, and a second that knocked him back again, and turned him dizzy and faint. To make all sure, he raised his voice in a frantic whine, not too loudly, but enough to cover the movements of one who must be already close: 'Don't! You're hurting me! Let me go! I'm sorry, I'm sorry . . . don't hit me . . .' Something of a crow about the tone, and his hackles erected all the time, but this creature did not know the difference, he was chuckling and quaking with merriment.

He was still laughing when the long arm took him about the face, muzzling his mouth, and jerked him backwards to the boards, and a long-legged, agile, youthful body dropped astride him, drove a knee into his belly, and therewith all the wind out of him, and jolting off his conical steel helmet, calmly hoisted him high enough to drive his skull back against the wood with stunning force, laying him out on the floor limp as a landed fish, and just as silent.

Yves dropped ecstatically upon the pair of them, like a half-trained hawk stooping, and fell to unbuckling the belt that held the guard's sword and dagger. His hands were shaking, but he went about it eagerly, peeled loose the arms, and shoved the belt towards the stranger, who was waiting for it with commending and commendable placidity and patience, and had it drawn tightly round the guard's upper arms, hobbling them behind his back, before he turned to look closely at his helper. He was smiling. The light here was only from a haze of stars, but very pure and clear, and the smile was unmistakable.

He reached a hand into the ample breast of the brown homespun cotte he wore, hauled out a long white roll of linen, and held it out to Yves.

'Wipe your face,' said a calm, low voice, in which both smile and praise were implicit, 'before I use it to make this loud mouth mute.'

12

Yves scrubbed the slime from his cheek and brow in awed and fascinated silence, round eyes fixed all the while upon the face that fronted him across the sprawled body of his tormentor. The faint starlight caught the gleam of white teeth, and bright eyes that shone like amber. The capuchon had fallen back from ruffled black hair that did not curl, but curved and clasped in a thick cap about a shapely, vigorous head. Every line and every movement cried out his youth and audacity. Yves gazed and lost his heart. He had had heroes before, his own father among them, but this one was new and young, and above all, present.

'Give!' said his ally briefly, and snapped demanding fingers for the length of linen, which Yves hastily surrendered. An end of the cloth was shoved briskly into the guard's open mouth, the length of it whipped about his head to make him blind as well as dumb, and secured round his shoulders to the belt with which his arms were already pinioned. For want of a cord to bind the prisoner's legs, the lacings of his leather jerkin were stripped out in a moment, made fast around his ankles, and doubled back to tie his feet to his wrists in the small of his back. He lay like a package made compact and neat to be slung one side of a pony for carriage. Yves watched, great-eyed, marvelling at the economy of the movements involved in the process.

They eyed each other, in the breathing space that followed, with mutual content. Yves opened his mouth to speak, and was hushed by a forbidding finger on lips still reassuringly smiling.

'Wait!' said the deep, serene voice, just above a whisper. Whispers have no identify, but carry alarmingly. This muted murmur reached no ears but the boy's. 'Let's see if we may leave the way I came.'

Yves crouched, charmed into stillness, ears pricked, listening and quivering. His companion lay flat over the trap, an ear to the wood, and after a few moments cautiously hoisted one edge to peer down into the timber-scented darkness of the tower below. From outside, about the bailey and the guardwalk along the stockade, came the sounds of movements and voices, from a garrison on the alert, but below among the shadowy beams there was silence and stillness.

'We may essay. Follow close and do as I do."

He lifted the trap and swung himself down the ladder by his hands, agile as a cat, and Yves scurried after him. In the dimness of the floor below they froze again, backs to the darkest wall, but nothing moved to threaten them. There were fixed stairs, rough but solid, from the corner of this level. They had reached the middle of the flight and could hear the hum and bustle of activity in the hall, and see the flickering of torches and firelight round the rim of a great door below. One more flight, and they would be in the base of the tower, and level with the hall, only that door between them and Alain le Gaucher and his outlaws. A long arm drew Yves close, and again held him still to listen and watch.

The base of the tower was half of rock and half of beaten earth, and the air that came up to them was colder here than between the massive timbers above. Peering down fearfully, Yves could see in a far corner the foot of a deep embrasure, and felt the strong draught that blew from it. There was a narrow outer door upon the night, surely the door by which his rescuer had entered, and if they could but reach it unobserved they might yet make their way back by the same route, out of this enemy stronghold. He would not be afraid, with this superb being as a guide, even to venture the traverse of the rocks in the dark. What one had done alone, surely two could do together.

It was the first tread of that final staircase that undid them. Until then all had been solid and silent, but as soon as a foot was set on this warped board it tilted and settled again with a loud clap, and the echoes took the impact and flung it about the tower in a chain of hollow reverberations. In the hall someone cried out an alarm, there was a rushing of feet, and the great door was flung open, spilling forth firelight and armed men.

'Back!' snapped the stranger instantly, and whipped round without hesitation to hoist the boy before him up the flight they had just descended. 'Up to the roof, quickly!' There was no other way of retreat, and the brief check below to accustom eyes to the darkness after the lighted hall could last only a moment. It was already over, the foremost man loosed a great bellow of alarm and rage, and came for the stairs in a bull's rush, with three or four more on his heels. The blast of the uproar they raised almost blew the fleeing pair up the steps of the tower.

Where the long flight ended, the ladder in sight, Yves felt himself lifted and flung halfway up to the open trap, and that was the height of a tall man. He gripped and climbed, but looking over his shoulder and hesitating, loth to leave his comrade behind, until he was ordered sharply. 'Go! Up, quickly!' He completed the climb in a wild scramble, and flung himself down on his belly by the trap, craning anxiously over the rim, just in time to see in a confusion of shadows further confused by the starlight through the trap, how the foremost pursuer came lurching up the narrow wooden treads of the stairway, drawn sword flailing. A big, bulky man, blocking off from view those who followed him.

Yves had not even noticed, until that moment, that his ally already wore a sword. The one they had taken from the guard still lay here on the roof, though Yves had possessed himself of the dagger and buckled it proudly to his belt as a substitute for the one taken from him. The brief flash of a blade, like distant lightning, stabbed the darkness below, a trick of starlight following its slashing course. The outlaw loosed an outraged yell, his short sword struck from his hand and flung below to clatter on the boards. The next moment a braced foot took him in the chest and hurled him backwards while he was off balance. Down he went in a long, echoing fall, and swept his followers down with him. The stairway was narrow and unguarded, two or three went backwards under their leader's massive weight, one at least went over the side, to a heavier fall below.

The young man turned without another glance, and sprang halfway up the ladder to the roof, and in a moment was beside Yves. The naked sword he swung glittering along the ice of the roof, and leaned to grip the uprights of the ladder with both muscular hands, and haul it aloft after him. As soon as Yves had recovered his wits he leaned eagerly to clutch from rung to rung and help to hoist the weight. With all his might, and all the breath he had regained, he heaved and exulted. The ladder had been braced against a wooden bar both below and above, but not fixed. It rose blithely, out of reach of the tallest long before the first of the attackers erupted furiously below and leaped to try and hold it.

The lower end rose clear, tilted aside and clattered on the roof, ringing a glassy cry from the splintered ice. The roars of anger below fumed out of the open trap, and Yves leaned to drag the cover over to shut them out, but his ally waved him aside, and the bewitched boy drew back obediently. Whatever his hero did would be right and wise.

And his hero, palpably smiling, though the smile was hidden in the dark, simply took their prisoner, now uneasily stirring in his bonds, by the cord that bound his feet to his wrists in the small of his back, dragged him to the trap, upended him judiciously so that his head should not take the impact below, and tipped him almost gently through the trap to fall upon his friends, and lay two or three of them flat on the boards. Their startled and aggrieved outcry was cut off when the trap was clapped into place above.

'Quick, now,' said the placid voice almost chidingly, 'here with the ladder, here over the trap. So! Now you lie there upon that end, and I upon this, and who will shift us?'

Yves lay as he had been ordered, flat on his belly on the ladder, his face buried in his arms, panting and shivering, for a long time. The boards under him throbbed to the din below, spent in ugly fury six feet short of reaching the trap. And if they did rear something that would enable them to reach it, how were they to shift it or penetrate it? The trap fitted close, no lance nor sword could be thrust through the cracks. Even if they should climb up and batter a way through with an axe, only one could emerge at a time, and they two above were armed and ready. Yves lay braced, willing his weight to be double, spreading arms and legs, holding his breath. For all the bitter cold, he was in a lavish sweat.

'Look up, my heart,' said the voice at the other end of the ladder, almost gaily, 'and show me that gallant face again, bruises, grime and all. Let me look at my prize!'

Yves lifted his head from his arms and stared dazedly along the ladder into bright, gold-gleaming eyes and an indulgent, glittering smile. A young, oval face under that thick, close cap of black hair, high-cheekboned, thin-black-browed, long-lipped, and with a lean, arrogant beak of a nose, like a scimitar. Smooth-shaven as a Norman, smooth-skinned as a girl, but of an olive, glossy smoothness.

'Take breath, and let them rave, they'll tire of it. If we failed to get past them, neither can they get at us. We have time to think. Only keep well below the parapet. They know their ground, and might think it worth setting their archers to watch for an unwary head.'

'How if they set fire to the tower and burn us out?' wondered Yves, trembling as much with excitement as fear.

'They're no such fools. They could not, without setting the hall ablaze with it. Moreover, why be in haste to do anything, when they know we cannot break out? Here in the cold or in a cell below, they have us cornered. As at this moment, true enough. You and I, Messire Yves Hugonin, have some thinking of our own to do.' He cocked his head, raising a hand for silence, to listen to the babel of voices below, which had sunk into a low, conspiratorial muttering. 'They grow content. We're securely trapped up here, they'll leave us to freeze. They're needed below, all that's wanted here is a couple of men to watch our only way out. They can wait to flay us.'

The prospect did not seem to dismay him at all, he stated it serenely. Below them the hum of consultation receded and stilled. He had judged accurately, Alain le Gaucher knew how to concentrate on what was most urgent, and needed all his company to man his stockade. Let his

151

prisoners, lords though they might be of a tower-top some dozen or so paces square, enjoy their lordship until it chilled them into helplessness, and if need be, killed them. Whatever they did, they could not get away.

A wary, suspicious stillness fell below. And the cold, no question of it, was biting sharply, congealing into the deepest, darkest and deadliest of the night.

The young man eased from his braced listening, and turned to reach a long arm towards the boy. 'Come close, let's share what warmth we have. Come! In a while we may move, but now we'll hold down the lid together over hell a little longer. While we consider what to do next.'

Yves wriggled thankfully along the ladder and was drawn warmly into the embracing arm. They settled together until they found mutual ease, and fitted snugly into one comforting mass. Yves drew breath deep into him, and leaned his cheek almost shyly into this admired and welcoming shoulder.

'You know me, sir,' he said hesitantly. 'I do not know you.'

'You shall, Yves, you shall. I had no leisure until now to present myself respectfully to your lordship. To any but you, my friend, I am Robert, son to one of the foresters of Clee Forest. To you . . .' He turned his head to meet the boy's round-eyed, earnest stare, and smiled. 'To you I can freely be what I really am, if you can keep a blank face and a still tongue when needed. I am one of the newest and least of the esquires of your uncle, Laurence d'Angers, and my name is Olivier de Bretagne. My lord is waiting anxiously in Gloucester for news of you. I am sent to find you, and I have found you. And be sure, I will not now lose you again.'

Yves sat speechless, lost between bewilderment, joy and apprehension. 'Truly? My uncle sent you to find us and take us to him? They did tell me in Bromfield that he was seeking us—my sister and me.' The thought of Ermina made him tremble and falter, for what was the use of being found while she remained lost? 'She—my sister . . . She left us! I don't know where she is!' It ended in a forlorn wisp of sound.

'Ah, but I have the better of you there, for I do know! Make your mind easy about Ermina. She is safe and well in the Bromfield you abandoned. True, believe me! Would

I lie to you? I myself took her there to join you, only to find before ever we reached the gate that you were away again on a quest of your own.'

'I couldn't help it, I had to go . . .'

It was almost too much to take in, so suddenly. Yves gulped down wonder and grew coherent. Now that he need no longer worry and grieve over Ermina's fate, whatever the perils hanging over his own, he recoiled for support into resentment against her for ever bringing him and so many others to this pass. 'You don't know her! She won't be bidden,' he warned indignantly. 'When she finds I'm gone she may do *anything!* It was she who caused all this, and if the fit takes her she'll fly off again on some mad folly. You don't know her as I do!'

He thought it an innocent stranger's over-confidence that Olivier laughed, however softly and amiably. 'She'll be bidden! Never fret, she'll be waiting in Bromfield. But I think you have a story to tell me, before I tell mine. Heave it off your heart! You may, we had better not move from here yet. I hear someone stirring below.' Yves had heard nothing. 'You left Worcester a fugitive, that I know, and how your sister left you, and why, that I know, too. She has told me, and made no secret of it. And if it please you to know the best, no, she is not married, nor like to be yet, but thinks herself well out of a foolish mistake. And now what of you, after her going?'

Yves nestled into the rough homespun shoulder, and poured out the whole of it, from his first wanderings in the forest to the remembered comfort and kindness of Father Leonard and Brother Cadfael at Bromfield, the tragedy of Sister Hilaria, and the desperate sally after poor, possessed Elayas.

'And I left him there, never thinking . . .' Yves shrank from remembering the words Brother Elyas had spoken, as they lay side by side in the night. That was something he could not share, even with this admirable being. 'I'm afraid for him. But I did leave the door unbarred. Do you think they would find him? In good time?'

'In God's time,' said Olivier positively, 'which is always good. Your God cares for the sick in mind, and will see to it the lost are found.'

Yves was quick to note the strangeness of the chosen

words. '*My* God?' he said, looking up with sharp curiosity into the dark face so close above his own.

'Oh, mine also, though I came to Christendom somewhat roundabout. My mother, Yves, was a Muslim woman of Syria, my father was a crusader of Robert of Normandy's following, from this same England, and sailed for home again before ever I was born. I took his faith and went to join his people in Jerusalem as soon as I came a man. That's where I found service with my lord your uncle, and when he returned here I came back with him. I am a christian soul like you, though I chose it, where you were born to it. And I feel in my bones, Yves, that you will encounter your Brother Elyas again none the worse for the cold night you spent. We'd best be giving our minds rather to how you and I are to get safely out of here.'

'How did you ever get in?' wondered Yves. 'How did you know I was here?'

'I did not *know* it, until this rogue lord of yours hoisted you on the wall there with a knife at your throat. But I saw them pass by with their booty, at some distance, and thought it worth tracking such a company to its den. If they were harrying the countryside by night, and you lost by night . . . It was possible they might take prisoners, if there was profit to be made out of them.'

'Then you saw, you know, that we have an army of our friends close at hand,' said Yves, suddenly glowing with a new and wonderful idea.

'Of your friends, surely. But mine? Friends better avoided, no blame to them. Have you not understood that I am your uncle's man, and your uncle is liegeman to the Empress Maud? I have no wish to fall into the sheriff's hands and sit drumming my heels in a Shropshire prison. Though I owe them a favour, too, for it was under cover of their onslaught that I made my way round and on to the rocks below unnoticed, while these vermin within rushed to slam the gates. I should never have succeeded but for the distraction they provided. And once round the stockade in the dark, what difference between one lumpish ruffian stalking the bailey and all the others? I knew where they had left you. I saw your guard relieved.'

'Then you saw that the only reason Hugh Beringar drew his men off was because they threatened to kill me.

And he is not gone far, I know it, he would not give up so easily. And now, don't you see, there is no one holding a knife at my throat, and no reason why they should not attack!'

Olivier had caught his drift, and was eyeing him with respect and amusement. His gaze roved speculatively from the guard's discarded sword, lying in its sheath under the wall, to the battered conical steel helmet which had rolled into a corner beside it. The amber eyes in their deep, black-lashed settings, came back to Yves, dancing.

'A pity we have no trumpets to sound the onset, but the makings of a very servicable drum we certainly have. Under the wall with it, then, and try what you can do, while I stand guard here. They'll have a matter of minutes to spend trying to hack their way through at us, after that they'll be busy below, if your friends out there are as quick-witted as you.'

13

Brother Cadfael had spent the entire day prowling through the belt of trees, from one end of the crescent to the other, and back again, studying every fold of ground between him and the stockade, in search of even the most tenuous cover by which, once darkness came, a man might hope to approach nearer. Hugh would not allow any man to show himself in the open, and had gone to great pains, while deploying his forces as widely as possible, to keep them well out of sight. Alain le Gaucher could not get out, and the sheriff's powers could not get in, and absolute deadlock had Hugh gnawing his knuckles in frustration. Small doubt but there were lavish supplies of stolen meat and grain within, enough to keep the garrison snugly for some time. Starving them out would be a long business, and starve the unfortunate boy in the process. Le Gaucher might be willing to surrender him in return for free passage out for himself and all his men, but that would only be to place some other unhappy region under the same scourge. Not even a last resort! It was Hugh's business to restore order and do justice in this shire, and he meant to see it done.

He had singled out from his ranks a number of men who claimed skill in climbing, and were born and bred in hill country, and drawn them back out of the ravine, to pros-

156

pect round the summit in both directions, and see if they could find a level where it might be possible to climb out and penetrate the enclosure from the rear without being seen from above. The slight rise of the lip of land behind the fortress afforded cover, but from below it was seen to be cover for a sheer drop where only birds could hope to find foothold. The only remaining possibility was where they could not reconnoitre without being seen, and provoking a blade at the boy's throat yet again. Close to the stockade there might just be ground enough to let a man inch his way round to the rear, if he had a good head for heights. But to make the assay he would have had to cross a part of that bleak expanse of open rock, making Yves' death likely and his own certain.

But in the darkness, yes, perhaps. If the covering of snow complicated movement, yet there were places where bare rock cropped out to break the betraying pallor. But the night came all too tranquilly, lambent light from snow and stars, a clear sky, crackling with frost. This one night when fresh snow and driving winds might have made vision delusive, and covered dark garments with their own protective veil, no gale blew and no flake descended. And the stillness and silence were such that even the snapping of a buried branch underfoot might carry as far as the stockade.

Cadfael was just reflecting ruefully on this hush when it was abruptly shattered, blasted apart with a violence that made him jump almost out of his skin. Reverberating across from the summit came a loud metallic clanging like a great, ill-made bell, stroke on jarring stroke beating out a merciless peal that went on and on, piercing, demanding, a pain to the ears. Back among the trees men started to their feet, and ventured as near as they dared to the open, to stare across at the castle, and within the stockade, no less, arose shouts and bellowing and clamour that told Cadfael this music was none of theirs, had not been planned, was neither welcomed nor understood. If something had gone wrong within, then something profitable might yet be made of it without.

The din was coming from the top of the tower. Someone up there was industriously thrashing away at a shield, or a gong of some kind, however improvised. Why should any man of the garrison be sounding so furious a tocsin, when no attack had been threatened? And the noise had provoked other noises within the stockade, muffled and wordless but unmistakably angry, dismayed and vengeful. A great voice that could only belong to le Gaucher was roaring orders. Surely all attention had been diverted from the enemy without to the unexpected onslaught within.

Cadfael acted almost without thought. There was an undulation in the rock surface halfway to the stockade, a narrow black blot breaking the uniform whiteness. He broke from the shelter of the trees and ran for it, and dropped full-length along it, where his black habit could lie motionless and pass unremarked if anyone was still keeping guard. He doubted if they were. The relentless clanging continued tirelessly, though someone's arm must be beginning to ache by this time. Cautiously he raised his head to watch the serrated crest of the tower, clear against the sky. The rhythm of the discordant bell faltered and changed, and as it halted for a moment Cadfael saw a head peep cautiously out between the merlons. There were ominous splintering, crashing sounds now, dulled by the thick timbering of the tower, as though someone was wielding an axe. The head appeared a second time. Cadfael waved an arm, black sleeve plain against the snow, and shouted: 'Yves!'

Doubtful if he was heard, though the clear air carried sounds with meticulous accuracy. Certainly he was seen. The head—it barely topped the parapet—craned into view recklessly for a moment, to shriek in shrillest excitement. 'Come on! Bid them come on! We hold the tower! We are two, and armed!' Then he vanished behind the merlon, and none too soon, for at least one bowman within the stockade had been watching the same serrated outline, and his arrow struck the edge of the embrasure, and stuck there quivering. Defiantly the clangour from the tower resumed its resolute beat.

Cadfael picked himself up from his niche in the rock, regardless of danger, and ran for the trees. At least one arrow followed him, but fell short, somewhat to his surprise when he heard its shuddering flight extinguished in the snow behind him. He must still have a better turn of speed then he had thought, at least when running for his own life and many others. He plunged breathless into

158

cover, and into the arms of Hugh Beringar, and was aware by the stir and quiver all along the fringe of the trees that Hugh also had employed these few minutes to good effect, for his lines were drawn ready for action, waiting only the urgent word.

'Set on!' said Cadfael, puffing for breath. 'That's Yves sounding for us, he says he holds the tower. Someone has reached him, God knows how. No danger now but from our delay.'

There was no more delay. Hugh was away on the instant, and into the saddle before the words were spent. He from the left and Josce de Dinan from the right broke from the trees and drove in upon the gates of Alain le Gaucher's castle, with all their foot-men streaming full tilt behind them, and a file of torches spluttering into life after, to fire the fringe buildings within.

Brother Cadfael, left unceremoniously thus, stood for a while to get his breath back, and then, almost resentfully, resigned himself to the recollected fact that he had long ago forsworn arms. No matter, there was nothing in his vows to prevent him from following unarmed where the armed men led. Cadfael was striding purposefully across the open expanse of snow, torn up now by many hooves and many feet, by the time the assault converged in a spear-head to hurtle against the gates, and drive them in.

For all the industrious din he himself was making, Yves heard the charge of the sheriff's men, and felt the tower shake as they hit the gate like a sledge-hammer, and burst the holding timbers in a shower of flying splinters. The clamour of hand-to-hand battle filled the bailey, but about that he could do nothing; but here the very boards under them were heaving and groaning to a fury of axe-blows from below, and Olivier, sword drawn and long legs spread, was holding down ladder and trap against the onslaught. The ladder heaved at every blow, but while it held its place the trap could not be raised, and even if it should be breached, only a hand or a head could be first exposed, and either would be at Olivier's mercy. And at this extreme, Olivier would have no mercy. Braced from crown to heel, he bestrode the enemy's entry, balancing his weight, sword poised to pierce or slash the first flesh that offered.

159

Yves dropped his aching arm, and let the steel helmet roll away from between his feet, but then, with a better thought, scrambled after it and clapped it on his head. Why refuse any degree of protection that offered? He even remembered to stoop well below the parapet as he flexed his cramped hand, took a fresh grip on the hilt of the sword, and plunged across the roof to embrace Olivier, and plant his own feet on the rungs of the ladder that held them secure, to add his weight to the barrier. There were already splits visible in the wood of the trap, and splinters flew both above and below, but there was nowhere yet that a blade could be thrust through.

'Nor will be,' said Olivier in confident reassurance. 'You hear that?' It was the roaring voice of Alain le Gaucher himself, echoing hollowly up the dark spaces of the tower. 'He's calling off his hounds, they're needed more desperately below.'

The axe struck once more, a mighty blow that clove clean through an already splintered board, and sent a long triangle of shining blade into view beneath the ladder. But that was the last. The striker had trouble freeing his blade again, and cursed over it, but made no further assault. They heard a great scurrying down the stairs, and then all was quiet within the tower. Beneath, in the bailey, the whole enclosure was filled with the babel and struggle and clamour of arms, but up here under the starry calm of the sky the two of them stood and looked at each other in the sudden languor of relief, no longer threatened.

'Not that he would not make the same foul use of you,' said Olivier, sheathing his sword, 'if he could but get his hands on you. But if he spends time on hewing you out of your lair, he will already have lost what your throat might save. He'll seek to fight off this attack before he troubles you again.'

'He will not do it!' said Yves, glowing. 'Listen? They are well within. They'll never give back now, they have him in a noose.' He peered out from behind a merlon over the confused fighting below. All the space of the bailey seethed and swayed with struggling men, a churning, tumultuous darkness like a stormy night sea, but lit by fiery glimpses where the torches still burned. 'They've fired the gatehouse. They're leading out all the horses and cattle—and fetching down all the archers from the walls . . . Should we not go down and help them?'

'No,' said Olivier firmly. 'Not unless we must, not until we must. If you fell into the wrong hands now, all this would be thrown away, all to do again. The best you can do for your friends is to stay out of reach, and deny this rogue baron the one weapon that could save him.'

It was good sense, though none too welcome to an excited boy longing for prodigies to perform. But if Olivier ordered it, Yves accepted it.

'You may be a hero some other day,' said Olivier drily, 'when there's less at stake and you can put only your own neck in peril. Your part now is to wait in patience, even if it cost you more. And since we have time now, and may be mortally short of it before long, listen to me carefully. When we are loosed from here, and all over, I shall leave you. Go back to join your sister at Bromfield, let your friends have the satisfaction of uniting you in safety. I have no doubt they would send you with a good escort to your uncle in Gloucester, as they promised, but I have a fancy to finish my work and deliver you myself, as I was sent out to do. This mission is mine, and I'll complete it.'

'But how will you manage?' Yves wondered anxiously.

'With your help—and certain other help which I know where to find. Give me two days, and I will have horses and supplies ready for us. If all goes well, two nights from this night that's wearing away under us, I will come to Bromfield for you. Tell your sister so. After Compline, when the brothers will be bound for their beds, and you will be thought to be in yours. Ask no more questions, but tell her I shall come. And should I be forced to have speech here with the sheriff's men, or should you be asked about me after I vanish—tell me, Yves, who was it made his way in here to find you?'

Yves understood. He said at once: 'It was Robert, the forester's son who brought Ermina to Bromfield, and happened on this place while he was searching for me.' He added dubiously: 'But they'll wonder at such a deed in a forester, when all the sheriff's men were already searching. Unless,' he went on, curling a disdainful lip, 'they think that every man living will risk his life for Ermina, just because she is handsome. She *is* handsome,' he con-

161

ceded generously, 'but all too well she knows it and makes use of it. Don't ever let her make a fool of *you!*'

Olivier was peering out over the battlefield below, where a long tongue of fire had sprung from the burning gates and reached the roof of one of the byres. His dark and private smile was hidden from the boy. 'You may let them think me her besotted slave, if it convinces them,' he said. 'Tell them what you please that will serve the purpose. And bear my message, and be ready when I come for you.'

'I will!' vowed Yves fervently. 'I will do all as you tell me.'

They watched the fire spread along the stockade from roof to roof, while the fighting within continued as fiercely and confusedly as ever. The garrison had poured out to the defence greater numbers than anyone had suspected, and all too many of them experienced and powerful fighters. Yves and Olivier looked on from their eyrie intently, as the serpent of fire began to burn uncomfortably near to the corner of the hall itself. If it touched the tower, all that draughty, beam-braced interior would act as a chimney, and they would be isolated at the top of a ferocious blaze. Already the crackling and exploding of burning beams threatened to drown out the din of fighting.

'This grows too hot,' said Olivier, frowning. 'Better brave the devil below than wait for the one that's coming to us here.'

They hauled the ladder aside, and heaved up the mangled trap. Splinters jutted and fell, and a thin curl of smoke, hardly a breath as yet, coiled up out of the recesses of the tower. Olivier did not wait to lower the ladder, but slid through to hang by his hands, and dropped lightly to the floor below, and Yves followed him valiantly, to be caught neatly in mid-air by the waist, and set down silently. Olivier set off down the staircase, a hand extended behind him to hold the boy close. The air here was still cold, but from somewhere smoke was drifting steadily, obscuring the edges of the steps so that they were constrained to feel their way at every tread. The babel of battle grew more distant, a constant buzzing from without the thick walls. Even when they reached the rock floor of the tower, and saw by the dim remains of torches and firelight the outline of the great door to the hall, standing ajar, there was no stir of foot or sound of voices within. Every man must be out in the bailey, battling to fend off the sheriff's forces, or else, by this time just as possibly, to break through the circle somehow and make his escape.

Olivier made for the narrow outer door by which he had entered in the first place, lifted the heavy latch and tugged, but the door did not give. He braced a foot against the wall and heaved again, but the door remained fast shut.

'The devil damn them! They've barred it without, after they treed us. Through the hall, and keep close behind me.'

The very act of thrusting the great door open wide enough for them to slip through, as silently as possible, for fear some cautious or wounded outlaw should still be lurking, brought into play a cross-draught, and a sudden tongue of fire leaped up in the far corner of the hall, licked its way up the beams of the roof, and spat burning splinters below to smoulder in Alain le Gaucher's tapestried chairs, and bring to life three or four new buds of flame that opened marvellously into great crimson flowers. Those red and gold blazons were all they could see clearly through the smoke that thickened as abruptly as the fire had burst in. They groped and stumbled through a deserted wilderness of overturned benches and trampled and spilled dishes, trestle tables fallen aslant, hangings dragged down, torches burned out and adding to the pall of smoke that stung their eyes and was drawn chokingly into their throats. Before them, beyond this obscure and perilous wilderness the pandemonium of struggle and violence blew in on a freezing draught through the half-open main door of the hall. At the top of the sliver of open air thus uncovered, a single star showed, unbelievably pure and distant. They covered their mouths and nostrils and made for it, with eyes streaming and smarting.

They were almost at the doorway when a ripple of flame flowed suddenly along the surface of a roof-beam, peeling off the unplaned surface in a flurry of sparks, and caught the coarse homespun curtain that served to shut out the cold wind when the doors were closed and the household home at night. The dry, hairy cloth went up in a gush of flame, and fell in their path, a great folded cushion of fire. Olivier kicked it furiously aside, and swung Yves before him round the billowing bonfire towards the doorway.

'Out! Get to the open, and hide!'

If Yves had obeyed him to the letter, he might well have escaped notice, but having reached clear air, with the sweep of the steps and the loud turmoil of the bailey before him, he turned to look back anxiously, for fear the fire, blazing now to a man's height, had trapped Olivier within. The pause cost him and his friends all that they had gained together, for more than half the bailey was then in Beringar's hands, and the remnant of the garrison driven back into a tight knot of fighting round the hall, and while Yves' back was turned upon his enemies, and he hung hesitating whether to rush back to stretch a hand to his friend, Alain le Gaucher, hard-pressed at the foot of the steps to his own hall, cut a wide swathe before him to clear his ground, and leaped backwards up the wide timber stiarway. They all but collided, back to back. Yves turned to run, too late. A great hand shot out and gripped him by the hair, and a roar of triumph and defiance rose even above the clamour of arms and the thunderous crackling of bursting beams. In a moment le Gaucher had his back against the pillar of his doorway, secure from attack from the rear, and the boy clamped to his body before him, with a naked sword, already red, braced across his throat.

'Stand, every man! Down arms and draw off!' bellowed the lion, his tawny mane bristling and glaring in the flickering light of the fires. 'Back! Further, I say! Let me see a clear space before me. If any man so much as draw bow, this imp dies first. I have got my warranty again! Now, king's man, where are you? What will you pay for his life? A fresh horse, free passage out, and no pursuit, on your oath, or I slit his throat, and his blood be on your head!'

Hugh Beringar thrust through to the fore and stood, eyes levelled upon le Gaucher. 'Draw back,' he said without turning his head. 'Do as he says.'

The entire circle, king's men and outlaw's men together, drew back inch by inch and left a great space of trampled and stained snow before the steps of the hall.

Hugh moved back with them, though keeping his place in front. What else could he do? The boy's head was strained back against his captor's body, the steel touching his stretched neck. A false move and he would be dead. A few of the garrison began to edge out of the press, backwards towards the stockade and the gate, in the hope of finding a way out while all eyes were on the pair isolated at the top of the steps. The guard on the gate would deal with them, but who would deal with this ruthless and desperate creature? Everyone retreated before him.

Not everyone! Through the press, unnoticed by any until he reached the open space, came lurching a strange and solitary figure, limping and wavering, but marching ahead out of the crowd without pause, straight towards the steps. The red light of the fires trembled over him. A tall, emaciated man in a black habit, the cowl dropped back on his shoulders. Two puckered scars crossed his tonsured head. There was blood on his sandalled feet—he left stains on the snow as he trod—and blood on his brow from a fall in the rocky ground. Great, hollow eyes in a livid face stared upon Alain le Gaucher. A pointing hand accused him. A loud, imperious voice cried out at him:

'Leave go of the boy! I have come for him, he is mine.'

Intent upon Hugh Beringar, le Gaucher had not seen the newcomer until then. His head jerked round, astonished that anyone should break the silence he had imposed, or dare to cross the neutral ground he had exacted.

The shock was brief, but shattering while it lasted, and it lasted long enough. For one moment Alain le Gaucher saw his dead man advancing on him, terrible, invulnerable and fearless, saw the wounds he himself had inflicted still bloody, and the face he had murdered corpse-pale. He forgot the hostage. His hands sank nervelessly, and the sword with them. The next instant he knew past doubt that the dead do not rise, and recovered himself with a scream of rage and scorn, but too late to recover his ascendancy. Yves had slid from between his hands like an eel, dived under his arm and darted away down the steps.

Running blindly, he collided with a welcome solidity and warmth, and clung panting and spent, his eyes closed. Brother Cadfael's voice said in his ear: 'Softly, now, you're safe enough. Come and help me with Brother Elyas, for he'll go nowhere without you, now he's found you. Come, let's get him out of this, you and I together, and do what we can for him.'

Yves opened his eyes, still panting and trembling, and turned to stare back at the doorway of the hall. 'My friend is in there . . . my friend who helped me!'

He broke off there, drawing in breath to heave a huge, hopeful, fearful sigh. For Hugh Beringar, the instant the hostage was free, had darted forward to do battle, but another was before him. Out of the smoke and fire-shot blackness of the doorway surged Olivier, soiled and singed and sword in hand, sprang past le Gaucher to find elbow-room, and in passing struck him on the cheek with the flat of the blade, by way of notice of intent. The tawny mane flew as le Gaucher sprang round to face him. The silence that had exploded in shudderings of wonder at the apparition of Brother Elyas fell again like a stone. Everyone heard clearly the voice that trumpeted disdainfully: 'Now have ado with a man!'

There would be no moving Yves now, not until this last duel was resolved. Cadfael kept hold of him thankfully, though he need not have troubled, for the boy's small fists were clenched in his sleeve for mortal reassurance. Brother Elyas, his bearings lost, looked about him for his boy, and came limping painfully to touch, to comfort and be comforted, and Yves, without for an instant taking his worshipping eyes from Olivier, detached one hand from his hold on Cadfael to accept Elyas' clasp just as fiercely. For him everything now depended on this man to man encounter, from head to foot he was quivering with partisan passion. Both Cadfael and Elyas felt it and were infected by it, and stared as he stared upon this tall, agile, slender person poised with spread feet at the top of the steps. For all his smoke-soiled visage and common country garments, Cadfael knew him again.

And no one meddled, not even Hugh, who might have intervened by virtue of his office. Between his men and these thieves and murderers there would be no more fighting until this fight was over. There was that about the challenge that forbade interference.

It did not appear a very even combat, le Gaucher double his opponent in age and weight and experience, if not in reach and agility. And it did not last long. Le Gaucher, once he had viewed his challenger, came on confidently in a steady, battering onslaught, bent on driving the young man from his stance and backwards down the steps. Yet after long, increasingly furious attacks the boy—a mere half-trained peasant, at that!—had scarcely shifted his balance, not given back a pace, and everywhere the hacking blade crashed in, his sword was there to turn it aside. He stood and seemed at ease, while his adversary flailed at him and wasted energy. Yves gazed with huge, praying eyes, rigid from crown to toe. Elyas clung mutely to the hand he clasped, and quivered to its tension. Brother Cadfael watched the young man Olivier, and recalled disciplines he had almost forgotten, a manner of sword-play bred from the clash of east and west, and borrowing from both.

There was no moving this swordsman, if he gave an inch one moment he regained it the next, added to it the next. It was le Gaucher who was being edged back by degrees to the rim of the steps, while he wasted his strength to no avail.

The lion lunged once more, with all his weight. His heel was too near the edge of the icy stair, his lunge too reckless, the forward pressure slid his rearward foot from under him, and he hung out of balance, struggling for recovery. Olivier sprang forward like a hunting leopard, and drove down with all his weight, clean through the disrupted guard and into the exposed breast. The sword went in halfway to the hilt, and he braced both feet and leaned back on his heel to hoist his blade clear.

The lion's carcase dropped from the withdrawing point, arms spread, flew outwards on its back, landed three steps lower, and rolled ponderously, with an awful dignity, from stair to stair, to come to rest on its face at Hugh Beringar's feet, and bleed what was left of its life away into the defiled snow.

14

It was over, once their leader was dead, and seen to be dead. They broke in all directions, some running to try and find a way of escape, some fighting to the death, some bargaining vainly, some having the sense to surrender and hope to make a passable case for themselves thereafter. There were over sixty prisoners to be rounded up, besides the dead, any amount of plunder to drag out from hall and stores before all went up in fire, a passable flock of stolen sheep and herd of cattle to feed and water until they could be driven down to better lodging. Dinan undertook the custody of the prisoners, captured within his lordship. No need to doubt his adherence to law where his own writ was challenged.

The fire spread, and when all that was savable was brought out, they spread the flames of intent. The castle stood solitary, clear of the trees, on solid rock, it could burn to the bone and threaten nothing else. It had been a stain upon the countryside in its short and ignoble life, it might well be a passing blemish in its death.

The strangest thing, though unremarked by most in the general turmoil, was the disappearance of the unknown champion only minutes after he had felled the castellan. Every eye had followed that prodigious fall, and by the time they had stirred out of their daze and looked about, the chaos of flight and capture had broken out all around, and no one had seen the young countryman make off silently into the night.

'Gone like a shadow,' said Hugh, 'when I should have liked to know him better. And never a word as to where he may be found, when the king's Grace owes him a debt any sane man would be eager to collect. You are the only one who has spoken with him, Yves. Who is this paladin?'

Half-drunk with the lassitude of relief after stress, and the exhaustion of safety after terror, Yves said what he had been taught to say, and fronted Hugh with a clear stare and guileless face as he did so. 'That was the forester's son who sheltered Ermina, and brought her to Bromfield. It was he told me she's there. I knew nothing of that until then. She is really there?'

'She is, safe enough. And what is the name of this forester's son? And more to the purpose,' said Hugh thoughtfully, 'where did he learn his swordcraft?'

'His name is Robert. He told me he was searching for me, as he promised Ermina he would, and he saw the raiders coming back here, and followed their tracks. I know no more about him,' said Yves stoutly, and if he blushed as he said it, the night covered the blush.

'Certainly we seem to breed redoubtable foresters in these parts,' said Hugh drily. But he did not press it further.

'And now,' said Cadfael, intent on his own business, 'if you'll lend me four good men, and let us have the use of all these fresh horses, they'll be better on the move to the Bromfield stables, now they've no roof over their heads here, and I can get these two home to their beds. I can leave you my scrip. We'll rig a litter for Brother Elyas, and purloin whatever blankets and brychans are still unburned to wrap him up on the way.'

'Take what you need,' said Hugh. There were seven horses fresh from the stable, besides the common hillponies Yves had seen used to bring home plunder. 'Stolen, all or most of them,' said Hugh, looking them over. 'I'll have Dinan give it out wherever they've had losses, they can come to Bromfield and claim their own. The cattle and sheep we'll bring into Ludlow later, after the fellow at Cleeton has picked out his. But best get Brother

Elyas away as fast as you can, if he's to live. The marvel is he's survived even this far.'

Cadfael marshalled his helpers to good effect, and took his pick of the furnishings dragged out of the burning hall, to swaddle Brother Elyas in a cocoon of blankets, and fashion a secure cradle for him between two horses. He took thought to load, also, two sacks of fodder from the ransacked stores, in case the sudden arrival of seven horses should tax the resources of Bromfield. The spurt of energy and authority that had animated Elyas when there was most need of him had deserted him as soon as his work was done, and his boy delivered. He yielded himself into their hands docilely, and let them do what they would with him, astray between apathy and exhaustion, and half dead with cold. Cadfael eyed him with much concern. Unless some new fire could be kindled in him, to make life an imperative as it had been when he saw Yves threatened, Elyas would die.

Cadfael took Yves on his own saddle-bow, as once before, for the child was now so weary that he could not walk without stumbling, and if allowed to ride would probably fall asleep in the saddle. A good Welsh brychan wrapped him for warmth, and before they had wound their way down the spiral path and into easier country, as briskly as was safe in the dark, his chin was on his chest, and his breathing had eased and lengthened into deep sleep. Cadfael shifted him gently to rest in the hollow of his shoulder, and Yves stretched a little, turned his face warmly into the breast of Cadfael's habit, and slept all the way back to Bromfield.

Once well away into the fields, Cadfael looked back. The sheer bulk of the hill rose blackly, crested with a coronal of fire. It would take Beringar and Dinan the rest of the night to round up all their prisoners, and shift the beasts down to Cleeton, where John Druel might know his own, and thence on to Ludlow. The terror was over, and more economically than might have been expected. Over for this time, thought Cadfael. Over, perhaps, for his shire, if Prestcote and Hugh can keep their grip as firm in the future. But where royal kinsfolk are tearing each other for a crown, lesser men will ride the time for their own gain, without scruple or mercy.

And where they did so, he reflected, every villainy for

miles around would be laid at their door, and some of the crimes might well be laid there unjustly. Even villains should bear only the guilt that belongs to them. And never, now, could Alain le Gaucher speak up in his own defence, and say: 'This, and this I have done—but this, this despoiling and murder of a young nun, this deed is none of mine.'

They came to Bromfield about Prime, and rode in at the gatehouse into a court swept clear. No new snow had fallen in the night. The change was coming, by noon there might even be the brief promise of a thaw. Yves awoke, yawned, stretched and remembered. He was wide awake in a moment, unwinding himself from his wrappings and scrambling down to help carry Brother Elyas back to his forsaken bed. Hugh's men-at-arms took the horses to stable. And Brother Cadfael, glancing up towards the guest-hall, saw the door flung open, and Ermina peering out across the twilit court.

The torch above the door lit up a face utterly vulnerable in its wild mingling of hope and dread. She had heard the horses, and rushed out just as she was, barefoot, her hair loose about her shoulders. Her eyes lit upon Yves, busy unloosing the bindings of Brother Elyas' litter, and suddenly her face softened and glowed into so dazzling a radiance of joy and gratitude that Cadfael stood and stared from pure pleasure. The worst shadow soared from her like a bird rising, and was gone. She still had a brother.

Yves, perhaps fortunately, was so busy with his sick protégé and protector that he never glanced in her direction. And Cadfael was not in any way surprised when she did not rush to welcome and embrace, but withdrew softly and stealthily into the guest-hall, and closed the door.

Accordingly, he did not hurry the boy away too hastily from the small infirmary room where they had brought Brother Elyas, and Yves did not run to be embraced, either. He knew, he had been assured over and over, that she was here waiting for him. Both of them required a little time to prepare for the reunion. Only when he had dressed Brother Elyas' wounded and frost-pinched feet, packed them round with soft wool and warmed tiles,

171

bathed his face and hands and fed him spiced and honeyed wine, and heaped him with the lightest covering he had to hand, did Cadfael take Yves firmly by the shoulder, and steer him towards the guest-hall.

She was sitting by the fire, sewing at a gown brought for her from Ludlow, to alter it to her own measure, and none too willingly to judge by her scowl, when Yves entered with Brother Cadfael's hand on his shoulder. She put her work aside, and rose. Perhaps she saw attack in her brother's jutting lip and levelled eye, for she stepped forward briskly, and kissed him in a chill, admonishing, female manner.

'And a fine dance *you* have led everyone,' she said severely, 'running off into the night like that, without a word to a soul.'

'That *you* should be the one to say so, who have caused all this pother!' Yves retorted loftily. '*I* have brought *my* affair to success, madam. *You* ran off into the night without a word to a soul, and come back profitless and as arrogant as ever, but you had better sing a lower tune if you want to be listened to here. *We* have had more urgent matters to think about.'

'You'll have plenty to say to each other,' said Brother Cadfael, benignly blind and deaf to bickering, 'and plenty of time hereafter to say it. But now Yves should be in his bed, for he's had a couple of nights that could wear out any man. He needs a long day's sleep, and if I have a physician's authority, I order it.'

She rose to it with alacrity, though still scowling. She had his bed ready, probably smoothed with her own hands, she would shoo him into it like a hen-wife harrying her chicks, and when he was in it, and fast asleep, she would probably hang over him possessively, and have food ready for him when he stirred. But never, never would she admit that she had grieved and fretted over him, even wept, or that she had bitterly repented her rash departure. And surely that was well, for the boy would be dismayed and embarrassed if ever she bent her neck to him and begged forgiveness.

'Leave well alone until this evening,' said Cadfael contentedly, and went away and left them to argue their way to a truce. He returned to Brother Elyas, sat beside him a careful while, saw that he slept, corpse-like but deeply,

172

and went to his own bed. Even physicians have need of the simple medicines, now and then.

Ermina came looking for him before Vespers, for which office he had asked Prior Leonard to call him. Hugh Beringar had not yet returned, no doubt he was still busy at Ludlow with the bestowal of the prisoners and the storage of the stock and other plunder brought down from Clee. This day was an interlude of thanksgiving for one peril past, but also a breathing-space in preparation for tasks still to be completed.

'Brother Cadfael,' said Ermina, very neat, grave and quiet in the doorway of the infirmary, 'Yves is asking for you. There is still something on his mind, and I know he will not tell me, of all people. But you he wants. Will you come to him after Vespers? He will have had his supper then, and be ready for you.'

'I will come,' said Cadfael.

'And I have been wondering,' she said, and hesitated. 'Those horses you brought back this morning . . . they came from that thieves' nest there?'

'They did. Stolen from all these local holdings they have preyed on. Hugh Beringar is sending out to all who have had such losses to come and claim their own. The cattle and sheep are penned in Ludlow. John Durel may have picked out already some that are his. The horses I borrowed, they were fresh and ready for work. Why? What's in your mind concerning them?'

'There is one I believe belongs to Evrard.' It was a long time since she had spoken his name, it sounded almost strange on her tongue, as if she remembered him from many years past, and after long forgetfulness. 'They will be sending word to him, too?'

'Surely. Callowleas was stripped bare, there may well be other stock of his to be reclaimed.'

'If he does not already know that I am here,' said Ermina, 'I hope no one will tell him. It is not that I mind him knowing I am safe and well. But I would as soon he did not expect to see me.'

There was nothing strange in that. She had put that whole mistaken episode behind her, she might well wish to avoid the embarrassment and pain of meeting him

173

again face to face, and having to make vain play with words over something already dead.

'I doubt there'll have been any message sent but the same to all,' said Cadfael. 'Come and speak for your stolen property. And come they will. A pity there are losses that can never be made good.'

'Yes,' she said, 'great pity. We can't restore them their dead—only their cattle.'

Yves had risen from his long sleep cleansed of every fear for himself or his sister, and secure in his complete trust in Olivier to accomplish every miracle to which he turned his hand. He had washed and brushed and combed himself fittingly as for a thanksgiving festival, and observed with surprised approval that while he slept, Ermina had mended the rent in the knee of his hose, and laundered his only shirt and dried it by the fire. Her actions often failed to match her words, though he had never really noticed it before.

And then, not forgotten but only put aside while more desperate matters still hounded him, the question of Brother Elyas rose unresolved into his mind, and took possession of it wholly. It grew so monstrous and so insistent that he could not long contain it alone, and though Hugh Beringar was fair and approachable, Hugh Beringar was also the law, and bound by his office. But Brother Cadfael was not the law, and would listen with an open mind and a sympathetic ear.

Yves had finished his supper when Cadfael came, and Ermina wisely took her sewing and went away into the hall to have a better light for her work, leaving them together.

Yves found no way of beginning but directly, a leap into the cold and terror of remembrance. 'Brother Cadfael,' he blurted wretchedly, 'I'm frightened for Brother Elyas. I want to tell you. I don't know what we ought to do. I haven't said a word to anyone yet. He has told me things— no, he was not speaking to me, he did not *tell* me, but I heard. I couldn't choose but hear!'

'There's been no time yet for you to tell what happened when he led you away in the night,' said Cadfael reasonably, 'but you may tell it now. But first, there are things I have not yet told you. If I tell them first, it may be a help

174

to you. I know where he led you, and I know how you left him in the hut, hoping for help, and fell into the hands of outlaws and murderers. Was it there in the hut that he spoke out these things that so trouble you?'

'In his sleep,' said Yves unhappily. 'It is not fair dealing to listen to what a man says in his sleep, but I couldn't help it. I was so anxious about him, I needed to know, if there was any way of helping him . . . Even before, when I was sitting by his bed . . . It was because I spoke of Sister Hilaria, and told him she was dead. Nothing else had touched him, but her name . . . It was terrible! It was as if he had not known till then that she was dead, and yet he blamed himself for her death. He cried out to the stones of the house to fall on him and bury him. And he got up . . . I couldn't stop or hold him. I ran to find you, but everyone was at Compline.'

'And when you ran back to him,' said Cadfael mildly, 'he was gone. And so you went after him.'

'I had to, I was left to care for him. I thought in time he would tire, and I could turn him and lead him back, but I couldn't. So what could I do but go with him?'

'And he led you to the hut—yes, that we understood. And there these words passed, that so torment you. Don't be afraid to speak them. All that you did was done for his sake, believe that this, too, you may be doing for his sake.'

'But he accused himself,' whispered Yves, trembling at the memory. 'He said—he said that it was he who killed Sister Hilaria!'

The very quietness with which this was received shook him into despairing tears. 'He was in such anguish, so torn . . . How can we give him up to be branded a murderer? But how can we hide the truth? Himself he said it. And yet I am sure he is not evil, he is good. Oh, Brother Cadfael, what are we to do?'

Cadfael leaned across the narrow trestle and took firm hold of the boy's tight-clasped hands between his own. 'Look at me, Yves, and I'll tell you what we shall do. What *you* have to do is to put away all fears, and try to remember the very words he used. All of them, if you can. "He said that it was he who killed Sister Hilaria!" Did he indeed say that? Or is that what you understood by what he said? Give me the man's own words, and what *I* have to do is listen to those words, and to no others, and see what

175

can be made of them. Now! Go back to that night in the hut. Elyas spoke in his sleep. Begin there. Take your time, there is no haste.'

Yves scrubbed a moist cheek against his shoulder, and raised doubtful but trusting eyes to Cadfael's face. He thought back dutifully, gnawed an unsteady lip, and began hesitantly: 'I was asleep, I think, though I was trying not to sleep. He was lying on his face, but I could hear his voice clearly. He said: My sister—forgive me all my sin, my weakness. I, who have been your death! he said. That I'm sure of, that is word for word. I, who have been your death!' He shook and halted there, afraid that that alone might be enough. But Cadfael held him by the hands and nodded understanding, and waited.

'Yes, and then?'

'Then—do you remember how he called on Hunydd? And you said you thought she was his wife, who died? Well, next he said: Hunydd! She was like you, warm and trusting in my arms. After six months starving, he said, such hunger. *I could not bear the burning*, he said, *body and soul . . .*'

The words were returning in full now, as if they had been carved into his memory. Until now he had wished only to forget them, now, when he consented to remember, they came clearly.

'Go on. There was more.'

'Yes. He changed then, he said no, don't forgive me, bury me and put me out of mind. I am unworthy, he said, weak, inconstant . . .' There was a long pause, as there had been that night, before Brother Elyas cried out his mortal frailty aloud. 'He said: She clung to me, she had no fear, being with me. And then he said: Merciful God, I am a man, full of blood, with a man's body and a man's desires. And she is dead, he said, who trusted me!'

He stared, white-faced, amazed to see Brother Cadfael unshaken, thoughtful and calm, considering him across the table with a grave smile.

'Don't you believe me? I've told you truly. All those things he said.'

'I do believe you. Surely he said them. But think—his travelling cloak was there in the hut, together with her cloak and habit. And hidden! And she taken away from that place, and put into the brook, and he found some distance away, also. If he had not led you back to the hut we should not have known the half of these things. Surely I believe all that you have told me, even so you must believe and consider those things I have been able to tell you. It is not enough to say that a thing is so because of one fragment of knowledge, even so clear as a confession, and put away out of sight those other things known, because they cannot be explained. An answer to a matter of life and death must be an answer that explains all.'

Yves gazed blankly, understanding the words, but seeing no hope or help in them. 'But how can we find such an answer? And if we find it, and it is the wrong answer . . .' he faltered, and shook again.

'Truth is never a wrong answer. We will find it, Yves, by asking the one who knows.' Cadfael rose briskly, and drew the boy up with him. 'Take heart, nothing is ever quite what it seems. You and I will go and speak yet again with Brother Elyas.' Brother Elyas lay weak and mute as before, yet not as before, for his eyes were open, intelligent and illusionless, windows on a great, contained grief for which there was no cure. He had a memory again, though it brought him nothing but pain. He knew them, when they sat down one on either side his bed, the boy hopelessly astray and afraid of what might come of this, Cadfael solid and practical and ready with an offered drink, and a fresh dressing for the frost-gnawed feet. The fierce strength of a man in his robust prime had stood Brother Elyas, physically at least, in good stead, he would not even lose toes, and his chest was clear. Only his grieved mind rejected healing.

'The boy here tells me,' said Cadfael simply, 'that you have recovered the part of your memory that was lost. That's well. A man should possess all his past, it is waste to mislay any. Now that you know all that happened, the night they left you for dead, now you can come back from the dead a whole man, not the half of a man. Here is this boy of yours to prove the world had need of you last night, and has need of you still.'

The hollow eyes watched him from the pillow, and the face was wrung with a bitter spasm of rejection and pain.

'I have been at your hut,' said Cadfael. 'I know that you and Sister Hilaria took shelter there when the snowstorm was at its worst. A bad night, one of the worst of this bad

177

December. It grows more clement now, we shall have a thaw. But that night was bitter frost. Poor souls caught out in it must lie in each other's arms to live through it. And so did you with her, to keep her woman alive.' The dark eyes had burned into fierce life, even the wandering mind grew intent. 'I, too,' said Cadfael with deliberation, 'have known women, in my time. Never unwilling, never without love. I know what I'm saying.'

A voice harsh with disuse, but intelligent and aware, said faintly: 'She is dead. The boy told me. I am the cause. Let me go after her and fall at her feet. So beautiful she was, and trusted me. Little and soft in my arms, and clung, and confided . . . Oh, God!' pleaded Brother Elyas, 'was it well done to try me so sorely, and I emptied and starving? I could not bear the burning . . .'

'That I comprehend,' said Cadfael. 'Neither could I have borne it. I should have been forced to do as you did. In my fear for her if I stayed, and for my own soul's salvation, which is not such a noble motive as all that, I should have left her there asleep, and gone out into the snow and frost of that night, far away from her, to watch the night out as best I could, and return to her in the dawn, when we could go forth together and finish that journey. As you did.'

Yves leaned forward glittering with enlightenment, holding his breath for the answer. And Brother Elyas, turning his head tormentedly on his pillow, mourned aloud: 'Oh, God, that ever I left her so! That I had not the steadfastness and faith to endure the longing . . . Where was the peace they promised me? I crept away and left her alone. And she is dead!'

'The dead are in God's hand,' said Cadfael, 'Hunydd and Hilaria both. You may not wish them back. You have an advocate there. Do you suppose that she forgets that when you went out into the cold you left her your cloak, wrapped about her for warmth, and fled from her with only your habit, to bear the rigour of the winter all those hours to dawn? It was a killing night.'

The voice from the bed said harshly: 'It was not enough to help or save. I should have been strong enough in faith to bear the temptation laid on me, to stay with her though I burned . . .'

'So you may tell your confessor,' said Cadfael firmly,

'when you are well enough to return to Pershore. But you shall, you must shun the presumption of condemning yourself beyond what he sees as your due. All that you did was done out of care for her. What was amiss may be judged. What was done well will be approved. If you had stayed with her, there is no certainty that you could have changed what befell.'

'At worst I could have died with her,' said Brother Elyas.

'But so you did in essence. Death from violence fell upon you in your loneliness that same night, as death of cold you had accepted already. And if you were delivered from both, and find you must suffer still many years of this life,' said Cadfael, 'it is because God willed to have you so survive and so suffer. Beware of questioning the lot dealt out to you. Say it now, to God and us who hear you, say that you left her living, and meant to return to her with the morning, if you lived out the night, and to bring her safely where she would be. What more was required of you?'

'More courage,' lamented the gaunt mask on the pillow, and wrung out a bitter but human smile. 'All was done and undone as you have said. All was well-meant. God forgive me what was badly done.'

The lines of his face had softened into humility, the stress of his voice eased into submission. There was no more he had to remember or confess, everything was said and understood. Brother Elyas stretched his long body from crown to imperilled toes, shuddered and collapsed into peace. His very feebleness came to his aid, he sank without resistance into sleep. The large eyelids expanded, lines melted from about brow and mouth and deep eye-sockets. He floated down into a prodigious profound of penitence and forgiveness.

'Is it true?' asked Yves in an awed whisper, as soon as they had closed the door softly upon Brother Elyas' sleep.

'It is, surely. A passionate soul, who asks too much of himself, and under-values what he gives. He braved the frosty night and the blinding snow without his cloak, rather than sully Sister Hilaria with even the tormented presence of desire. He will live, he will be reconciled with

179

both his body and his soul. It takes time,' said Brother Cadfael tolerantly.

If a thirteen-year-old boy understood less than all of this, or understood it only in the academic way of one instructed in an art never yet practised, Yves gave no sign of it. The eyes fixed brightly upon Cadfael's face were sharply intelligent. Grateful, reassured and happy, he put the last burden away from him.

'Then it was the outlaw raiders who found her, after all,' he said, 'alone as she was, after Brother Elyas had left her.'

Cadfael shook his head. 'They found and struck down Brother Elyas, as I think it was their way to kill any who by chance encountered them on their forays, and might bear witness against them. But her—no, I think not. Before dawn followed that same night they had time to strike at Druel's farmstead. I do not believe they went half a mile out of their way to reach the hut. Why should they? They knew of nothing there for them. And besides, they would not have troubled to move her body elsewhere, and the good gowns they would have taken with them. No, someone came by the hut because it *was* on his way, and entered it, I fancy, because the blizzard was at its height, and he thought fit to shelter through the worst of it.'

'Then it could have been *anyone*,' said Yves, indignant and dismayed at the affront to justice, 'and we may never know.'

It was in Cadfael's mind then that there was already one person who knew, and the morrow would see it put to the proof. But he did not say so. 'Well, at least,' he said instead, 'you need have no more anxiety for Brother Elyas. He is as good as shriven, and he will live and thrive, and do honour to our order. And if you are not sleepy again yet, you may sit with him for a while. He claimed you for his boy in a good hour, and you may be his servicable boy still, while you are here.'

Ermina was sitting by the hall fire, still stitching relentlessly at a sleeve of the gown. Working against time, thought Cadfael, when she looked up only briefly, and at once returned to labour unaccustomed and uncongenial. She gave him a smile, but it was a grave and shadowy one.

180

'All is well with Yves,' said Cadfael simply. 'He was fretting over words Brother Elyas spoke in his sleep, that seemed to be confession of murder, but were no such thing.' He told her the whole of it. Why not? She was becoming a woman before his eyes, fettered by responsibilities suddenly realised and heroically accepted. 'There is nothing weighing on his heart now, except the fear that the true murderer may go undiscovered.'

'He need not fear,' said Ermina, and looked up and smiled, a different smile, at once secretive and confiding. 'God's justice must be infallible, it would be sin to doubt it.'

'At least,' said Cadfael noncommittally, 'he will be ready and willing to go with you now. Even eager. Your Olivier has a worshipper who would follow him to the world's end.'

The bright, proud stare of her eyes came up to him sharply, the firelight waking sparks of deep red in the depths. 'He has two,' she said.

'When is it to be?'

'How did you know?' she asked, with a little curiosity but no surprise or consternation.

'Would such a man leave his work unfinished, and let another send home, however gallantly, the charges he was sent to find? Of course he means to complete the task himself. What else?'

'You will not stand in his way?' But she waved that aside with the hand that held the needle. 'Pardon! I know you will not. You have seen him now, you know how to recognize a man! He sent me word by Yves. He will come tomorrow, about Compline, when the household makes ready for bed.'

Cadfael thought it over, and said judicially: 'I would leave departure until the brothers rise for Matins and Lauds, there will then be no porter on the gate, he will be in church with the rest. And no further stir until Prime. You and the boy could sleep some hours before riding. I would wake you and see you safe from the gate. And if he comes during Compline, I can bring him within until time to leave. If you will trust me with the charge?'

'And thank you for it,' she said without hesitation. 'We will do as you advise.'

'And you,' said Brother Cadfael, watching her seam

181

lengthen with fierce stitch after stitch, 'will you be as ready as Yves to leave this place by tomorrow's midnight?'

She looked up yet again, without haste or concealment, but without confiding, either, and the sinking firelight caught the red glow again in her eyes, while her face was a pure mask. 'Yes, I shall be ready,' she said, and glanced down at the sewing in her lap before she added: 'My work here will be done.'

15

The night was clear, starry and still, barely on the edge of frost. The sun emerged with dawn, and for the second night there had been no fresh snow. The drifts dwindled, even before the slow, quiet thaw set in, the kind of thaw that clears paths by gradual, almost stealthy erosion, and causes no floods.

Hugh Beringar had got back late in the evening, after overseeing the total destruction of what the fire had left, and the removal of a startling collection of plunder. The clutter of lean-to cells along the stockade had yielded up the remains of two murdered prisoners, tortured until they surrendered whatever they had of value, and three more still alive after the same treatment. They were being nursed in Ludlow, where Josce de Dinan had secured the survivors of the garrison in chains. Of the attacking force, there were some eighteen wounded, many more with minor grazes, but none dead. It might have been a deal more costly.

Prior Leonard strode radiantly about his court in the chill but brilliant sunlight, glittering with relief that his region was delivered from a pestilence, the missing pair safe within his walls, and Brother Elyas mute with wonder and grace in his bed, and bent upon life, whether blissful or baleful. He looked up with clear, patient eyes now, and took exhortation and reproof alike with humility and gladness. His mind was whole, his body would not be long in following.

Not long after High Mass the claimants began to come in to look for their horses, as doubtless they were flocking to Ludlow to pick out their own cows and sheep. Some, no doubt, would be claimed by more than one, and give rise to great quarrels and the calling in of neighbours to identify the disputed stock. But here there were only a handful of horses, and little ground for the opportunist greed of the cunning. Horses know their owners as well as the owners know their horses. Even the cows in Ludlow would have plenty to say about where they belonged.

John Druel was among the first to come, having walked all the way from Cleeton, and he had no need to urge his ownership, for the stout brown mountain cob strained and cried after him as soon as he showed his face in the stable-yard, and their meeting was an embrace. The cob blew sweetly in John's ear, and John hugged him about the neck, looked him over from head to hocks, and wept on his cheek. The cob was his only horse, worth a fortune to him. Yves had seen him come, and ran to tell Ermina, and the pair of them came flying to greet him and force on him such favours as they still had about them to give.

A wife from Whitbache, came to claim her dead husband's mare. A thin, grave boy from the same manor came in shyly and humbly to call a solid work-horse of hill stock, and it went to him hesitantly, wanting his sire, but acknowledged the child of the same blood with a human sigh.

Not until dinner was over in the refectory, and Brother Cadfael emerged again into the midday sparkle of sun on snow, did Evrard Boterel ride in at the gatehouse, dismount, and look round him for someone to whom he might most properly address himself. He was still somewhat pale and lean from his fever, but much recovered in the vigour of his movements and the clarity of his eye, and he stood with reared head and imperious stare, even frowning a little that no groom ran at once to take his bridle. A fine figure of a young man, fair as his horse's mane, and well aware of his handsome appearance and his dominant nobility. Such comeliness might well take any young woman's fancy. What did a young fellow with these advantages have to do to lose his hold? Reality, Ermina had said, had rudely invaded her idyllic fantasy. Well! But was that enough?

Prior Leonard, all goodwill, came beaming down the court with his gangling stride, to greet the visitor civilly, and conduct him into the stable-yard. One of Hugh's men, seeing the saddled horse untended, and being himself at leisure, came to take the bridle, and Boterel relinquished his mount as to a servant, without a further glance, and went with the prior.

He had come alone. If he had indeed a stolen horse to reclaim, he must take him home on a leading rein.

Brother Cadfael looked round at the guest-hall, very thoughtfully, and saw Ermina in her peasant gown come forth from the doorway and cross to the church, rapid and light, and bearing something rolled up beneath her arm. The dark arch of the porch swallowed her, as the walled enclosure of the stables had swallowed her sometime suitor. Yves would certainly be sitting now with Brother Elyas, his jealously guarded protégé and patient, on whom he waited with proprietorial zeal. Out of sight and out of peril. No arrows loosed here could strike at him.

Without haste, Cadfael stepped out into the cleared court and crossed towards the church, but tempered his going so judiciously that his path converged upon that by which Evrard Boterel and Hugh together emerged from the stables and made for the gatehouse. They, too, were taking their time, and Evrard was sunning into vivacity and smiles; the deputy sheriff was a study worth cultivating. Behind them a lay groom led a fine bay mare, chestnut-maned.

Cadfael reached the spot where their paths would cross, and there halted before the open, dim doorway of the church, so that they, too, came naturally to a halt. Boterel recognised the brother who had dressed his wound once in the manor of Ledwyche, and made gracious acknowledgement.

'I trust I see you fully restored to health,' said Cadfael civilly. His eye was on Hugh, curious to see if he had taken note of the waiting horse, which the man-at-arms was walking to and fro about the court, with an admiring eye on his gait and a gentling hand on his neck. There was not much escaped Beringar's eye, but his face gave away

185

nothing of his thoughts. Cadfael's thumbs pricked. He had no part to play here, on the face of it, yet his instinct drew him into a complex affair as yet only partly understood.

'I thank you, brother, I am indeed mending, if not mended,' said Evrard buoyantly.

'Little enough to thank me for,' said Cadfael. 'But have you yet thanked God? It would be a fair return for mercies, from one preserved in life and limb, and in recovery of so fine a property as this mare of yours. After coils and cruelties in which so many have died, honest men and innocent virgins.' He was facing the open door of the church, he caught the dark quiver of movement within, that froze again into stillness. 'For grace, come within now, and say a prayer for those less fortunate—even the one we have coffined here, ready for burial.'

He feared he had said too much, and was relieved to see Boterel confident and unshaken, turning towards the doorway with the light smile of one humouring a well-meaning churchman by consenting to a harmless gesture without significance.

'Very willingly, brother!' Why not? There had been dead left behind to the care of these or others in every rogue raid from Clee, small wonder if one of the last of them lay here newly coffined. He stepped jauntily up the stone stair and into the dim, cold nave, Cadfael close at his shoulder. Hugh Beringar, dark brows drawn down, followed as far as the threshold, and there stood astride, closing the way back.

The radiance of the sunlit snow fell behind them, turning them momentarily half-blind. The great, cold, twilit bulk enclosed them, the lamp on the high altar made an eye of fire ahead, very small and distant, and the only other light within was from the narrow windows, which laid pale bars across the tiles of the floor.

The red eye of the lamp went out suddenly. She must have come quite rapidly the few yards from the mortuary chapel to stand between, but in the brief darkness her movements had been silent and invisible. She came forward in a sweeping, hushed glide, advancing upon Evrard Boterel with hand extended, as in a vain entreaty that turned abruptly into a stabbing accusation. He hardly knew what caused the dim air to vibrate until she surged

186

into the first pallid bar of light, veil and cowl drawn close about her face, a slender Benedictine nun in a habit crumpled and soiled from the straw of the hut, the right breast and shoulder clotted and stiffened into a rusty blot of congealed blood. The pale grey light took her and showed every seamed fold, even the smears that marred her sleeve, as she had fought him and ripped his young wound open again while he lay upon her. She never made a sound, only flew towards him silently along the tiles of the floor.

He gave a great lurch backwards into Brother Cadfael's shoulder, and uttered a muffled moan of terror, whipping up a hand to cross his body against the unbelievable assault. Under the close-drawn hood great eyes blazed at him, and still she came on.

'No—no! Keep from me! You are dead . . .'

It was only a strangled whisper in his throat, as her voice might have been quenched under his hands; but Cadfael heard it. And it was enough, even though Evrard had gathered himself the next moment, and braced himself to stand his ground, stiffening almost breast to breast with her as she stepped into the light and became flesh, tangible and vulnerable.

'What fool's play is this? Do you shelter madwomen here? Who is this creature?'

She flung back the cowl from her head and dragged off the wimple, shaking out her great burden of black hair over the befouled breast of Sister Hilaria's gown, and showed him the fierce, marble face and burning eyes of Ermina Hugonin.

He was as little prepared for that apparition as for the other. Perhaps he had been thinking her safely dead somewhere under the forest drifts, since he had received no news of her. Perhaps he had concluded that he had nothing now to fear from anything she might have to urge against him, at least not in this world, and he had little consideration for any other. He gave back one hasty step before her, but could give no more, because Cadfael and Hugh stood one on either side between him and the open door. But he gathered himself together gallantly, and faced her with a hurt, bewildered countenance, appealing against inexplicable ill-usage.

'Ermina! What can this mean? If you live, why have you

187

not sent me word? What is this you are trying to do to me? Have I deserved it? Surely you know I have been wearing out myself and all my household, searching for you?'

'I know it,' she said, in a voice small and hard, cold as the ice that had prisoned and preserved Sister Hilaria. 'And if you had found me, and no other by, I should have gone the same way my dearest friend went, since you knew by then you would never get me to wed you. Married or buried, there was no third way for me, else I could tell all too much for your comfort and honour. And I have never said one word here to bring you to account, never a word for myself, since I brought it on myself, and was as much to blame as you. But knowing what I know now, and for her—Yes, yes, yes, a thousand times, I accuse you, murderer, ravisher, I name you, Evrard Boterel, as the killer of my sweet Hilaria . . .'

'You are out of your wits!' he cried, riding indignantly over her accusation. 'Who is this woman you speak of? What do I know of any such person? Since the day you left me I've lain in fever and sickness. All my household will say so . . .'

'Oh, no! Oh, no! Not that night! You rode out after me, to recover me for your honour's sake, to silence me, either by marriage or murder. Never deny it! I saw you ride! You think I was fool enough to believe I could outrun you on foot? Or terrified enough to lose my wits and run like a fool hare, zigzag, leaving tracks plain for you? I laid my traces no further than the trees, towards the Ludlow road where you would expect me to run, and made my way back roundabout to hide half the night among the timber you had stacked for your coward defences. I saw you go, Evrard, and I saw you return, with your wound fresh-broken and bloodied on you. I did not run until you were helped within to your bed and the worst of the blizzard over, and I knew I could run at my own pace, with the dawn barely an hour away. And while I was hiding from you, you killed her!' she wrung out, burning up like a bitter fire of thorns. 'On your way back from a fruitless hunt, you found a lone woman, and took your revenge for what I did to you, and all that you could not do to me. We killed her!' cried Ermina. 'You and I between us! I am as guilty as you!'

'What are you saying?' He had called up a little courage, a little confidence. If she had raved, he would have become soothing, solicitous, sure of himself, and even in her cold assurance he could find a foothold for his own. 'Certainly I rode out to look for you, how could I leave you to die in the frost? I had a fall, weak from my wound as I was, and broke it open again and bled—yes, that is truth. But the rest? I hunted you all that night, as long as I could endure, and never did I halt in my search for you. If I came back empty-handed and bleeding, do you accuse me of that? I know nothing of this woman you speak of . . .'

'Nothing?' said Cadfael at his shoulder. 'Nothing of a shepherd's hut close to the track you would be riding, back from the Ludlow road towards Ledwyche? I know, for I've ridden it the opposite way. Nothing of a young nun asleep in the hay there, wrapped in a good man's cloak? Nothing of a freezing brook handy on your way home, afterwards? It was not a fall that ripped your wound open again, it was the doughty fight she made for her honour in the cold night, where you had out your fury and lust upon her for want of another prey, more profitable to your ambitions. Nothing of the cloaks and habit hidden under the straw, to cast the crime on those guilty of everything else that cried to heaven here? Everything but this!'

The cold, pale light cast all shapes into marble, the shadows withdrew and left them stark. It was not long past noon of a sunlit day without. It was moon-chill and white here within. Ermina stood like a carving in stone, staring now in silence upon the three men before her. She had done what she had to do.

'This is folly,' said Evrard Boterel arduously, as against great odds. 'I rode out swathed, after the wounds I got in the storming of Callowleas, I rode back home bleeding through my bindings, what of that? A freezing night of blizzard and snow, and I had taken a fall. But this woman, this nun—the shepherd's hut—these mean nothing to me, I never was there, I do not even know where it is . . .'

'I have been there,' said Brother Cadfael, 'and found in the snow the droppings of a horse. A tall horse, that left a fistful of his mane roven in the rough boards under the eaves. Here it is!' He had the wavy cream-coloured strands in his hand. 'Shall I match them with your geld-

189

ing, there without? Shall we stretch you over the habit you see before you, and match your wound with the blood that soils it? Sister Hilaria did not bleed. Your wound I have seen, and know.'

Evrard hung for one long moment motionless, drawn up tall like a strung doll between the woman before him and the men behind. Then he shrank and sank, with a long, despairing moan, and collapsed on his knees on the tiles of the nave, fists clutched hard to his heart, and fair hair fallen forward over his face, the palest point in the bar of light where he kneeled.

'Oh, God forgive, God forgive . . . I only meant to hush her, not to kill . . . not to kill . . .'

'And it may even be true,' said Ermina sitting hunched and stiff by the fire in the hall, the storm of her tears past, and nothing left but a great weariness. 'He may not have meant to kill. What he says may be sooth.'

What he said, bestirring himself out of despair to make the best case he could for his life, was that he had turned for home again from his search by reason of the blizzard, and been driven to take shelter through the worst of it when he came to the hut, never thinking to find anyone there before him. But presented with a sleeping woman at his mercy, he had taken her out of spite and rage against all women for Ermina's sake. And when she awoke and fought him, he owned he had not been gentle. But he never meant to kill! Only to silence her, with the skirts of her habit pressed over her face. And then she lay limp and lifeless, and he could not revive her, and he stripped the gown from her, and hid all the garments under the straw, and took her with him as far as the brook, to make of here merely one more victim of the outlaws who had sacked Callowleas.

'Where he first came by that eloquent wound,' said Brother Cadfael, watching her pale face, and marking the convulsion of a bitter smile, that came and went like a grimace of pain on her mouth.

'I know—so he told you! And I let it stand! In gallant defence of his manor and his men! I tell you, he never drew sword, he left his people to be slaughtered, and ran like a rat. And forced me with him! No man of my blood ever before turned his back and abandoned his own people to die!

190

This he did to me, and I cannot forgive it. And I had thought I loved him! I will tell you,' she said, 'how he got that wound of his that betrayed him in the end. All that first day at Ledwyche he drove his men at cutting fence-pales and building barricades, and he with never a scratch on him. And all that day I brooded and was shamed, and in the evening, when he came, I told him I would not marry him, that I would not match with a coward. He had not touched me until then, he had been all duty and service, but when he saw he would lose both me and my lands, then it was another story.'

Cadfael understood. Marriage by rape, once the thing was done, and privately, would be accepted by most families as preferable to causing an ugly scandal and starting a feud. No uncommon practice to take first and marry after.

'I had a dagger,' she said grimly. 'I have it still. It was I who wounded him, and I struck for his heart, but it went astray and ripped down from shoulder to arm. Well, you have seen . . .' She looked down at the folded habit that lay beside her on the bench. 'And while he was raving and cursing and dripping blood, and they were running to staunch his wound and bandage him, I slipped out into the night and ran. He would follow me, that I knew. He could not afford to let me escape him, after that, marry or bury were the only ways. He would expect me to run towards the road and the town. Where else? So I did, but only until the woods covered my traces, and then I circled back and hid. I told you, I saw him ride out, weakened as he was, in a great rage, the way I knew he would go.'

'Alone?'

'Of course alone. He would not want witnesses for either rape or murder. Those within had their orders. And I saw him ride back, freshly bloodied through his bandages, though I thought nothing of it then but that he had exerted himself too rashly.' She shuddered at the thought of that exertion. 'When he was cheated of me, he took out his venom on the first woman who fell in his way, and so avenged himself. For myself I would not have accused him. I had the better of him, and I had brought it on myself. But what had *she* done?'

It was the eternal question, and the one to which there exists no answer. Why do the innocent suffer?

191

'And yet,' she said doubtfully, 'it may be true what he says. He was not used to being thwarted, it made him mad . . . He had a devil's temper. God forgive me, I used almost to admire him for it once . . .'

Yes, it might be true that he had killed without meaning to, and in panic sought to cover up his deed. Or it might be that he had reasoned coldly that a dead woman could never accuse him, and made sure of her eternal silence. Let those judge who were appointed to do the judging, here in this world.

'Don't tell Yves!' said Ermina. 'I will do that, when the time comes. But not here. Not now!'

No, there was no need to say any word to the boy of the battle that was over. Evrard Boterel was gone to Ludlow under armed escort, and there was no sign in the great court that ever a crime had been uncovered. Peace came back to Bromfield very softly, almost stealthily. In less than half an hour it would be time for Vespers.

'After supper,' said Cadfael, 'you should go to your bed, and get some hours of sleep, and the boy also. I will keep watch and let your squire in.'

He had chosen his words well. It was like the coming of the thaw outside. She lifted her face to him like a flower opening, and all the bitter sadness of guilt and folly regretted melted away and fell from her before such a radiance that Cadfael's eyes dazzled. From death and the past she leaned eagerly to life and the future. He did not think she was making any mistake this time, nor that any power would now turn her from her allegiance.

There was a small congregation in the parish part of the church even at Compline that night, a dozen or so goodmen of the district, come to offer devout thanks for deliverance from terror. Even the weather partook of the general grace, for there was barely a touch of frost in the air, and the sky was clear and starry. Not a bad night for setting out on a journey.

Cadfael knew what to look for by now, but for all that it took him a little time to single out the bowed black head for which he was searching. Marvellous that a creature so remarkable could become at will so unremarked. When Compline ended, it was no surprise to count the villagers leaving, and make them one less than had entered. Olivier

192

could not only look like a local lad when he pleased, he could also vanish into shadow without a sound, and remain as still as the stones about him.

They were all gone, the villagers to their homes, the brothers to the warming-room for half an hour of relaxation before bed. The chill dark bulk of the church was silent.

'Olivier,' said Brother Cadfael, 'come forth and be easy. Your wards are getting their rest until midnight, and have trusted you to me.'

The shadows stirred, and gave forth the shape of a lean, lissome, youthful body, instantly advancing to be seen. He had not thought wise or fit to bring his sword with him into a sacred place. He trod without sound, light as a cat. 'You know me?'

'From her I know you. If the boy promised silence, be content, he has kept his word. She chose to trust me.'

'Then so can I,' said the young man, and drew nearer. 'You have privilege here? For I see you come and go as you please.'

'I am not a brother of the house, but of Shrewsbury. I have a patient here mending, my justification for an irregular life. At the battle up there you saw him—the same distraught soul who marched into peril of his life and gave Yves the chance to break free.'

'I am much in his debt.' The voice was low, earnest and assured. 'And in yours, too, I think, for you must be the brother to whom the boy ran, the same of whom he spoke, the one who first brought him safe to this house. The name he gave you I do not remember.'

'My name is Cadfael. Wait but a moment, till I look out and see if all are within . . .' In the sinking glow of torchlight, the last of the evening, the court showed its pattern of black and white as the paths crossed, empty, quiet and still. 'Come!' said Cadfael. 'We can offer you a warmer place to wait, if not a holier. I advised leaving while the brethren are at Matins and Lauds, for the porter will also attend, and I can let you out at the wicket in peace. But your horses?'

'They are handy, and in shelter,' said Olivier serenely. 'There is a boy goes with me, orphaned at Whitbache, he has them in charge. He will wait until we come. I will go with you, Brother Cadfael.' He tasted the name delicately if inaccurately, finding it strange on his tongue. He laughed, very softly, surrendering his hand to be led half-blind wherever his guide wished. Thus hand in hand they went out by the cloister, and threaded the maze to the infirmary door.

In the inner room Brother Elyas lay monumentally asleep, long, splendid and calm, stretched on his back, with lean hands easy on his breast, and face serene and handsome. A tomb-figure carved to flatter and ennoble the dead man beneath, but this man lived and breathed evenly, and the large, rounded lids over his sleeping eyes were placid as a child's. Brother Elyas gathered within him the grace that healed body and mind, and made no overwheening claim on a guilt beyond his due.

No need to agonise any more over Brother Elyas. Cadfael closed the door on him, and sat down in the dim ante-room with his guest. They had, perhaps, as much as two hours before midnight and Matins.

The small room, bare and stony and lit by only one candle had a secret intimacy about it at this late hour. They were quiet together, the young man and the elder, eyeing each other with open and amiable curiosity. Long silences did not disturb them, and when they spoke their voices were low, reflective and at peace. They might have known each other life long. Life long? The one of them could surely be no more than five or six and twenty, and a stranger from a strange land.

'You may have a hazardous journey yet,' said Cadfael. 'In your shoes I would leave the highways after Leominster, and avoid Hereford.' He grew enthusiastic, and went into some detail about the route to be preferred, even drawing a plan of the ways as he remembered them, with a charcoal stick on the stones of the floor. The boy leaned and peered, all willing attention, and looked up into Cadfael's face at close quarters with a mettlesome lift of the head and a swift, brilliant smile. Everything about him was stirring and strange, and yet from time to time Cadfael caught his breath as at a fleeting glimpse of something familiar, but so long past that the illusion was gone before he could grasp it, and search back in his memory for the place and the time where it belonged.

'All this you are doing in pure goodwill,' said Olivier,

his smile at once challenging and amused, 'and you know nothing of me! How can you be sure I am fit to be trusted with this errand, and take no advantage for my lord and my empress?'

'Ah, but I do know something of you, more than you may think. I know that you are called Olivier de Bretagne, and that you came with Laurence d'Angers from Tripoli. I know that you have been in his service six years, and are his most trusted squire. I know that you were born in Syria, of a Syrian mother and a Frankish knight, and that you made your way to Jerusalem to join your father's people and your father's faith.' And I know more, he thought, recalling the girl's rapt face and devout voice as she praised her paladin. I know that Ermina Hugonin, who is well worth winning, has set her heart on you, and will not easily give up, and by that amber stare of yours, and the blood mounting to your brow, I know that you have set your heart on her, and that you will not undervalue your own worth by comparison with her, or let any other make it a barrier between you, no matter in what obscure way you came into this world. Between the two of you, it would be a bold uncle who would stand in your way.

'She does indeed trust you!' said Olivier, intent and solemn.

'So she may, and so may you. You are here on an honourable quest, and have done well in it. I am for you, and for them, sister and brother both. I have seen their mettle and yours.'

'But for all that,' owned Olivier, relaxing into a rueful smile, 'she has somewhat deceived you and herself. For her every Frankish soldier of the Crusade could be nothing less than a noble knight. And the most of them were none, but runaway younger sons, romantic boys from the byre and the field, rogues one leap ahead of the officers for theft or highway robbery or breaking open some church almsbox. No worse than most other men, but no better. Not even every lord with a horse and a lance was another Godfrey of Bouillon or Guimar de Massard. And my father was no knight, but a simple man-at-arms of Robert of Normandy's force. And my mother was a poor widow who had a booth in the market of Antioch. And I am their bastard, got between faiths, between peoples, a

195

mongrel afterthought before they parted. But for all that, she was beautiful and loving, and he was brave and kind, and I think myself well mothered and fathered, and the equal of any man living. And I shall make that good before Ermina's kin, and they will acknowledge it and give her to me!' His deep, soft voice had grown urgent, and his hawk-face passionately earnest, and at the end of it he drew breath deep, and smiled. 'I do not know why I tell you all this, except that I have seen you care for her, and wish her the future she deserves. I should like you to think well of me.'

'I am a common man myself,' said Cadfael comfortably, 'and have found as good in the kennel as in the court. She is dead, your mother?'

'Else I would not have left her. I was fourteen years old when she died.'

'And your father?'

'I never knew him, nor he me. He sailed for England from St Symeon after their last meeting, and never knew he had left her a son. They had been lovers long before, when he came fresh to Syria. She never would tell me his name, though often she praised him. There cannot be much amiss,' said Olivier thoughtfully, 'with a mating that left her such fondness and pride.'

'Half mankind matches without ritual blessing,' said Cadfael, surprised at the stirring of his own thoughts. 'Not necessarily the worse half. At least no money passes then, and no lands are prized before the woman.'

Olivier looked up, suddenly aware of the oddity of these exchanges, and laughed, but softly, not to disturb the sleeper next door. 'Brother, these walls are hearing curious confidences, and I am learning how wide is the Benedictine scope. I might well imagine you speak of your own knowledge.'

'I was in the world forty years,' said Cadfael simply, 'before I chose this discipline for my cure. I have been soldier, sailor and sinner. Even crusader! At least that was pure, however the cause fell short of my hopes. I was very young then. I knew both Tripoli and Antioch, once. I knew Jerusalem. They will all have changed now, that was long ago.'

Long ago, yes—twenty-seven years since he had left those shores!

196

The young man grew talkative at finding so knowledge-
able a companion. For all his knightly ambitions and his
dedication to a new faith, a part of him leaned back with
longing to his native land. He began to talk of the royal
city, and of old campaigns, to question eagerly of events
before ever he was born, and to extol the charm of remembered places.

'I wonder, though,' admitted Cadfael wryly, recalling
how far his own cause had often fallen short, and how
often the paynim against whom he had fought had seemed
to him the nobler and the braver, 'I wonder, born into
such a faith, that you should find it easy to leave it, even
for a father.' He rose as he spoke, recollecting how time
must be passing. 'I should be waking them. It cannot be
long to the Matins bell.'

'It was not easy at all,' said Olivier, pondering in some
surprise that the same doubt had so seldom troubled him.
'I was torn, a long time. It was from my mother I had, as
it were, the sign that turned the scale. Given the difference in our tongues, my mother bore the same name as
your Lady Mary . . .'

Behind Cadfael's back the door of the little room had
opened very softly. He turned his head to see Ermina,
flushed and young from sleep, standing in the doorway.

'. . . she was called Mariam,' said Olivier.

'I have roused Yves,' said Ermina, just above a whisper. 'I am ready.'

Her eyes, huge and clear, all the agonising of the day
washed away by sleep, clung to Olivier's face, and at the
sound of her voice he flung up his head and answered the
look as nakedly as if they had embraced heart to heart.
Brother Cadfael stood amazed and enlightened. It was
not the name the boy had spoken, it was the wild rise of
his head, the softened light over his cheek and brow, the
unveiled, unguarded blaze of love, turning the proud male
face momentarily into a woman's face, one known and remembered through twenty-seven years of absence.

Cadfael turned like a man in a dream, and left them together, and went to help a sleepy Yves to dress and make
ready for his journey.

He let them out by the wicket door while the brothers
were at Matins. The girl took a grave and dignified leave,

and asked his prayers. The boy, still half asleep, lifted his face for the kiss proper between respected elder and departing child, and the young man, in generous innocence and in acknowledgement of a parting probably lifelong, copied the tribute and offered an olive cheek. He did not wonder at Cadfael's silence, for after all, the night demanded silence and discretion.

Cadfael did not stand to watch them go, but closed the wicket again, and went back to sit beside Brother Elyas, and let the wonder and the triumph wash over him in wave on wave of exultation. *Nunc dimittis!* No need to speak, no need to make any claim, or trouble in any way the course Olivier had set himself. What need had he now of that father of his? But I have seen him, rejoiced Cadfael, I have had him by the hand in the darkness, I have sat with him and talked of time past, I have kissed him, I have had cause to be glad of him, and shall have cause to be glad lifelong. There is a marvellous creature in the world with my blood in his veins, and Mariam's blood, and what does it matter whether these eyes ever see him again? And yet they may, even in this world! Who knows?

The night passed sweetly over him. He fell asleep where he sat, and dreamed of unimaginable and undeserved mercies until the bell rang for Prime.

He thought it politic, on reflection, to be the first to discover the defection and raise the mild alarm. There was a search, but the guests were gone, and it was not the business of the brothers to confine or pursue them, and the only anxiety Prior Leonard expressed was for the fugitives themselves, that they might go in safety, and come safely to their proper guardian. Indeed, Prior Leonard received the whole affair with a degree of complacency that Cadfael found faintly suspicious, though it might have been only a reflection of the distracted elation he himself could not quite dissemble. The discovery that Ermina had stripped the rings from her fingers and left them, with the carefully folded habit, on Sister Hilaria's sealed coffin as an offering, absolved the runaways from the charge of ingratitude.

'But what the deputy sheriff will say is another matter,' sighed Prior Leonard, shaking an apprehensive head.

Hugh did not present himself until it was time for High Mass, and heard the news with a very appropriate and official show of displeasure, only to shrug it off as of secondary importance, considering the weightier matters he had dealt with successfully.

'Well, they have saved us an escort, then, and so they get safe to d'Angers, so much the better if it's at his expense. We have rooted out the lair of wolves, and sent a murderer off this morning towards Shrewsbury, and that was the chief of my business here. And I'm off after my men within the hour, and you may as well ride with me, Cadfael, for I fancy your business here is just as well concluded as mine.'

Brother Cadfael thought so, too. Elyas had no more need of him, and to linger where those three had been had no more meaning now. At noon he saddled up and took his leave of Leonard, and rode with Hugh Beringar for Shrewsbury.

The sky was veiled but benign, the air cold but still and clear, a good day for going home well content. They had not ridden thus knee to knee in peace and without haste for some time, and the companionship was good, whether in speech or silence.

'So you got your children away without a hitch,' said Hugh innocently. 'I thought it could safely be left to you.'

Cadfael gave him a measuring and mildly resentful look, and could feel no great surprise. 'I should have known! I *thought* you made and kept yourself very scarce overnight. I suppose it wouldn't have done for a deputy sheriff with your reputation for sharpness to sleep the night through while his hostages slipped away quietly for Gloucester.' Not to speak of their escort, he thought, but did not say. Hugh had noted the quality of the supposed forester's son, and even guessed at his purpose, but Hugh did not know his name and lineage. Some day, when wars ended and England became one again, some day Hugh might be told what now Cadfael hugged to his heart in secret. But not yet! It was too new a visitation, he could spare none of the miraculous, the astonishing grace. 'From Ludlow,' he said, 'I grant you could hardly be expected to hear the wicket at Bromfield open and close at midnight. You did not leave Boterel in Dinan's care, then?'

'I was none too sure there would not be another departure in the night,' said Hugh. 'He is Dinan's tenant. We have taken confession from him, but I would rather have him safe under lock and key in Shrewsbury castle.'

'Will he hang, do you think?'

'I doubt it. Let those judge whose work is judging. My work is to hold the ways safe for travellers, as far as man can, and apprehend murderers. And let honest men, women and children go their ways freely, with my goodwill.'

They were more than halfway to Shrewsbury, and the light still good, and Hugh's pace began to quicken, and his gaze to prick eagerly ahead, hungry for the first sight of the hill-top towers within the wall. Aline would be waiting for him, proud and fond, and deep in happy preparations for the Christmas feast.

'My son will be grown out of knowledge during these days I've been away. All must be very well with them both, or Constance would have been sending after me. And you have not even seen my son yet, Cadfael!'

But you have seen mine, thought Cadfael, rapt and silent beside him, though you do not know it.

'Long-boned and strong—he'll be taller than his father by a head . . .'

He *is* taller by a head, Cadfael exulted. Taller by a head and something to spare. And what paragons of beauty and gallantry may not spring from his union with that imperial girl!

'Wait until you see him! A son to be proud of!'

Cadfael rode mute and content, still full of the wonder and astonishment, all elation and all humility. Eleven more days to the Christmas feast, and no shadow hanging over it now, only a great light. A time of births, of triumphant begettings, and this year how richly celebrated— the son of the young woman from Worcester, the son of Aline and Hugh, the son of Mariam, the Son of Man . . .

A son to be proud of! Yes, amen!

ABOUT THE AUTHOR

Ellis Peters is a pseudonym for Edith Pargeter, author of many books under her own name. The recipient of the C.W.A. Silver Dagger Award, she is also well known as a translator of poetry and prose from the Czech. Miss Pargeter makes her home in Shropshire, England.